I0593675

Truth Be told

Copyright © 2023, Vince Craig.

First published 2022.
Reprint 2023.

Published by Harvest Publishing for Larkspur Press
Melbourne, Victoria, Australia.
Email: harvestpublishing@houseofjt.com.au.
Phone: + 61 3 9079 6955
Publisher URL: https://harvestpublishing.com.au
Publication URL: https://harvestpublishing.com.au/truth-be-told

Layout and Typesetting: The Good Black Sheep

All rights reserved. Without limiting the rights under copyright reserved above, no part of this publication may be reproduced, stored in or introduced into a database and retrieval system or transmitted in any form or any means (electronic, mechanical, photocopying, recording or otherwise) without the prior written permission of both the owner of copyright and the above publishers.

Truth Be Told By Vince Craig
Printed Edition Paperback ISBN 978-0-6454431-1-0
Printed Edition Hardback ISBN 978-0-6454431-2-7
Digital Edition ISBN 978-0-6454431-0-3

VINCE CRAIG

Vince Craig is a pseudonym.

He is a former Special Forces soldier who spent over 15 years with the Australian Army and has worked with the Green Beret, Navy Seals and British SAS.

Vince is a former academic who has taught students at college and university level. Vince spent time in Iraq as a Private Military Contractor and now enjoys music and fitness training in his retirement. Vince currently resides in Majorca.

Truth Be Told

Chapter 1

THE DISCOVERY

t was early morning and the beginning of spring when a thickset man in his 40s produced a metal detector from his 4x4 with the intention of sweeping the ground for shiny specks of gold. The dew was thick, which meant the wild bush grass had sodden the cuffs of his worn cargo trousers and old tan army boots; his calves were damp also. The mild discomfort did not faze the *Prospector* as he enjoyed, or to be more precise, relished being in the Australian bush, with a myriad of birds chirping, a view of an occasional grey kangaroo but more importantly the unencumbered freedom of isolation. The *Prospector* was a military veteran who had turned his back on civilisation for reasons only he knew and cared about. Anyway, the weather was perfect for his cause – not too hot or cold and the morning was beginning to warm a little;

perspiration began to dampen the inside sweat band of his raggedy bush hat. He thought - *'time to remove the polar fleece'*.

The *Prospector* had taken note of a thin quartz trail, always a solid indicator of gold and decided this is where he would start. As he gestured his detector in a slow, sweeping motion, from left to right, his machine would emit high-pitched screams into his headphones that indicated potential gold or metal bits and pieces, followed by low buzzing sounds when no metal objects were present. This demanding, methodical process was punctuated by ferocious digging with his short pick when the high tone resonated and a rigorous fossicking of the soil with his other detecting implements. Sometimes, he had to dig deep into the heavy clay soil, a metre or two only to find old shotgun pellets, dull brass buttons or spent bullet cases from long ago. Nevertheless, it was the thrill of the chase, the physical exertion, and the slight chance of finding gold that was an adventure too good to miss, or so he convinced himself. It had been difficult, if not impossible, finding gainful employment after his discharge from the military. Gold prospecting had given him *a new lease on life.*

The area was not much to look at now, quite ugly in fact, what with the rural landscape dotted with 'mullock heaps', essentially large burial type mounds created from the diggings by miners 160 years ago. Most of these dirt and rock mounds were 5, 10, 15 metres high, and the same measurement at ground level. The expanse had that dug-up feel and scarred look about it, as there were old, lengthy sluice trenches and deep water-filled holes that resembled the devastation of the Somme battlefield from *World War One*. Based on what the *Prospector* now saw, it was impossible to imagine the entire area had been a massive canvas tent city. For a five-mile radius, calico-coloured tents, fiery hurricane lamps and noisy diggings filled the bush vista. At a distance, the blossoming tent city, in the evening, looked enchanting, even magical with its mushroom like canopies, firefly lighting and raucous folk music. Yet, these tents housed industrious but mostly struggling miners, some with their large families. There were tents where provisions were sold at incredibly inflated prices and tents where miners could buy grog, opium or solicit 'fallen women'. The area was a veritable multi-cultural 'melting pot' and a hive of physical activity as the population consisted of all the nationalities from Europe, the Americas and a large Chinese contingent – population around 10,000 inhabitants.

However, when the gold went so did the prospectors, and their families, the goods purveyors and the 'working girls'. Today it is commonly known as an old 'Ghost Town' and more renowned as an area where people go rabbit hunting. But, with the poisoning of the rabbit plagues, the only thing left was the odd, rusty rabbit trap, an abundance of lead shotgun pellets and deadly, unrecorded mine shafts, which is why most prospectors left the area well alone. His prospecting mates had tried to warn the *Prospector* off this patch – *'don't waste your bloody time looking there,'* or *'you're a goose if you think you'll find anything'* was all he heard, but he thought *'what the hell'*. The *Prospector* had not made a decent find for some time, months in fact, but believed the area was worth a second look with 'fresh' eyes. He had nothing to lose... After poking at a few holes and hardly hearing a sound from his machine in an hour or so, an intense beeping noise echoed in his headphones on the next sweep with his reliable detector. The exasperating tone grew louder and aggressive as he strolled onwards, very slowly, but he ventured forward with genuine hope. The *Prospector* cautiously walked five more metres towards a small, darkish depression in the soil, flanked by low, dense bush. It was on his third, deliberate step forward that the earth he stood on suddenly and violently collapsed and he fell, so effortlessly, *into the void*...

The shaken *Prospector* was not certain how long he had been 'out' for or exactly where he was. His old military training kicked in and he took stock of his situation. He checked himself thoroughly all over for injuries and inspected what gear he had; his new and expensive gold detector was missing, and his cell phone had zero reception, and the battery was dangerously low. He looked all around and upward and could only barely make out a faint light, where the surface would be. What he did ascertain was that he had fallen down a narrow mineshaft, around ten metres high by his reckoning and wide enough for two stout men. The shaft had been built so long ago that tree roots and shrubby bush had grown out from the moist clay walls and was the only reason he was still intact – this clingy vegetation had buffeted and slowed his descent and the bottom of the shaft was wet and spongy, which is why he hadn't been seriously hurt. The only wound he had was a small, solid oedema that he could feel developing on the left side of his forehead, like a giant, painful pimple. Despite this injury, he did not have a headache or blurred vision. He knew he was in decent shape, and, for a moment, he thought how lucky he was. It quickly dawned on him he could have been killed! The *Prospector* tested the closest logs that shore up the shaft, but these beams were too rotten or unstable to sustain his weight or even attempt a climb. For a second or so, he started to worry and think of how he would get out – *he also wished he had left his green fleece on*! At this moment, he noticed, for the first time, a beach ball sized shadow to his right. He fumbled in his trouser pocket and found his pack of crushed cigarettes, but eventually located his trusty *Zippo* lighter, the one he had always carried on his military deployments. One flick and the *Zippo's* iridescent flame illuminated this small area to expose a horizontal shaft that had been concealed by old canvas sacking, now tattered and rotten by mildew. Upon careful examination, he could see the newer shaft had been constructed with heavy concrete roof braces, corrugated iron siding, and led away ten metres or more from his position. The *Prospector* sat in the damp mud perplexed. He did not have to ask himself a series of complex questions to know that this shaft had been constructed in the last twenty years or so and certainly wasn't made by old, sweaty miners!

The passage looked sturdy enough and was his only way out, so he took the plunge and began crawling on his hands and knees down its length. Every few metres he paused and fired his *Zippo*, waved away two or three cobwebs, took in his surroundings, and then continued forward. The journey was slow and painful on his knees, but soon he came to a solid metal object blocking his way. Again, he ignited his lighter to find a metal door with a wheel in the centre, as you would see on a hatch in a submarine. He pocketed the *Zippo* and worked on the door wheel. The cold, corroding wheel, immovable at first, ever so slowly began to turn. The *Prospector* felt buoyed with his progress and then the door opened...

The *Prospector* turned quickly away from the blinding luminescence and grimaced for a second or two until his eyes were accustomed to the light. He could now see into a large cave. The cavern walls were glossy with condensation but comprised of solid quartz, which gave the cave its incredible strength. Much to the *Prospector's* amazement, in the cave's centre, rested four massive forty-foot-shipping containers, stacked in twos with small floodlights on every corner. Straight away, this alerted the *Prospector* to the dimensions of this cavern – 40+ feet in length, 20+ feet in height and fifteen feet in width, with an additional five feet above the highest container to the ceiling of the cave and to its sides. He immediately realised, '*this isn't a cave but a bloody bunker!*' The *Prospector* slowly moved forward, his mind racing with rudimentary questions that, in his mind, demanded an answer: '*Who built this place?*' '*What's its purpose?*' and '*Is anyone living here now?*'

Besides the outer illumination that lit the cave, a fuzzy glow emanated from inside all the shipping containers. The *Prospector* edged forward, very gradually, all the while suspiciously scanning the enormous cave. Part of him wanted to yell out, a quick, *'hello, is there anyone there?'* but his inquisitiveness was tempered by suspicion and a slight fear of the unknown. As he got closer, he discovered all the containers had a dozen tiny windows on the sides of their brown, rusting hulls, and they were each about the size of your average dinner plate. These large metal boxes had been carefully configured to create four living spaces: laboratory – bottom left; library – top left; kitchen/bathroom – bottom right and bedroom – top right. A large exhaust fan protruded from the kitchen container and its ducting extended to the roof of the cave and to the surface, or so he presumed; bulky ventilation tubing descended from the cave's ceiling back towards the bedroom container.

The *Prospector* had been crouching in a good observation position for around five minutes but had not heard anything nor did he see anyone. He crept forward, in inches, to the closest container – the laboratory, looked in the window and then quickly entered. The *Prospector* could see the room had been furnished with all the sophisticated implements of its time, including state-of-the-art computers. It could easily pass for a university laboratory, circa 2000, except all the equipment was housed in a bulky steel shell underground that was now in slow decay. Scrawled drawings and scientific calculations were abandoned on the solid workbenches whilst dust and mouse droppings lay about with equal disregard for the scientific work that had been conducted there. He picked up a small but weighty rock hammer, for protection, and then decided to move cautiously upstairs via the metal ladder that went from the bottom container to the container housing the upstairs library. Still, no one to be seen and only silence. He thought this is how a crypt must be - *silent, creepy,* and *very cold.* The library contained shelving from wall to wall and had a small wooden table and chair in the centre, but this room was even messier. Fifteen or twenty academic books and journals were strewn across the room and a stale, damp-like redolence hung in the air.

At the upper level, a double sliding door, the type you would commonly find leading to a patio, connected the library to the bedroom, which was semi-lit. The *Prospector* scanned the half-lit room briefly before he cautiously ventured in and, when he moved forward, he looked to his left in the half-light. What he saw came as a jolt - *he instinctively leapt a metre to his right*! The subjection of abject fear was so great he began to physically shake. What had terrified the *Prospector* so intensely was a spectral figure sitting in a corner chair next to a double bed, decayed badly by mould. The reliable *Zippo* flashed once more and he could clearly make out that the body had been there for some time, many years in fact. It reminded him of the scary mummy-like characters that he had seen in movies: gaunt sunken face, blackened tight skin, matted stringy hair, with a torso of rotting clothing that hung off dirty, discoloured bones. He was further surprised to notice a small terrier-type dog lay, obediently at the feet of the skeleton and was in the same state of natural decay as, he presumed, its owner. On what remained of the decomposing and tattered lab coat, there existed a name, sewn in black cotton above the left pocket in one-inch cursive letters: *Prof. Hamish MacMillan*. The name was of no consequence to the *Prospector* as he was more interested in the .22 semi-automatic pistol that lay at the dead man's feet. To the *Prospector*, the stark image made a plain statement. It was in this chair that this intelligent, but desperate man grappled with the decision to shoot the dog and for him to take his own life. The *Prospector* spoke out incredulously: *'Why the hell would you shoot your dog and do yourself in?' 'What would make someone do this?'* A further brisk but thorough inspection of the room shed no light on these circumstances, so the *Prospector* decided to make his way downstairs, via the steel ladder that connected the two living spaces.

The kitchen was very barren in its design, only a single gas burner, a round wooden bench - complete with a cup and plate, cutlery, white plastic chairs, and a few cupboards up against the outer facing wall. Again, nothing much to report here until he noticed, at the far end of the room a solid, rusting metal door with an ageing metal sign in black and white writing - *Battery Room*. The *Prospector* walked very quietly to the door and opened it, cautiously.

The 'Battery Room' was still part of the container but had been re-configured as a small, separate room with its own ventilation system that disappeared out into the cave. The batteries in this room were about the size of small black *Fender* 15-Watt guitar amplifiers and there were ten of these, stacked regimentally side by side. These batteries were cabled to a lunch box sized panel that simply announced the word - *Solar*. So, this underground system had been running for years based on a miniature, sophisticated solar configuration, and ultra-deep cell capacity batteries? The *Prospector* could hardly believe this. His own detecting machinery ran on an advanced lithium battery system, but this subterranean enterprise was nothing he had ever seen or heard of. He spoke out loud in a cynical tone to himself, '*Wonders never cease*'.

At the end of this room and the container there existed a standard dark grey roller door, as you would find in any car garage. The *Prospector* still took slow vigilant steps to this door and once there, stopped and listened. Nothing. He quickly jerked the door's large central handle and raised the door. To his astonishment, there was a terraced stone pathway leading upward to the surface. The pathway was lit either side by small lights recessed into the walls and resembled the stone stairway one would find ascending from a chamber in an Egyptian Pyramid. The *Prospector* thought that this must've been the main entrance with the other shaft acting as an auxiliary channel. This durable stone stairway was on a 45-degree angle but clearly manageable in height for an average sized man and easily convenient for bringing in all sorts of equipment and supplies. The main difference in this clever passage was that it was shored with thick metal beams and concrete lined walls. This construction would have taken place after the cavern had been dug out and the containers positioned. The *Prospector* was convinced he had seen enough of the cave and its mysteries and decided to follow the light beams upward to the surface. After nine or ten metres he came to a sliding roof that had been locked from the inside by a sliding bolt contraption that ran from one side of the door to the other. Much to his surprise, when he slid the bolt, the roof door that it was attached it slid back with ease, displaying the bright welcoming light of the afternoon and a burst of fresh, country air. He looked at his watch for the first time in ages, *'My God,'* he thought, *'I've been in that cave for nearly three hours!'*

Once more, on the surface, he realised the top of the sliding door's roof had been decorated with a succulent type of plant and small native ground covers. Floral camouflage, coupled with the roof's black, green, and brown resin structure would always guarantee concealment to the bunker's entrance, even in the event of a bush fire. 'Pretty clever,' he thought. He also noticed dark green wiring that led upward to the solar panels, adjacent to the sliding roof door, which were responsible for the bunker's enduring power. These panels where fashioned as a group of ten or fifteen football-sized rocks and logs, concealing their true purpose. Someone would have to walk directly upon the camouflage to shatter the illusion. He closed the sliding door and locked it by its sliding bolt on the surface, restoring the chameleon effect. Still impressed by this deception, the *Prospector* thought, 'What cunning bastards!' Quickly, he took a GPS app reading on his phone of the secret entrance location, re-orientated himself to his bush surroundings and made his way the short distance back to his vehicle; at this point he wasn't worried about his detector, he would locate that later. He was more committed to making a phone call to a dear old friend who may shine some light on this mystery. At his vehicle, he noticed his phone reception was exceptionally good, but he connected the phone to a cigarette lighter charger. He then punched the speed dial. The phone connected almost instantly, and the *Prospector* spoke rapidly, in fact, he gushed with unbridled excitement down the line; *'Hey, Nathan, it's Danny. Man, have I got some things to tell you...?'*

Chapter 2

THE CALL

'*For Fucks sake*' was all Nathan could say, in a loud, irritated voice as the phone rang. As always, he was in the middle of something important, this time practicing his C Barre chord on his *Gretsch Jetliner* custom guitar. He had taken up the instrument again after many decades - his former military life had little use for guitars and such an extravagant waste of his time. He practised daily and had acquired several expensive instruments, such as a *Fender Stratocaster* and *Gibson Les Paul*. He was never going to be *Eddie Van Halen* or *Joe Walsh*, but he was on *his* musical journey and enjoyed the musical and intellectual discoveries he found in this art form. Nathan had not heard from Danny in a long time, a year or so, but ex-military veterans can pick up a conversation with an old comrade as if it were yesterday. He listened intently to the one-sided dialogue of excitement and animated conversation for

around twenty minutes and, as he took careful note of Danny's story, he perused the walls of his cosy sitting room. Photographic reminders of former adventures and long-lost glory festooned every wall. There were snapshots of military free-fallers lined up at the ramp of a parked *Hercules C-130* at some remote airfield; hiking adventures along the torturous and steamy *Kokoda Track*; team photos with Iraqis he had trained in the desert and a variety of challenge coins from *US Special Forces*, *Navy Seals*, and other 'special' militaria laying about the place. His cabin was not a 'man cave,' with your average beer posters and automobile company emblems, nor was it a shrine to a former way-of-life. The photos and mementoes were simple but significant reminders of good friends, great times, and worthy causes - notably absent were pictures of loved ones - especially a wife or partner.

Nathan Philips was around 50 years of age and was in splendid physical shape for a man who had crammed so much adventure into his short life. As he jokingly told people, 'Remember what Indiana Jones said- *"It's not the years but the mileage"*' and Nathan had many, many miles on his biological clock. As a result, he worked out most days in his purpose-built gym, which he affectionately called the 'house of pain.' He gravitated between *Concept 2* rowing, treadmill running and his '*Spartan routine*': working six different muscle groups, performing 50 repetitions per group at a time and completing 300 reps per group, hence the '300' *Spartan* classification. Nathan was more in tune with his body these days and knew when to ease off, go hard or train ridiculously hard. Experience affords that knowledge and wisdom. His only vices were copious amounts of chocolate and a limited amount of alcohol. Nevertheless, he was good at keeping things in moderation. He had always picked at his food and was told he 'Ate like a schoolboy,' frequently consuming sausage rolls, cereal, and donuts. Nathan was not a 'foodie.' To him, cuisine was just fuel and his demanding exercise routine burnt off the carbohydrates, so it didn't really matter to him what he ate. As he would say in jest, *'stodge built the British Empire, so what's wrong with my diet?'*

Even so, he was in better condition now than when he was twenty, and only a fraction slower. He was muscular in build but deceptive in physical stature when wearing a T-shirt or jacket. As he was of average height, his opponents had always underestimated his strength and physicality. Balding for some time, he shaved his head every couple of weeks; he had always preferred short hair anyway and only shaved his face every second day or so. His face was perpetually tanned, which matched his swarthy complexion; he was often taken for an Italian, but the blue eyes were a giveaway. At a distance, he had that rough *Jason Statham* look about him. Nathan wasn't worried about the lines on his face, or crow's-feet around his eyes; he would frequently refer to these small creases as the 'roadmap of his life.' And, unlike most people, he was proud of his wrinkles - they were his history, sacrifices, successes, and failures.

After leaving the Australian *Special Air Service Regiment* (SAS) in his late twenties, he sought further challenges and went to university where he completed a doctorate in History. Deep down he had always wanted to be an archaeologist ever since he was a boy, mostly because he was obsessed with dinosaurs, and this was as close as he got. Still, not bad for someone who hadn't finished high school and a guy who had worked night jobs to put himself through his studies. Nathan did the usual 'security circuit' along the way, working in close protection jobs, high-end surveillance work and a stint as a Private Military Contractor (PMC) in Iraq during *Gulf War Two*. However, he was far from being a 'Mercenary.' Money was never an issue and certainly not his life's purpose – it was always the challenge of adventure that mattered, the defence of a righteous principle or the support of a worthy cause. In a previous life, he may have been an adventurer in darkest Africa or a British soldier on the Indian sub-continent, guarding the Khyber Pass. At his life's end, he did not want to go out knowing he had not given it a 'good crack.' Most of his friends and military clique felt the same way and they conducted their lives in a similar, daring but noble fashion.

So far, he didn't have to worry about any self-interrogatory questions waiting for him at his mortal end. He certainly did not expect to see some guiding angel or a devilish entity waiting to steer him to the other world; *the only hell he had encountered was on Earth!* Moreover, Nathan didn't see life as a series of 'wins' or 'failures' but a platform for opportunities, contests, and experiences. That was his treasure, and his legacy to the world – do the honourable deed, always and leave the world in better shape than when you found it. This is also, why many of his relationships in the last few years had failed. His lifestyle didn't lend itself to being home on a regular basis, working a 9-5 job, or helping a partner select swanky manchester at a big city department store. Former girlfriends could not understand Nathan's philosophy, which was a knight's creed to put others before himself and profit. After listening to Danny blurt out his story for so long, he politely asked his old friend how he was keeping, had he found any gold lately and finished by saying, 'Leave this to me, I know some people who may be able to help us with this. And then I'll come with you tomorrow to look at *your* cave.' Sure, Danny could have reported the find to the local police. However, the sound of the elaborate bunker, the dead scientist and the sophisticated power systems made Nathan inquisitive. He couldn't resist not looking. Once satisfied, they could ring the cops. Besides, he wasn't doing anything all that important the next few days...

Nathan sat in his leather recliner chair for a brief time, taking in Danny's remarkable story. He made himself another plunger coffee, scratched his shaven head and patted *Moochee*, his pet and resilient moggie. He enjoyed the company of cats and always thought them to be independently more intelligent than canines. This frequently led to arguments with dog owners. In defence of this opinion he would justifiably say, 'you wouldn't have seen a cat sitting on the Tucker Box, would you? A cat would have already selected a new owner and would've been long gone! *That's a real sign of intelligence!*' As far as his occupation went, he had been around long enough to cultivate dozens of contacts in the various Police agencies, Government departments and the university sector, and he still had many comrades serving in the military. This is how he remained semi-retired and able to pick the employment he was interested in or select the 'right' people to work with. Nathan had his standards. He wouldn't do anything or work with anyone. Many of these contacts had been created and nurtured when he was still in 'the Regiment,' as *SAS* members called it. He slightly digressed for a moment and thought how it seemed strange how people couldn't do enough to help the *SAS* so they could say they had a friend in the Regiment or assisted the unit in its various 'special' roles. 'People's egos work in various ways;' he had always thought. With a complex mystery such as this, he needed to make discrete inquiries, but to the right people. Firstly, he decided he would make some general internet and database searches on 'Hamish MacMillan.'

Nathan was surprised that after thirty minutes on the internet all he could find was a brief reference to a MacMillan who had been the hapless victim of a boating mishap on *Port Phillip Bay*, twenty years ago – the body was never recovered. *Well, that's remarkably interesting and convenient*, he thought. There wasn't even a photo connected to the news article! This seemed unconvincing and highly suspicious to Nathan. He knew that any no-name *schlep* can rack up a multitude of references on the internet and everyone is a star on social media these days, yet why was there little, if any, information on a prominent scientist? Time to make a phone call. Nathan dialled the number only to receive the standard: 'You know whom you have called, leave a message.' *'Fucking Brian Leyland - you can never get on to this guy,'* he thought with a degree of irritation. 'I'll give it five minutes and try again. In the meantime, I'll prep my grab bag.'

The one constant element of *Special Forces* training, (along with the *Boy Scouts*) is the creation of a mindset that forces the operator to be prepared for anything - forever. Nathan always took a small, black military denier bag that he would throw in the car or carry with him on all his unique jobs. The bag contained incredibly useful things like a flashlight, *Leatherman* multi-tool, small binoculars, water, protein bars and rain poncho; a handgun and spare magazines could easily be accommodated as with other utensils or small weapons. He judiciously decided to include the latter items for insurance on this trip. Again, he tried to ring Brian. Brian Leyland was an ex-Warrant Officer who served in the *Australian Army* for forty years. He had started in the *Corps of Infantry* but finished his career in Intelligence. His security clearance went all the way to 'top secret' and his network quadrupled that of Nathan's. However, he was a hard man to reach and was an arrogant piece of work. Twenty years as a Warrant Officer does that to a man, so you had to catch him on a good day when he didn't have that enormous chip on his shoulder. Since leaving the military, Brian had become part conspiracy theorist/ doomsday prepper, misogynist, and Mr. Anti-social; he lived in a grubby caravan, engaged excessively in the rantings of socio-political theorists on-line, smoked incessantly and moved his whole production every couple of days, for safety. Always hard to hit a moving target was his mantra. After four rings, Brian answered in a slow, condescending, 'yes....' 'Brian, glad to hear you're having one your better days, you wanker.' *'Fuck off,'* was the curt reply. Brian knew exactly who was at the other end of the line.

Both men commenced their long association when they were young soldiers and would go out drinking and partying and were good mates until they went down different career paths. Unfortunately, people part as friends and aren't always the same chums when they are re-acquainted. As well, 'life' also takes a heavier toll on some people. Nevertheless, they had history and banter and that maintained their cordial friendship. 'Mate, I need some info on a scientist dude called Hamish MacMillan, ever heard of him?' There was a pause at the other end for about 10 seconds. 'Are you still there?' asked Nathan. The memory cogs in Brian's mind had been working overtime. He recollected a scientist by that name who had been connected to a covert science division of the *Department of Defence*. This division was tasked with developing new strategic concepts and weapons for the military. 'I remember talk of this guy being there one day and gone the next. Some scandal too. Secret documents or a prototype weapon missing and stuff like that.' The excitement factor had gone up two notches for Nathan and he asked Brian if he could find out more. Brian replied, 'I'll see what I can do but it has been some time and a lot of that crowd are long gone. I'm talking decades.' Nathan said 'thanks' and hung up. Although it wasn't said, they were both glad to hear from one another and Nathan knew Brian would try his best to gather any credible information. Nathan rang Danny to arrange a time and rendezvous point for the next day. After a brief exchange and a timing agreed upon, he hung up. He had also emailed several contacts to garnish more information on MacMillan and was now awaiting replies.

By now, it was well into the evening and the cabin on his bush block was starting to get a tad chilly. He lit a tiny fire in the small stone fireplace, aggressively poking around the tinder and kindling until the flames burst into life, all the while pondering on what he had learnt from the day's conversations. The one thing he did gleam from his chat with Brian was the likelihood that secret Government forces were at work here. This was concerning but it didn't frighten Nathan. He had a way of dealing with 'big dogs.' *Moochee* jumped onto his lap, and, in a little while, they both fell asleep in front of the obliging warmth of the fire. 🦎

Chapter 3

THE SEARCH FOR SECRETS

The drive to the RV site to meet Danny took nearly 90 minutes and was nothing short of boring. Along the way, Nathan pulled into a Maccas drive-through and bought a coffee, standard NATO as the military called it –flat white with two sugars. His white *Hyundai* I-load was effortless to drive for a van and never aroused any suspicions; the public, would guess his occupation to be a delivery guy or tradesman. To the police, it was a different matter. He had been told by an Army mate who had joined the *New South Wales Police* that his vehicle, age, and his single disposition fitted the profile of most pedophiles. The vehicle had never raised any concerns with the public, unlike his other vehicle, a 1967 GT *Mustang Fastback*, which turned heads everywhere it went. Nathan didn't drive the *Mustang* as much as he liked but when he did - he drove hard. Once, in the north of the state, on a deserted road, he pushed the car out to 120 miles an hour, roughly 200 kilometres per hour. Not bad for a car that is well over 50 years old! Another police friend said if he were caught speeding, the car would be impounded, he would lose his licence and he would go to court for further punishment. He always imagined he could outrun the cops if they tried to arrest him and say the car had been stolen. For convenience, self-preservation and for the sake of continued *Mustang* ownership, he mostly drove the van.

As a precaution, Nathan parked his vehicle 500 metres from the pre-arranged meeting place and arrived 20 minutes before time. The vehicle sat safely in a busy lay-by whilst he walked slowly and assuredly through the bush and pulled up 50 metres short of the meeting point. From concealment, he sat silently and observed. Wildlife flew, buzzed, slithered, and hopped about, all oblivious to his presence. This is what he loved so much about being in the bush, connecting with nature and its wonders, all in serene harmony. Danny's 4x4 arrived just on time and he got out and lit a cigarette. Nathan watched Danny and the area for a further 5 minutes before slowly gliding out of the bush, behind Danny. Danny jumped to one side, obviously startled. *'For fuck's sake,* Nathan, will you cut that 'sneaky Pete' shit out?' 'Just being careful, that's all' was Nathan's reply. They talked for a minute or two about the weather and other mundane things, like the football, and then Danny guided Nathan the short distance to the entrance of the cave, where he slid open the camouflaged top hatch and led Nathan down to the *Battery Room.*

Nathan was immensely impressed by the advanced technology of the lights, the progressive batteries, the technical construction of the bunker and the selective concealment protocols; his level of excitement and interest increased with each step forward. They were now in the kitchen area. This time Danny had brought his large patrolman's Maglite and along with Nathan's flashlight, they moved with ease upstairs to the bedroom where the decomposed body of Hamish MacMillan was waiting. 'Okay,' said Nathan, 'show me this dead body of yours.' The Maglite's large beam passed quickly across the room to where the corpse was supposed to be located, but *it wasn't there!* Danny stood in mute silence and began to flash his Maglite frantically around, as if it were Merlin's magic wand that could conjure up the dead. Even the dog was missing! Before either man could comment, a metallic, crashing sound came from the battery room area and they both knew they were not alone. They could hear muffled voices and quiet, purposeful footsteps in the kitchen, slowly edging their way to the stairs that would lead up to their position.

Nathan quickly took control of the situation as Danny was perplexed. He gestured for him to follow him. Until they knew who these people were, invisibility and guile were their best two options. They moved swiftly into the study next to the bedroom and descended the stairwell to the laboratory, oh so quietly; lights were beginning to flash up into the bedroom from the stairwell below, bouncing off the walls and ceiling. Danny whispered that there wasn't an entrance connecting the kitchen to the laboratory. 'Thank God for that,' Nathan thought. At the same time, he grabbed a Bunsen burner on a bench top and turned it on. He was in luck, the gas hissed with intensity from the burner. They could hear, what they thought were three or four people moving about, rummaging in the bedroom, tearing it apart in their search but at this point no one had ventured into the study or attempted to walk down the stairs. The gas was slowly filling the confined space and it was at this point that Nathan led Danny to the door that led outwards. He produced a small box of safety matches from his grab bag, shielded a match, lit one on a single strike and placed it upright so that it would burn down slowly, like a fuse until it ignited the box and created a small fireball. The key here was to use quality matches.

He had seen this trick in an old war movie called 'Stalag 17', tried it and it worked, like most simple things. Nathan placed the lit match and the box low on the wooden container floor next to the door that led out and said to Danny, *'okay old mate, show me where this bloody auxiliary shaft is?'*

Both men moved very slowly in the half-light of the cave, as the heavy gas began to rapidly fill the room and very quietly, to where the 'submarine hatch' was. Suddenly, they could hear loud voices downstairs but before they could gauge what was being said a small explosion briefly lit the entire cavern. The fireball affirmed the two men's purpose to move faster, and they launched themselves into the cold auxiliary shaft, secured the hatch and moved rapidly along the tunnel to where Danny had fallen the day before. They waited and steeled themselves for a pursuit, and a battle. Nathan coolly produced his 9mm *Browning Hi-Power* from his grab bag and aimed the black pistol back down the shaft. Danny lifted his weighty Maglite - the torch hovered menacingly above his head waiting to crash down on someone, if it had to. *No one came! There was no more noise!* They both thought, 'these people mustn't have come across the auxiliary shaft or did not know about it. Most probably they needed to lick their wounds because of the explosion and re-group and re-assess what had just occurred.' Still, the two men waited for 20 minutes before they next spoke to one another. Danny uttered the first words, 'mate, how are we going to get out? I don't fancy going back into the cave, so the only way is up.' Nathan shone his flashlight up, down and about the shaft and said to Danny, 'piece of piss, I'll free climb my way up, run to the car, grab a rope, and get you out.' 'Piece of piss' Danny thought, but Nathan was versed in mountain climbing from his *Special Forces* days.

There is a technique called 'lay backing' where you use the opposing wall to push off with your feet whilst using your back to maintain contact and friction on the opposing wall; arms are used to grip, push, and lift the body. Physically strenuous but not too difficult for an experienced climber. True to his word, Nathan commenced his ascent, which was made easier as there were branches, sticks and some hand holds to help him along the way. Danny was amazed at the speed in which Nathan climbed, disappeared, and re-appeared after twenty minutes. Nathan cheekily called out to Danny – 'Domino's Pizza delivery!' A bowline had been fashioned at the end of the rope and lowered down, so Danny placed this around his torso and clambered up the shaft while Nathan hauled him out.

As soon as Danny reached the top Nathan suggested they both go somewhere public and safe and de-brief what had just happened. The decision was to go to the closest *McDonalds*. It may sound like a silly idea, but Nathan reminded Danny there are plenty of security cameras in-store and cops and families frequent the restaurants and, this is Australia, not Sicily, no-one guns down families at Maccas! Both men were cautiously excited and collected their cars quickly for the twenty-minute drive to the fast-food restaurant. Neither man saw the black coloured stealth drone rise above the gum trees, assume a height of 300 feet and follow Danny's 4x4. The female operator was incredibly pleased with herself and ordered her driver to keep their black *Ford Everest* 200 metres away - for the time being. 🦎

Chapter 4

CONFRONTATION

Both Nathan and Danny pulled into the highway Maccas at the same time, went in and ordered coffee. Nathan also ordered a large chocolate donut. He gestured for them to sit near the toilets after they had collected their order. This area offered them protection, a safe distance from the front doors, and a room where they could retreat to and fight from; there was also a frosted window in the parents/kiddies change room facing the car park, which could be easily kicked out for an escape. Nathan was always in 'situational awareness' mode, especially when he felt threatened or was unsure of the odds. He had been here on many occasions and instinctively scoped out this site for what he considered his 'special requirements,' like he did to most buildings he always re-visited. Danny looked about the half-filled restaurant quickly, leaned across and blurted his frustrations out to Nathan in a loud voice. *'What the hell is going on and who were those people?'* Nathan paused for a short while after Danny had spoken and explained that the 'people' who had entered the bunker after them were mostly probably one of the Government's secret 'clean up' squads. 'Do you think only America, the Russians and other Governments have goon squads, that not even the military or most politicians know of? We had entered after they had removed the body and they came back looking for other information and to probably secure the site for all time.'

He went on to say he suspected the secret bunker had been a remnant of the latter part of the Cold War, particularly when Australia had concluded its involvement in Vietnam. 'It's amazing what you can do when you compulsory acquire land, like the Government does, announce the area to be an Aboriginal 'sacred site' or dig under the pretext of mineral exploration, in the supposed interest of all Australians.' 'You gotta remember that people and Government were shit scared of an idea called the "Domino Principle," where the military, analysts and the Government thought the Communists would roll down through Asia and take us out.' 'Damn, we even had an infantry Rifle Company at airbase Butterworth in Malaysia after the Vietnam debacle. Although it was publicly presented by Government as training, the Diggers were there to keep the Communist Terrorists in check as well as securing a "Forward Operating Base" (FOB), if needed.' Nathan was on a roll and kept talking, excitedly, at a furious rate. 'I can tell you the Regiment created so many hidden arms and supply caches in Northern Australia and Western Australia because of this fear. We learnt this trick from the wily *Afika Corps* in *World War Two*, who had caches all over North Africa that had been set up by archaeologists in the 1930s. Archaeological digs, yeah right!'

'Why do you think the Government and Army created *Norforce* and the *Pilbara Regiment*?' 'For a while there, the Regiment went full "Lawrence of Arabia" and had troopers learning to ride and care for camels in the strong belief the Northern Australian deserts would be the next battlefield.' Nathan continued to educate Danny on the mysterious and bizarre workings of Government. 'I've even heard rumours that the Government has now quietly recruited thousands of crazy old military guys and Private Military Contractors form Iraq and Afghanistan to take up *Barrett* 50 calibre rifles and act as snipers against any foreign invader. This would slow down the opposition and give our military time to get their act together. In any case, the country is full of these secret bunkers for a host of reasons – science, security, the storage of military assets and keeping people on the down-low. Damn, I've seen old RAAF Mirages completely wrapped in plastic, ready to be used again, in military aircraft hangers in central Australia! *You don't really think all that funding goes to Australia's Olympic program, do you, or schools, hospitals or the building of roads?'* Danny considered Nathan's last words and said, 'yeah, the roads are pretty shit.' Nathan concluded by saying, 'you most probably tripped an alarm and by the time they had put a team together both our universes collided.'

Just as Nathan was about to continue the conversation, a thirty-something woman strode confidently into the busy restaurant. A mousey haired brunette who was attractive in a brooding Rachel Weisz kind-of-way. She wore a dark plum business ensemble and shiny black patent leather shoes. The only jewellery was a thin gold chain that adorned her slender neck, no watch or wedding ring. Three serious looking men appeared just behind her, and they could have passed for clones of one another. The men were physically solid and built like boxing middleweights, wore similar Gazman type casual clothing but all permeated a confidence in their ability to perform any function asked of them. Most probably recruited from the military or police, elite sporting codes or rejects from an Olympic program, they had gone over to the 'dark side' and were now 'hatchet men' for the woman in the dark plum suit. The small but sinister group sat at the opposite end of the restaurant and stared intently at Nathan and Danny.

This made Danny jittery. He hadn't smoked a cigarette for some time and his nerves were bare, he was fidgety like a strung-out junkie, and he began to look like he wanted to get up and run. Nathan leaned across to Danny and whispered in a calm but confident manner, '*keep your shit together* - they are just sussing us out. They want to know who they are up against.' All the while, Nathan's hand remained in his pocket, wrapped tightly around the *Browning*. 'Mate, they won't have a go at us here, too public, be all over the news, not their form. Their *modus operandi* is to mix you a drug cocktail when you're not looking or kill you in an alley and make it look like a robbery gone wrong, – or create a boating accident.' He paused briefly, looked around and spoke with firm assurance to Danny, 'When I nudge your leg under the table, knock your coffee over and make a really big fuss.' Danny's frown signalled he wasn't sure what Nathan's intentions were, but he bided his time to be kicked. The blow came a few seconds later and the coffee was intentionally spilt all over the table, Danny jumped up and carried on, so much so that a young Maccas employee came over to assist with the clean up. Whilst all this was going on,

Nathan had secretly screen shot the woman and her entourage. The woman and her 'hatchet men' thought this was a suitable time to exit and they proceeded quietly and quickly out the door. The time wasn't right to grab Nathan and Danny. Maybe they were satisfied with the information they now had. Maybe they held a belief both Danny and Nathan were 'lightweights' who could be killed at some other time of their choosing. Nonetheless, they were gone in their vehicle before Nathan had crossed the room halfway to identify their ride, but he still felt smug and thought, *you might know what we look like lady but I sure as hell know what you look like and who you represent.*

Nathan told Danny to leave his 4x4 at Maccas, it would be perfectly safe there and to go with him – safety in numbers and all that. He was certain his vehicle hadn't been bugged as he had parked his van in plain view and inline with his position inside the restaurant. It was the ideal time to leave as traffic was building on the adjacent highway and this would afford them some protection and opportunities to throw off any 'tails,' or for their vehicle to be 'taken out.' The engine pitch of the Hyundai slowly increased as they took off. The van might look like a white slug on tiny wheels but with the right driver and motivation it could go very, very fast. Nathan frequently enjoyed passing *BMW* and *Mercedes*

Benz drivers in the van for kicks. He would look at these posers and then say condescendingly - 'high performance cars, low performance drivers.' They travelled for an hour without speaking, with both men trying to grapple, in their own way, with all that had occurred and what they now knew. In a noticeably brief time, the country greenery slowly fell away as the concrete and big city lights appeared. Nathan turned to Danny and said in a cheerful, re-assuring tone, 'I think it's time to visit Uncle Phil.'

Chapter 5

DEAR OLD FRIENDS

Nathan knew it was time to call in some excessively big favours. He had no choice, and he knew he could not go back to the cabin. It was probably trashed or, at least, was under some form of surveillance. He knew Danny's house was probably turned over as well. Nathan was certain the 'opposition' would by now have their names, backgrounds, tax file numbers, dental records, military history, and anything else they wanted, which would be easy with all the information stored in various Government and supposedly 'private' databases. It was time to reach out to the 'brotherhood' – Nathan's extended network of military comrades and security contacts. Nathan chose to park the van in the 'long term parking section' of an underground car park in a major shopping complex in the city and then walk up a floor or two, mingle with the crowd and then depart. They bought some cheap cotton jackets and baseball caps with cash. These they would don before they left the complex, in the dark of the evening for some protection from the elements but primarily to aid concealment. Nathan felt safe in this busy location. Contrary to a widely held belief, not all video, live stream or phone taps can be readily accessed by Government or spy agencies, you only see that happen in *James Bond* movies.

Although tempting, it was more prudent not to call 'Uncle Phil' but to arrive unannounced. The pavement was wet, which contributed to an icy breeze that cut through their flimsy jackets as Nathan and Danny walked the easy ten blocks to Uncle Phil's city apartment. The *art deco* apartment block was owned by Uncle Phil, and he lived in floors two and three of the five block apartment, looking south he had great views of the *Yarra River* and the remarkable *Flinders Street Station*. The top floor was his nightclub. His baby. The bottom floor was rented to independent businesses. Uncle Phil had joined the *Army* with Nathan but left after three years. This recruit was the fittest and fastest soldier the instructors had seen for years – all lean muscle and taut sinew, but the *Army* really wasn't his thing - too much discipline and attitude, especially from people who hid behind their rank. Like most young guys, he went from job to job hoping to find his niche. By chance, Phil had made good and long-lasting friends with bikers from the local outlaw motorcycle club – *The Cossacks*. Phil was a magician with motorcycles and would repair, restore and re-build bikes for club members and the public. Although he wasn't a club member, he earned their trust and they reciprocated by passing business his way and involving him in some of their criminal activities, the usual drugs, guns, prostitution, and stand-over rackets. Over time, Phil had slowly distanced himself from the more nefarious money-spinners and had invested heavily into motorcycle restoration, his building, and the nightclub, but he was still an ally of the local MC. Like the IRA say, 'once in, never out.' Nathan pushed the button of the intercom looked up at the surveillance camera and poked his tongue out. Suddenly, the door flew open and a man, who could easily pass for Nathan's twin yelled out – '*mate......*' in a raucous, happy-to-see-you voice.

Both men strongly embraced and slapped each other fiercely on the back, repeatedly, before being ushered into the apartment. The friendly warmth of the room instantly hit Danny and Nathan. 'Pink Floyd's *'Great Gig in the Sky'* played softly on a turntable in a corner and the room was bathed in soft lighting and warm central heating. The pungent smell of a joint pervaded the large rectangle living space that comprised of three large leather couches and a huge coffee table. Decades before, Phil and Nathan were like brothers, and inseparable. However, we each have a destiny, and nothing stays the same forever. Nathan went north on a posting with the *Army* and Phil followed his hunches. They had lost contact for decades but were re-connected by the 'wonder' of social media. They kept in regular contact but like most ex-military mates they knew when to keep their distance. Nevertheless, there is nothing they wouldn't do for one another. Phil spoke first, in a serious tone, 'So, brother, what can I do for you?' Nathan introduced Danny and proceeded to outline what had occurred in the last twenty-four hours, not leaving out any details, whilst Phil poured the first shots of *Bundy Rum*.

Nathan began, 'As I see it, the only way we are going to get out of this alive is to get backup and to find out who Hamish MacMillan was and what it was he was doing. We must go to the press, put it on the internet, write it in the sky by crop-duster or put it up on the *Goodyear* blimp. *The country needs to know about this and the sort of people their tax dollars are funding. Only this will guarantee our safety.* "Bitchface" in the plum suit knows who we are, that's a certain, and those sorts of people are adept and making people vanish.' Without hesitation, Phil said,

'All I have is yours, brother, just ask. What I will do, is ask my good buddies at the MC to ride shotgun for you desperate boys. I know they will do this without question. They hate cops of all description, bureaucrats nearly as much and will help you out just out of sheer boredom.' Nathan and Danny let out a hearty laugh at the way Phil had made this offer. Phil continued, 'So until tomorrow, my place is yours, *mi casa es su casa*. Let's have a few more drinks, I've got some choice weed and there is a bedroom for everyone. Sorry, no bitches, another time, perhaps?' Nathan reached out and shook Phil's hand with some intensity and by the look on Phil's face he knew Nathan appreciated his efforts but most of all, their enduring friendship.

Danny began to relax as the alcohol and marijuana was taking effect, it was doing him good, as well as the good-humoured conversation over the pros and cons of *Led Zeppelin*, which by now was being played, albeit loudly, on the record player. Nathan paced himself with the alcohol and didn't touch the weed. He heard a faint 'ting' on his phone and saw a text message from one of the many contacts he had reached out to the day before. It read, 'meet you at our favourite coffee shop tomorrow for mornos. Have info that will interest you, Paul.' This information was just what Nathan wanted and needed and he visibly relaxed in his chair. He would meet Paul at 'Café Sicilio' in Lygon St. Carlton at 10 tomorrow for 'morno's or morning tea as 'civvies' call it. He casually informed Phil and Danny of the text and it was Phil who suggested they call it a night. He indicated where they could wash-up and sleep and set the alarm system. Phil had constructed a fortress out of his apartment, mostly because of some of the 'shady' people he knew or worked with. The windows were fitted with heavy gauge steel shutters, security cameras covered all the avenues and exits around the building and the main door could resist an *SAS* frame door charge! He chose the middle floors for their lack of easy access; the time it took to get to his apartment from the ground floor also gave him plenty of warning. Phil picked up his phone before he made for his room and rang the Sgt-at-Arms of *The Cossacks*. The conversation was brief but jovial and as he turned out his bedroom light, he reflected on how good it was to see his old mate again...

Chapter 6

IT'S THE LITTLE THINGS...

Nathan had always been an early riser and this morning was no exception. He decided to cook a generous breakfast for the 'boys.' Bacon, eggs, toast, juice, cereal, and coffee was his specialty, he had it laid on the breakfast table as Phil and Danny stumbled slowly into the kitchen around 8 am. The men talked about life in general whilst the radio played 'Life in the fast lane' by 'The Eagles;' Nathan thought, 'how appropriate.' It certainly felt like life had taken an accelerated turn compared to his usual routine. He had been cruising in his cabin the other day playing guitar, having workouts, and doing all the usual chores and now it was life at warp speed!

In the background, the sound of road works

emanated, annoyingly, from outside. The smell of coffee hung thick in the area as was the feeling of camaraderie. Phil blurted out that he was in the middle of a messy divorce, and he was hoping he wasn't going to be 'taken to the cleaners' by his ex. His wife had caught him flirting, among other things, with some pretty young thing at his nightclub. For Phil, this wasn't the first time... Phil inquired if Nathan was 'looking again' for someone to occupy his life. Nathan didn't say anything but turned his head ferociously towards Phil and he gave him an angry, foul look. Nathan had been married to Veronica, a beautiful English woman for twenty plus years. Tragically, she had developed early-onset Alzheimer's. They had met on a 'blind date' when he first went to the Regiment and he was captivated, in fact, enthralled by her cheeky smile, cute puffy cheeks and charisma. This was a wonder woman. The sort of person animals would congregate to, even in a room full of people. Veronica was the purest and most decent person he had ever met. Sure, life wasn't always rosy, but they were a great team and had a pretty good life together. It had been torture for him to see his beloved wife deteriorate to that of a helpless baby; it was still torture for him to think of all the times he should've been there with his wife when she had been healthy and loving and he had been off somewhere on some goddamn jolly! He would never forgive himself for his selfishness. He had met other women since but convinced himself that 'you only have one soul mate.' Phil turned away, wishing he had never brought up the subject. Danny had been married a couple of times but like so many military veterans, the burden of service is too difficult a journey for a family to navigate and endure and gold prospecting had become his mistress.

Amongst the small talk, Nathan indicated that he wanted to leave at around 9 am. It would only take them 15 or so minutes to get to the café but it was necessary to throw in a few anti-tracking measures in case they were being followed; they also needed some time to recon the café before entering and to identify an exit strategy in case things went 'pear-shaped'. With breakfast finished, Nathan and Danny grabbed their cheap jackets and met Phil near the front door of the apartment. Phil had spent the last five minutes observing the outside of his building via his surveillance system and it looked like everyday life was going on – shoppers on the prowl, people going about their business and workmen digging up a road. Angrily, he thought to himself, *'there is always some bastard in Victoria digging up a road!'* He turned to Nathan and said, 'Mate, I'm waiting on a confirmation call from *The Cossacks* who will meet you in Carlton around 9:30'. Nathan and Danny thanked Phil again for his hospitality and unfailing assistance at such a critical time and warned him to take care as he was now intertwined in their affairs. After backslaps and hugs all-round, Nathan and Danny walked the Victorian tiled stairs down to the ground floor. Nathan tried to avoid lifts as they are havens for ambush. He knew his fixation with personal security made people uneasy, but he didn't care. His obsession had kept him and others alive in the past.

They emerged on the street to find it drizzling, plain cold and dour. 'Typical bloody Melbourne,' Nathan thought. He then quickly and expertly scanned the area to identity any immediate and possible threats. Nothing out of the ordinary so far. He then re-scanned the streetscape and saw four workmen going through the motions of erecting barriers and running a large yellow compressor and he thought, 'these guys look too fit and work too fast to be road crew and their uniforms look too clean.' Not the usual longhaired, grotty, semi-intelligent slobs that work on your average road gang! He focussed his gaze to the 'stop and go' woman and realised simply from her body shape, composure, and facial outline that this was 'Bitchface,' even though she donned a safety helmet, work clothes and wore a football scarf around her mouth. *Nathan instinctively drew the Browning at the same time the 'road crew' knew their cover had been blown;* they drew their weapons – *H&K MP5s*, the shortened K variant. A taller and more solidly built workman produced a small but weighty 5.56 *Minimi* light machine gun, complete with paratrooper folding stock and box magazine from a large waterproof sports bag and commenced firing - the muzzle producing a bright orange flaming ring when it spat bullets.

Nathan ushered Danny back into the immediate safety of the apartment lobby as *bullets rained down and around their feeble position*, ricocheting off the brickwork and smashing windows. The firing of the automatic weapons, especially the light machine gun produced a 'jack hammer' noise: *thump, thump, thump*, as well as a *sharp cracking sound*, like the manipulation of a drover's leather bullwhip, as the bullets passed, perilously overhead. Nathan's *Browning* bucked in his hand as he double tapped one of Baker's crew. As the man fell, like a bleeding sack of potatoes, he aggressively thought, *'I bet you wished you had picked a better fire position!'* The loss of one of their team had the desired effect and they madly scattered to seek safety in and around their manufactured road works. They recommenced their assault, some took the opportunity to change magazines, slapping forward the cocking handle on their matt black German submachine guns. Danny had instinctively rung Phil who decided to send the lift down to the lobby. It was their only re-course currently and Nathan was on to his second, and last magazine.

The lift hadn't arrived – they never do when required, and *time was running out!* In 30 seconds, they would be *shot dead or over run!* If Nathan was lucky, it would descend to hand-to hand combat and a glimmer of survival. Suddenly, the unmistakable roar of big *Harley Davidson* engines invaded and amplified the narrow city street and *The Cossacks* appeared - to their rescue! The bikers brandished an array of handguns and automatic assault weapons – *Glocks, Sigs* and *AKs* and they knew instantly where to direct their fire and rage. Straight away their influence in the firefight took toll of one of the other workmen and they wounded another. 'Bitchface' screeched a series of orders and the work crew quickly picked up their fallen and made for their black SUVs in the nearby lane. Showing great anticipation, three *Cossack* members had positioned themselves at the getaway end of the street and opened fire. The SUVS charged down towards them, all weapons blazing. One of the MC members fell from this onslaught while the other two sought immediate shelter. 'Bitchface,' driving the lead SUV, crashed through the parked bikes, and deliberately targeted the head of the biker that had been slain. Danny would never forget the *booming* sound of the biker's head going '*pop*,' like a *burst brown paper bag* or the sight of bone and brains *becoming mush and a by-product of the road and pavement*. Here was a woman, thought Nathan, who didn't get her job because of some 'woke' campaign, BS 'affirmative action' program, or quota system for females. She had proved she was as conniving, dangerous, and vicious as the next man and *not to be taken lightly.*

As quickly as the battle commenced it subsided just as fast. Mad Dog, the tattoo festooned and bearded Sgt-at-Arms, introduced himself to Nathan just as Phil and Danny were emerging, sheepishly, onto the street. Nathan shook his hand firmly and said, 'Mate, thanks for your help but you better get your boys out here before VicPol arrives.' Mad Dog replied, 'no worries, we'll let it slip with the media that we had a beef with a rival crew. The cops mightn't fall for it, but Mr and Mrs Joe Public will, and life will be back to normal in a day or two.' Phil embraced his biker friend in the customary biker hug and thanked him again for saving his friends. Mad Dog called out as he rode off with his crew, 'we'll be around Carlton, keeping a low-profile but we'll be close, if you need us, just call.' As they were riding away, he reiterated the offer to Nathan by making the phone gesture with his hand and held it up to his face. Other club members had carried off the fallen biker and damaged motorbikes and the street was at it was before, except for some building barricades, a hissing compressor and small bone fragments in the gutter. Phil spoke to Nathan,

'Mate, I was lucky to call Mad Dog as he was en route to Carlton and close by.' Nathan didn't say anything but hugged Phil and said, *'we best be off. I don't want you to get into any trouble. And please be careful with these vicious arseholes about!'* He offered Phil his *Browning*, but Phil flashed a *Glock 19* from inside his jacket. And on that, Nathan and Danny slowly jogged down the street, caught a cab, and headed off towards Carlton. Not too far away, a black spy drone rose above the street and followed the cab...

Chapter 7

MORNING TEA IN CARLTON

All the while they sat in the taxi, Nathan thought about how they could have been compromised. He instantly discounted any of his friends and associates he had contacted via email because he always utilised a 'code' and a sophisticated computer firewall system on anything controversial. As it was, he hardly made any calls on his phone. Too damn risky. The internal GPS was always turned off and he didn't use it all that much; many a time *he left the damned annoying thing behind!* Nathan did not believe they had been tracked using planted devices, as the opportunity had not presented itself to bug his vehicle, their bodies, or personal accoutrements. So, the only other option was some form of aerial surveillance or vehicle plate recognition. He knew there were sophisticated drones that the Police and Fire Brigades used in the course of their duties and the military were using these sneaky buggers for combat operations. Facial recognition software had developed so much so that only a few facial identifiers where necessary to pinpoint Criminals, Terrorists, Paedophiles or to locate lost children via street 'security' cameras. The Police also parked Government vehicles fitted with special cameras to identify vehicles that were unregistered or had drivers with outstanding warrants.

Nathan thought about how we had all unwittingly assisted the Government to harvest and store this information by volunteering our personal identification, images and contact details and we instantly updated our descriptions and information at the Government's beck and call. Private firms, clubs and enterprises had also been roped into this deception. Why would or should a Rugby League Club or even your local Doctor have the need for such detailed and exhaustive information? The nail in the coffin will be when Australia becomes a 'cashless' society. You won't be able to scratch yourself without the Government knowing where you are, what you've bought, what you're doing and how you're doing it. They will input this information into some computer algorithm to exercise further trends, exert further control and maintain suppression. The Orwellian dictatorial 'Big Brother' society finally realised in the 'Lucky Country.' *Who would have thought?*

Such in-depth information had become a double-edged sword: benevolent in its general intent but malevolent when placed in the wrong hands. Some people had thought Nathan was paranoid, a wacky recluse but he had seen too much, knew too many sinister people and read too widely to dismiss such notions. He wasn't the only person who thought this way. Historically, every country has its spy agencies: MI5, MI6, NKVD, KGB, NSA, CIA, and the list goes on. Australia has ASIO and ASIS. But there are dark cells within all these agencies, rogue elements and dangerous people driven by personal agendas. As well, there are just some things State and Federal Governments don't want you to know. The public is naïve to think this country doesn't have agencies modelled on its foreign counterparts and their despicable ways of doing 'business.'

As they exited the taxi on Lygon Street, Nathan knew he had to be more careful, these people weren't amateurs he was dealing with, and the stakes were getting higher all the time. First, a dead scientist and now a shoot-out in broad daylight on a Melbourne City Street. What next? Both men walked down busy Lygon Street until they faced the public hotel, across the road on the corner of Elgin Street. Quickly crossing the road, they briskly walked in and followed the long hall to the outside toilets at the rear of the premises. Nathan quickly looked around and said to Danny, 'follow me.' Nathan jumped the fence to the right into a small tree shaded yard with Danny on his heels. He jumped the next fence, again to the right and was in the rear garden pergola area of Café Sicilio. A waitress was cleaning up the breakfast mess from some earlier patrons and was visibly startled by the intrusion. Nathan smiled at her and cheerfully stated, *we got lost.* They walked into the noisy café that reeked with the smell of freshly ground coffee and came upon Paul from behind. 'Sorry we're late,' Nathan announced, 'we had some issues along the way.' Danny was introduced to Paul, and they all sat down. A waiter appeared and coffee was ordered; Nathan also selected a chocolate éclair. Whilst they waited for their drinks, Nathan filled in Paul on what had occurred over the last few days. In the meantime, the spy drone flew about Carlton frantically attempting to identify Nathan and Danny's whereabouts.

None of what Nathan had said fazed Paul. Paul Burton was ex-police and had worked in most branches of Victoria Police: *Motorcycle Unit*, *Special Operations Group* and *Criminal Investigations*. He had also been a reservist in the Commandos and was a third Dan black belt in *Kyokushin* Karate. He had 'worked' all the 'mean streets' of Melbourne and left the force when knuckling crims wasn't popular anymore. The police force had rolled over to 'community expectations' and like the dinosaur, officers like Paul were relics of the past. And the Government wondered why public crime and social disorder was on the rise? Paul now made his living locating, buying, and selling antiques, militaria, and information. Like Nathan, he had kept close to his contacts in the State and Federal police forces. For Nathan, his fee would be the price of a coffee. Paul began the conversation by explaining how Prof. Hamish MacMillan had been connected with the atomic testing in central Australia during the late 50s and early 60s as a young and brilliant scientist. He was also involved in the 'over-the-horizon' surveillance radar, which Australia employed at Exmouth in Western Australia, at the 'Harold Holt Communications Base,' which was primarily run by the American military. He was working on low yield nuclear weapons that could be shielded by electromagnetic forces, therefore limiting danger to our military and damage to the wider environment.' '*Selective nukes*, if you will, shielded by a cone of safety.' 'I know this all sounds sci-fi, but the professor was at the forefront of this development,

working with a number of Government agencies and his university when he suddenly went missing.' A waitress appeared with their order and the men went silent. Nathan sat and stared at his coffee and added two sugars to it. He thought it sounded far-fetched, but Australia had produced some real geniuses over the years, people like Nobel Prize winner Florey, and the nation had invented highly sophisticated gadgets like the aircraft 'black box' and Wi-Fi. The 'Hills hoist' and *Vegemite* wasn't the nation's only principal achievements! Nathan finished stirring his coffee and slowly looked up at the two men. He looked at them intently, paused for two seconds and quietly stated, 'Did you know that Hitler had a penchant for éclairs? Not too many people know that.' '*Fuck Hitler*, have you been listening to what I just told you,' Paul said

with some annoyance. Nathan just smiled and Danny looked away, trying hard not to laugh. After regaining his composure, Paul then mentioned that the Professor didn't have any family living but there was a close friend, a Dr. Maxwell Ghent, who is still alive; he had only just retired from this field of work. He also had a country Victoria address, which he passed to Nathan in a note. Like Phil, Paul offered all assistance to Nathan and Danny – 'please, call me, anytime.' The coffee and cake were soon devoured, and Nathan left a 50-dollar note on the table. Paul was meeting some clients at the café and was going to stay.

All three men rose, shook their hands, and said their goodbyes. Just as he turned and started walking, Nathan stopped and went back to Paul. 'Mate, I've got a screen shot of the crew that's been chasing us. Paul looked at the grim faces in the phone's screen and then looked up, any cheerfulness having drained from his face. He went on to say that he recognised a few of the men, ex-military, and ex-cops, who worked in the Middle East, the Philippines, Nigeria, and most of the world's other shit holes.

The woman he recognised as Madison Baker, who he had come across on a secondment to the Federal Police. She had since moved on to a covert department in Government intelligence called the *Agency*. Those in the job called her 'Ma Baker,' after the vicious American gangster matriarch. This wasn't a term of endearment. Baker was one dangerous bitch. Her rise in the intelligence sector was astounding. Not only had she outperformed many of her male peers, but it was also rumoured she slept with anyone, got dirt on anyone, and would do anything to anyone just to get the top job. Being a 'hatchet lady' was just another rung on the way up. *'Gee, what you have to do to break through the glass ceiling,'* Nathan said with a half-smile. The two men further nodded at each other, nothing else had to be said. Nathan and Danny walked outside as the midday throng trundled up and down the busy Carlton Street. Nathan turned to Danny, let us walk a bit, I have some serious thinking to do...

Chapter 8

PICKING
YOUR MARK

The two men quickly skipped across the street and headed towards Lygon Central, a small shopping centre with one of the major food stores and some boutique shopping outlets. He knew they were 'dead men' if they came up against 'Ma Baker's' crew again - especially as they were on their own, but he wanted to take the heat off Phil and the bikers. He had bought a copy of the 'Women's Weekly' magazine and had rolled the thick publication until it resembled a small baton; this he could use in conjunction with the *Browning*, if need be. They needed time to lay low, come up with a plan or two and find out where Dr. Ghent was living. Danny knew Nathan was thinking intently and sat quietly. He carefully scanned the shopping centre for any threat, to make himself useful. Nathan

meticulously watched the shoppers coming and going for some time until he carefully picked his mark. An old Italian gentleman with a wrinkly, tanned and worn face and equally worn clothes exited from the food store with a small mesh bag of groceries. He slowly walked to the centre's back entrance and unleashed his small terrier from the railing. He took exceedingly small dottery steps as he negotiated the back lane, away from the shopping precinct, all the while speaking to his dog, 'Benito' as he went.

Nathan stood up and nodded to Danny for them to go. Nathan was adept at judging character. He learnt this skill very early on in the military. He chose the old Italian by his shabby appearance, lack of groceries and pet, which signalled to Nathan that he most likely lived on his own, his wife probably having long passed, and the level of threat was minimal. They casually followed the old Italian on the other side of the street for around 400 metres before the man halted outside a rusting wrought iron gate, by a terraced cottage and fished in his pockets for his house keys. *Nathan swiftly crossed the street, saddled up behind the man,* and said in a charming voice, 'here, I'll help you with your shopping.' Nathan grabbed the man's trousers in the small of his back and frog-marched him to the door. Before he had even a slight chance to remonstrate or the terrier a chance to react,

Nathan had snatched the keys out of the wrinkly hands, opened the door, guided the man and his dog inside, and proceeded straight ahead to the kitchen area of the house - all in a matter of seconds. He finished the drill by saying, 'Danny, close the door.' Danny was stunned. Nathan forcefully put his hand over the old man's mouth. The old dog attempted to jump and bite Nathan, but he pistol-whipped the pooch with the solid *Browning*, the dog now lay in a tight ball, whimpering in a corner. 'Okay, old man. You speak English?' The man slowly nodded yes, terribly frightened by the aggression to him and the violence towards his animal. Nathan continued, *'I will ask you a series of questions, you give me the right answers, and no-one gets hurt, capisce?'*

In the vein of an interrogation, Nathan enquired if anyone else lived there, was he expecting anyone, what was his night routine and what he did in the morning; was he expecting 'meals on wheels' or anything like that. He concluded by saying in a more menacing tone, 'we are only visitors for a few hours, we just need some space, that's all. I am not here to harm you, *but I will viciously hurt you, your fucking dog and anyone who comes here, if necessary.'* The old man understood and nodded his head. Nathan slowly released his hand and the man nervously sat down, quiet, and obedient in a wicker chair, an old portrait of Jesus adorned the wall above him. Here was the desired effect of Nathan's terrorism – stunned obedience! Danny looked at Nathan for answers to all this but Nathan's *'don't say a fucking word'* aggressive look prevented him form uttering a syllable. 'Go and check the rooms,' Nathan said angrily. Grabbing a house to bunker down in was standard operating procedure (SOP) in Iraq if things went to shit. *Lock it down, fight it out and wait until the cavalry arrives.* If nothing else, a place to make your last stand. Nathan wasn't happy that he had to resort to this type of action and treatment of the old gentlemen. However, the home invasion would give Nathan time to plan, and he needed a plan A, B and C, the way things were going. It would also take some of the 'heat' off Phil.

Fatigue was beginning to settle in, and Nathan felt slightly dehydrated. They had been on the go for a couple of days now and the repetitious waves of adrenaline was taking its toll. As the shaken old man sat in his chair, with one hand resting on the thinning hair on his head and the other stroking his submissive dog, Nathan went to the kitchen faucet, took a glass, and drank nearly two litres of water. Danny walked in and helped himself to some of the cool fluid. Nathan ushered his directions for the evening, 'I'll take the first watch for four hours, you better get some sleep. This old bloke doesn't go anywhere except to rack out on the couch in plain view or to take a piss and you watch him do that. *If the dog goes off its tree, club it!* We will leave early in the morning when I have more information and a plan. Just put today behind you.' Danny saw an element of Nathan's persona that he had never witnessed before, and if he was honest, it slightly frightened him. But he did realise that Nathan's SF pedigree cultivated a 'do what you need to do, when you have to do it' philosophy. He relaxed in one of the old man's well-worn chairs and slowly closed his eyes. He was asleep in seconds.

Chapter 9

TIME TO MOVE

The evening had passed without incident. Nathan had delicately placed and balanced some of the fine China plates, cups, and saucers he had found in the kitchen precariously against doors and windows as additional security, potentially for those within and most certainly for those on the outside. It was crude but the noise would have woken the dead! Nathan let Danny continue sleeping as he sought a way out of this mess. The old man had slept through the night, cradling his dog. Fear leads to worry; worry leads to exhaustion and profound sleep. He woke Danny and once he was cognisant of his surroundings, Nathan spoke in a quiet tone so only he could hear, 'Okay, we'll leave here in 5 minutes, whilst it is still dark. I've rung Mad Dog and he will rendezvous with us at the park, 6 streets away to the north. He will take you to their clubhouse for safekeeping. It is better this way; the two of us are a bigger target. Together

we can be used as leverage against one another, if captured. Phil has left a motorbike, three more streets away from the park to the east and I will take that and meet up with Brian Leyland. He has Intel on Ghent. *Any questions, doubtful points?'*

Nathan had checked the house for phones during the night and had cut the phone lines; he didn't want the old man ringing the cops or a friend the moment they trotted out. With Danny's movement, the old man had slowly woken up. Nathan told the old Italian not to go running for help the moment they walked out. Just to make sure, he bent close to the old man's ear and whispered, 'If the cops get us, I will, this man or another friend of mine will come back and give you and your dog a Sicilian necktie, *you do know what that means don't you?'* With this direct and menacing comment, he stood back and stared deeply into the old Italian's eyes. The frail, old man looked back into Nathan's eyes briefly and then swiftly looked away, he knew Nathan wasn't bluffing.

It was nearly five in the morning and the neighbourhood birds were starting to register their presence with a cacophony of shrills and whistles. Any lights in the house had been extinguished and Nathan peered with intense concentration into the shadowy half-light of the street for movement and danger.

Without warning, Nathan said to Danny - *'let's go.'* The two men were outside before the old man could register, they were leaving, not that he could do anything. He sat semi-paralysed in the kitchen, drained, and stunned from the night's tension, not really knowing what to do next. Their destination was 10 minutes away. Nathan began walking slowly, then faster until his legs had slightly warmed up, if he had to run, he didn't want to run cold. He had his share of soft-tissue injuries over the years, and like his *'67 Fastback*, he was slow to get moving but impossible to stop once warmed up. The streets were wet and mostly empty except for a few people on their way to work. They made it to the park in 8 minutes. Mad Dog had been waiting and had secured the park area with his crew; they hadn't brought the bikes this time but instead two Ford Transit vans – one for any passengers and the other carrying biker muscle and biker weapons. After the obligatory biker hug, Nathan quickly farewelled Danny, with a strong handshake, and his entourage and made his way to Phil's motorbike, some streets away. Time was of the essence. He ran at a good pace to bridge the distance and came across a Jet-Black *Triumph Bonneville* parked by the roadside; it was the newer version – electronic ignition instead of the old kick-start mechanism. The keys were hidden behind the rear licence plate, as Phil had promised. Not the fastest bike, but tough, dependable, and good fuel economy.

It was a *Triumph*, the motorbike made to look like a German bike, which negotiated the obstacle jumps in the movie, 'The Great Escape.' So, that tells you something about their abilities. On starting, the motorbike rumbled without the loud pretentiousness of a biker's *Harley Davidson*. The motorbike even looked classier than your average Harley, exuding a mechanical and stylistic confidence that was understated, but sexy. Nathan wriggled on the long seat until he was comfortable and then put on his black full-face helmet and leather biker gloves. He paused, took another look at his immediate surroundings, and then made a mental note of the route to where he would marry up with Brian Leyland. The bike started first time and Nathan took off. The bike accelerated through the gears effortlessly until all Nathan could see in his mirrors was the diminishing view of the city. As the bike sped on its way, it not only created a spatial but a mental distance from the dramas of the past few days. Nathan's focus was now on the coming days and what lay ahead... 🦎

Chapter 10

CATCH UP
IN THE COUNTRY

Nathan had agreed to meet Brian by the road, 10 minutes away from his bush block, which was on the eastern side of the central goldfields. He was only a minute or so away from the meeting point and wished he had more time to savour the majestic *Triumph*. He longed for the feeling of pure freedom that comes with a cruiser motorbike that you just don't get in a car; the grand vista of the open road viewed from the solitude of your helmet; the forces of nature tugging at your clothing and skin and the 'at one with the machine' feeling of pure exhilaration. He could see Brian's car and caravan in the distance and geared down the bike. Nathan stopped about five metres away, took of his helmet and walked over to Brian, who was resting against his car, smoking a cigarette – *as always*.

At first glance, the image of Brian, his dilapidated jalopy and his decrepit caravan wouldn't inspire anyone to think here was an intelligent man, a former Army Warrant Officer, and a font of information regarding the country's spy and security agencies. Brian had been married but his union also broke down due to service life. The sad thing was he hadn't seen his children in twenty years, nor was he interested in renewing his status as a father. A true stereotype of a bitter and twisted old man.

The two men shook hands, and it was Brian who initiated the conversation, 'As luck would have it, Ghent is about thirty minutes north of us and lives, semi-retired in a small country town called 'Green Hills,' of around 1500 inhabitants. I rang his home phone number purporting to be an insurance agent in the area. Through our conversation, I received enough clues to know it was Ghent and he was going to be there this afternoon and evening. He concluded his report by saying, *'Fucking academics, they are so naïve!'* Nathan said, 'Well done,' and suggested they go for a brew and discuss a quick plan for their meeting with Ghent. 'Let's go to 'Caroline's Coffee Caravan,' which is only minutes away. They could get something decent to eat and refreshing to drink, have a chat and be in better shape for tonight's 'activities. Nathan remarked, 'I also need to speak with Caroline as I have a small job for her....' They set off in their rides and travelled the short distance to the coffee caravan site. Caroline had her large silver airstream caravan parked in the blue stone gravel car park by the busy main road. The caravan had been modified to serve as a small but efficient kitchen. It had detachable red and yellow octagonal signage on the caravan's side that announced her business in large black and bold cursive lettering – *'Caroline's Coffee Caravan,'* and what food and drinks were being offered. The hectic road normally catered for interstate truckers, grey nomad caravan types and day-trippers to the country. Caroline was just finishing serving a truck driver burger and fries as Nathan and Brian arrived. Caroline exited the van and ran over to Nathan, giving him a big girly hug. They had been friends for many years, since when Caroline had worked in aged care and had helped nurse Nathan's elderly Mother. This seemed like an eon and a world away now. But the bond was created then and they couldn't do enough for each other.

Caroline was around 15 years younger than Nathan, a sassy attractive brunette in a Drew Barrymore 'Charlie's Angels' sort-of-way and had grown up in a large country family, where you give as good as you get. She had an enormous heart and was always helping those less fortunate; you couldn't measure her generosity. There had been men in her life, but she hadn't found 'Mr Right.' With a broad grin and white flashing teeth she said she was so happy to see 'Nath' as she called him, but only gave a cursory glance and hello to Brian. Caroline had met Brian at the funeral of Nathan's Veronica and thought he was uncouth, a dirty old man and couldn't fathom why Nathan would want anything to do with him. Brian knew Caroline didn't like him and the feeling was mutual. Men, especially ex-military, see qualities in people and value their friendships differently to women and here was the proof. It was most probably the bond of military service; having seen a lot of crazy things and done a lot of crazy shit together.

'Here's the thing, Caro,' as he affectionately called her, 'we have to go and see a man this evening and there maybe some nasty people who might pass this road junction looking for us, they may even come up the road from my place. You won't be able to miss these characters as they look like they came out of the movie "Men in Black," dark SUV and shit like that, except there is an evil bitch that leads these war dogs. *Please, be extremely careful,* but I would appreciate a veiled text a couple of minutes after they pass by, letting me know what road they've taken.' He smiled at her and pleaded, 'can you please do that for me?' Caroline asked, 'What if they use a helicopter?' Nathan reiterated they will come by SUV, no need to report flight plans or to turn up on Government radar, all subtle and no need for a grand entrance. This is what Nathan would do. Besides, half the country drives an SUV, less conspicuous. Caroline could see the logic in what he said. What he didn't mention was they were arrogant and had just fought it out with some extremely dangerous bikers, but he knew their arrogance would be their downfall. A nod of the head and a kiss on the cheek meant she wouldn't let him down.

Nathan ordered his usual coffee and some snacks and chatted to Caroline while the order was being prepared. Brian sat alone at a bench like some petulant child and chain-smoked cigarettes. Nathan could smell the greasy pungent stench of the 'chop chop' tobacco he was smoking and thought how it was bad enough to smoke but these 'coffin nails' would certainly put Brian into an early grave. It suddenly occurred to him that this may be what Brian was aiming for, an easy way out. The meal was soon prepared, and it was time to work out their strategy for the meeting with Ghent.

Firstly, they would travel to *Green Hills* individually. They would then recon Ghent's home and the surrounding area and make their move on dusk. If it got dark and they hadn't located their subject, Nathan would use the night vision scope he had bought some time ago and further recon the place. If they found Ghent in the open, they would 'convince' him using their friend *'Mr. Browning'* to come with them for a chat. That is if he didn't wish to come of his own accord. They would endeavour to assure him that's all they wanted, some chat and plenty of answers. If they had to play 'rough,' so be it. The many other scenarios, like friends and family present, dogs, and kids, they would play by ear. *They just had to get to Ghent first before the opposition!*

Caroline always had the radio on in her caravan. Suddenly, the cheerful strains of *Olivia Newton-John* ceased as a news headline blasted out over the radio waves. A male voice barked the following bulletin: '6 members of the Cossack Motorcycle Club have been gunned down on the streets of Melbourne by an alleged rival club. A number of bystanders have been wounded and police are investigating a possible turf war.' The voice trailed off, babbling about other aspects of the incident and other news but Nathan, Caro and Brian just sat at the bench, speechless. Nathan's phone suddenly rang, which brought him back to life. It was Phil and he told Nathan that Danny had been slain, along with the bikers, many of whom were involved in yesterday's street battle. It was obvious that a skilled adversary had ambushed them. They didn't know what hit them. It was a wonder that not all were gunned down. Mad

Dog and a few others had survived and said it had been the same crew they had encountered outside Phil's apartment block.

Phil had taken up permanent residence at MC headquarters until this all blew over. He paused and then said, 'mate, don't beat yourself up, Danny was a big boy, he knew what he was involved in,' and in finishing his report, he said, 'take care, I've got your back, let me know if you need anything, brother' and then hung up. '*Fuuuuck*', was all that Nathan could register, loudly, at this moment. He knew this was Baker's retribution. He also knew this said something about the psyche of the woman; she didn't like losing and had to impose her authority. Surprisingly, with this therapeutic expletive and a few moments to reflect in stunned silence, Nathan's anger quickly subsided and he re-focused on the task at hand. He looked confidently at both of his friends. 'Okay, the plan is the still same, *but we have to get our skates on.*' He kissed Caro on the forehead, started the bike and signalled Brian to go.

Vehicles and men took off for the short drive to *Green Hills*, leaving dust, noise, and a waving Caro behind them. Nathan had only tunnel vision now, like on Ops, do whatever necessary to achieve the mission but now he was committed to seriously hurt some people for the death of a close friend and the bikers. Besides solving the mystery of Hamish MacMillan, he was on an irreversible course for some serious payback... 🖋

Chapter 11

A MAN CALLED GHENT

They were at the rural outskirts of *Green Hills* before they knew it. The single lane country road had been clear, both ways. The men had decided to arrive in town a few minutes apart, so as not to make it look too suspicious. There was a reason for that. Whilst they may look like bumpkins, small town country people are adept at reading people and situations. As the old saying goes, 'they're not as stupid as they look.' In the case of the two strangers, Nathan looked like a guy on a day's bike ride, whilst Brian came across like any other 'grey nomad' on his way to another caravan site. As luck would have it, Ghent lived on the edge of town. Brian drove his caravan to the caravan courtesy station that resided by a small reservoir and discharged the caravan's septic tank

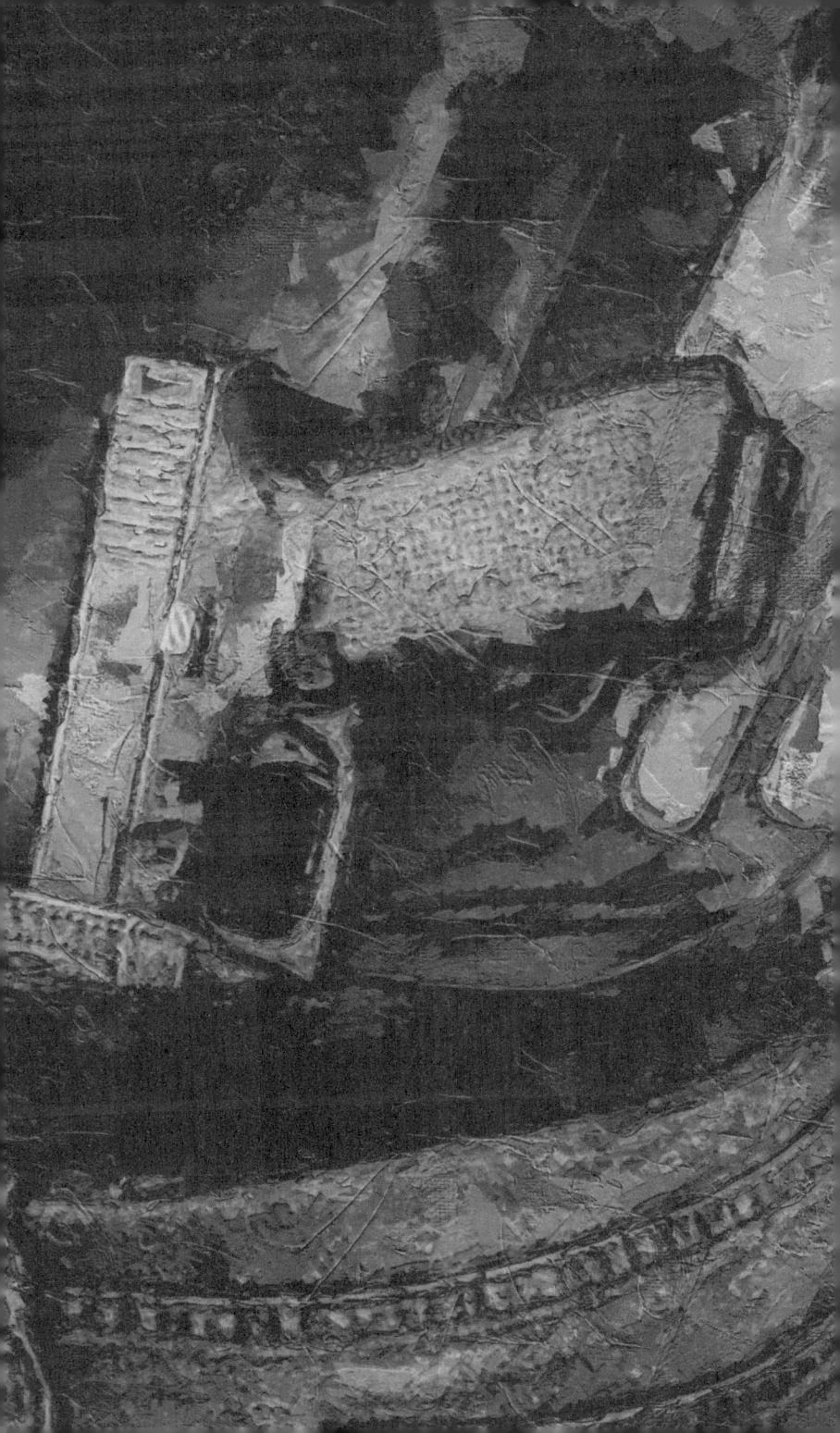

while Nathan re-fuelled the motorbike at the one petrol station. On completion, he rode the powerful bike around the town, like a tourist, and then to a parking spot at the reservoir. He took out his mobile phone and pretended to make a call.

Outside of a few people walking the reservoir's circular foot/running track, the area was empty. Ghent's residence was only minutes away, it was on dusk, and the temperature was dropping. A few kangaroos had ventured out in the evening and were feeding on native grass. Nathan looked across at Brian for 10 seconds and then headed towards Ghent's house, stealthily on foot, which resided on a bigger than average block. The property was the size of an acre. Nathan had casually ridden past the house when he entered Green Hills and saw the plain wooden letterbox, which simply announced 'D. Ghent' in glossy, black writing. The rear of the residence backed onto the reservoir, or more accurately was 50 metres away from the gravel walking track, whilst the front of his house presented itself to one of the quiet side streets of the town, which was built on a grid system. All the blocks were bigger than you would see in Melbourne and neighbours were at a considerable distance from one another. Nathan walked slowly to within 15 metres of the house, halted and purposefully went down on one knee behind a native shrub. Brian followed this patrol pattern and took position by a Wattyl bush to Nathan's right. They employed the 'one foot on the ground method' so Nathan and Brian could stealthily bug out if they were spotted, or more importantly return fire if attacked by Ma Baker and her crew.

The lights were on in the house, and they could see Ghent was washing dishes by the kitchen window. It appeared as if no one else was present in the home. Only one car was parked in the driveway. On seeing this, Nathan thought it was time to be decisive and he noticed an automatic sprinkler system that normally watered the backyard. He crept forward and turned it on. Water began cascading around the back lawn in huge jets, all the while making a shoosh-shooshing noise. Straightaway, there were quick footsteps in the house and a man's voice cursed. The back-fly screen door flew open, and Ghent appeared and walked as quickly as he could down the rear steps, on his way to the water tap and the automated watering system shut off system. As his hand turned off the tap, Nathan materialised through the shadows from behind and gripped the man's withered left wrist left, just above his watch, with his strong left hand. He placed the *Browning's* muzzle against the man's right temple and simply stated, '*don't say a fucking word.*' Nathan used the force of the wrist grip and gun pressure to the temple manoeuvre to usher Ghent back into the house;

Brian saw the move, anticipated the outcome, and quickly followed the two men into the house. The man was pushed down unceremoniously onto a vinyl seat and steel framed kitchen chair and, for the present, was too stunned to say a word. Brian quickly walked in, locked the back door, and scanned the backyard for 20 seconds through a white mesh curtain - all was quiet, not even a dog barked.

Nathan introduced himself and Brian and reassured Ghent that they were only there to discuss Hamish MacMillan. They hadn't had time for pleasantries, which is why the 'strong arm' tactics had been employed. Nathan outlined how Danny had found MacMillan dead and rotting in the bunker. MacMillan and his dog had since gone missing and there were ruthless Government agents now attempting to 'sanitise the situation,' a well-used euphemism for killing all those connected with the principal target; they were most possibly on their way to *Green Hills* now so no time for idle chit-chat. On hearing his old friend's name, Ghent perked up in his chair and calmly stated, 'what is it you wish to know?' Nathan wasn't trying to be a smartass but announced, 'well, basically all you know about MacMillan, how do you think he ended up in that underground bunker and what was he doing, in general, would be a good start.'

Nathan inspected this man as he carefully tried to remember events from long ago. Ghent was in his early seventies and besides a few pock marks his complexion was mostly free of blemishes and wrinkles, but he was pale, like he had been born in Europe or was sick in some way. He had spent most of his life in laboratories and classrooms where the only light was fluorescent. Physically, he looked like a man who had used his brains more than his limbs. A 'geeks' body. His clothes were plain and purely functional, not fashionable, again the trappings of an academic life. Ghent paused, took a deep breath, and began his story. Nathan and Brian felt they were in for a long narrative and both men pulled up a chair and sat down; Nathan rested the *Browning* uppermost on his thigh, pointing casually but menacingly at Ghent. Ghent went back to the beginning of his chronicles with MacMillan. Both young and brilliant men had met at academic conferences and were at the same university a few years later. This was in the 1960s. Both men shared the same interests – high-energy physics and alternate energy sources such as nuclear energy and solar power. An equal interest was the 'arms race' and the proliferation of nuclear weapons. MacMillan had been a pioneer in early solar power research, especially in the area of solar incineration. He had grown increasingly frustrated at the lack of Government and corporate funding and the recalcitrant attitude of most politicians to see that solar power was the future of Australia; a future where this unique, clean power would meet all the country's power needs, but only if the program commenced soon. Australia could be the world leader and eventually export its expertise and solar systems to other nations. The country would be able to phase out its dependence on coal and other non-renewable energies, but the Government had to act quickly, or we would miss the 'Solar' boat.

MacMillan's frustration and insistence with politicians and Government put him at odds with his university and his behaviour distanced himself from his academic cohort– he was starting to get a reputation as a 'troublemaker' and a 'quack.' He wrote long, aggressive diatribes to all politicians and frequented all the anti-nuke marches around the country. Instead of teaching his core subjects at the university, he would go off on rants about the 'system' and professed various plans that would make Australia, independent and 'neutral' on the world's stage. The university didn't want him to compromise their reputation, and funding so it was better to show MacMillan the door and pay him a stipend to stay away. The last time he saw MacMillan was over a coffee at the staff lounge, where he stated enthusiastically, he had been headhunted by a civilian 'think tank' that would fund his projects and realise 'all his dreams.' MacMillan pushed a sealed manuscript across the table at Ghent and asked him to keep this for him. *'It might come in handy one day...'* was all he said as he stood up, shook Ghent's hand, and walked out. That was the last he saw or heard of him, until the boating accident. Ghent had a quizzical look on his face and said, 'he didn't even like boats or the water,' so it was a surprise that he had presumably 'drowned,' body missing. Nathan quickly spoke, 'do you still possess the manuscript?' 'In fact, I still do, said Ghent. It is in my study in this house.'

Nathan felt satisfied he wouldn't get 'any tricks' from Ghent, he pocketed his gun and they followed him into his rather large study, which was a converted bedroom. Besides, he could quickly overpower the man if he chose to. Ghent moved a few books on a tall, wide pine shelf and produced the manuscript, still secure with its original binding. It had rested for many years in dust between a copy of H.G. Wells' *War of the Worlds* and Milton's *Paradise Lost*. Both texts had forecast the doom of mankind in contrasting philosophical ways, which made Nathan value the importance of the manuscript so much more. On the face of it, the manuscript didn't look much, a tan faux leather cover and scruffy paper, about 100 pages thick, or thereabouts. The men moved back to the kitchen as one. Nathan's phone 'tinged.' It was Caroline's text – *'Men in Black just passed on main road heading to*

Green Hills.' 'Good old Caro,' Nathan thought, she had come through like he knew she would. They had about 20 minutes up their sleeves, so the time to move was now. Nathan said to Ghent in an urgent tone, 'pack a few things and come with us, we'll get you somewhere safe. There are some dangerous people heading this way, right now.' Ghent slowly shook his head. 'If I die, it will be here. There isn't much these people can do to me; I have bone cancer, terminal, and mostly likely a result of the nuclear testing during the 1950s at Montebello. I am old, alone and have no family. If they kill me, it will be a blessing. I will try my best not to tell them anything.'

Nathan and Brian could see the rationale in the academic's comments. As they looked at him, they could detect a deep sadness in his eyes and a resolve for the man to be in charge for the final time. This happens to us all. There comes a time in every person's life when he or she is tired and done. Like the aging, worn-out boxer *that just can't get up for the last round.* This was Ghent's time. Nathan spoke quickly but respectfully, 'Okay, if that's the way you want it. Much obliged for your help but we must be off. Don't worry, I promise you, this manuscript will fall into the right hands.' They all vigorously shook hands in a solemn atmosphere of respect and the two men quickly exited from the back door. Nathan and Brian jogged to their modes of transport and headed due north, at speed. They knew all the roads and tracks back to his block, ones that weren't even registered on GPS or standard maps, but they were headed elsewhere... They needed time to read and digest the manuscript. Ghent, sat in the kitchen, looking forlorn and in a slight daydream, his eyes fixed on the tired and scuffed looking black and white chequered linoleum on the floor. He slowly raised a heavy head and listened. The winds had gotten up outside and threatening rain clouds, *like the evil forces in transit*, were moving quickly to *Green Hills* from the south. He slowly stirred himself from the chair, went over to the sink, picked up a glass of water, swallowed 20 *Valium* tablets from a plastic medicine bottle and waited for the coming storm...

Chapter 12

TIME OUT

he plan was simple: head north, lay low for the remainder of the night and for the next day or so and then double-back to Nathan's block. They hit the Murray Valley highway at around one is, just before the tiny town of Gunbower, 30 minutes Northwest of the port town of Echuca. They call it a highway when in fact it is just a two-lane bitumen road. They would continue to Lake Boga, around an hour away and then rest up there at one of the many caravan sites. Distance gave them time and the area opportunities for observation and concealment. The destination also gave them an ace up their sleeve.

Lake Boga had its own unique set of attractions. During the *Second World War* the lake had been utilised by the *Royal Australian Air Force* (RAAF) to train pilots from the Commonwealth to fly Catalina

Flying Boats. It was one of a number of secret bases that sprouted up in rural Australia. For decades, the area had been left to rot and the lake nothing more than a dry salt pan for kids to ride their dirt bikes on. Some bright spark had come up with the novel idea to restore an old Catalina and create a military museum on the original site. The lake was dredged so that it could be used for recreation and to encourage a return of the local flora and fauna. The area now boasts an award-winning winery, sizeable agricultural ventures, and a population of a thousand residents.

Brian had arranged accommodation, knowing they would be arriving in the wee hours, and he knew and could trust the manager as he had stayed there on many occasions. Gus, who not only looked well in his late 60s but cranky 'old' with it, was waiting for them and quickly and quietly escorted them to a 'bush allotment' on the far side of the lake – *one road in and the only road out*, approximately three kilometres from the caravan park entrance. Nathan parked the motorbike first and Brian was not far behind. Having positioned his caravan, Brian threw a 'used' sleeping bag, a bivvy bag and sleeping mat to Nathan, who instinctively brought the bag up to his nose for a whiff. *'You can fucking sleep on the ground, if you don't like it,'* said Brian in an indignant tone. *'Fuck,* said Nathan, *it smells like someone, or something died in this bag.* Do you have any *Vicks VapoRub* so I can bog up my nose from the stench?' They both exchanged the usual 'Fuck offs' and sorted themselves out to catch some sleep. Nathan picked a spot by a tree twenty metres form the caravan, facing the lake. The night was cool but still. No need to keep watch as the outlying terrain was dense, prickly and would make the noise of a *Banshee* if anyone was foolish enough to walk through it at night; they were protected on the other side by the lake.

Anyway, Nathan hadn't slept soundly for years. Age, coupled with military service and leading an adventurous life, had this effect on him and most veterans he knew. It wasn't always about where they went, what they saw or what they did. This was a misconception formed by politicians and the public. A way of re-directing the blame and guilt. A great deal of the posttraumatic stress had been created by the *Army* and Government and not what had occurred in some far-off land. Betrayal in the form of lies, broken promises and fighting bureaucrats for basic entitlements created the most casualties – serving one's country was easy! Nathan would enlighten people with examples of this political deception. He would tell them the longest serving court battle in Australian history concerned the 'Voyager Disaster' where an Australian aircraft carrier in 1964 had collided and sunk an Australian Navy Destroyer with the loss of

82 lives. The Federal Government continues to prefer litigation and complicating the process rather than paying compensation; there are around 130 cases still before the courts. It is akin to tobacco companies who wait for claimants to die so they can get out of their obligation. Then there is the sexual harassment, not just to women who served but men also. What makes the entire system even more incredulous is how successive Governments have 'talked up' the process of assisting veterans but really failed to deliver.

Nathan thought about the latest veteran benefits card, which supposedly gave Veterans discounts, and a way of saying 'thank you' for their service. 'Shit, I can get a better deal going to my local appliance store and haggling a deal on a new computer than what this card can do,' as he told another veteran. This was the Federal Government's way of getting corporate Australia to 'pay it forward' to veterans and for the Government to leave public money in the treasury coffers. It seemed obvious to Nathan that the bureaucratic battles were harder to fight than when he had to do run-through drills in the 'killing house' at Swanbourne. The sad reality was these issues played on the minds of most veterans, daily. 'No wonder veterans are killing themselves,' he thought as he lay toasty warm in his sleeping bag. Nathan was sleepy. He could vaguely make out the water of the lake lapping against the shore in the dim light, but he could feel the waves of tiredness washing over him and before he knew it, he was out. It felt like he had only been asleep a minute or two when Brian woke him, with a slight kick to his foot inside the sleeping bag. It was 9 am. Brian spoke, 'Brew's on'. Nathan scratched his head, dug the sleep gunge out of his eyes and crawled out of his warm sleeping bag, just as Brian passed him a large army canteen cup of steaming coffee. The weather forecast was good for most of the day except for some patchy rain that was expected later in the evening. Nathan sat on a campstool, quietly drinking his brew, and enjoying the early morning sun and its warmth. Brian had arranged for Gus to furnish breakfast, mostly bacon and egg rolls, and sandwiches for lunch. They had plenty of brew gear and Brian also had large supply of cigarettes. That was about as far as they had planned the day, except to sit down and delve into MacMillan's manuscript. Gus's vehicle soon approached and before they knew it, they were chomping down on their delectable breakfast rolls. At any other time, Nathan thought, this would be a great holiday but now was not the time to go on 'vacation.' They made another coffee and Brian settled in with his cigarettes. Nathan would read five pages of the manuscript and then pass then to Brian to read. This is how Diggers normally read the one book that is taken out bush on exercise. It would take the men around 3 hours to properly read the manuscript.

Nathan looked at the pages with an open mind and began to read. He didn't say anything but chose to remain quiet and to discuss the contents at reading's end. Brian could see Nathan's concentration levels were peaking as he appeared to be in another place, such was his focus. Nathan stopped, passed 5 pages to Brian, and resumed the process. This was the pattern for the next three hours. Make a quick brew, have a toilet break, or stand up and stretch. Toward the three-hour mark, Nathan finished and kept quiet so as not to disturb Brian, as he was coming to the end of his reading. Nathan was *stunned* by what he had just read. He sat, slightly bemused, and contemplated its significance, not only to the average Australian but also to the nation and to the world...

Besides the manuscript's content and main points of contention, what struck Nathan so profoundly was the narrative's psychology, which was, at times, disturbing but a true reflection of the genius and mental state of its author. He could sense the inherent frustration in MacMillan's writing and the manuscript's aggressive tone, which traversed from indifference to outright contempt for generational officialdom and its leaders. In the vein of Mein *Kampf*, it traversed from a rational argument to a pleading, beseeching condemnation of the socio-political elites who ran Australia. Brian finished his last five pages, looked up and announced, '*fuck me, this is dynamite.*' Nathan nodded in silent agreement and the two men made another brew and sat down to discuss what they had read, to see, if their thoughts coalesced.

The manuscript had not gone into too much technical detail. It was more a 'grandiose ideas' project, based on a monumental concept, in the vein of a H.G. Wells trope and not the technical sophistication of a Jules Verne treatise. Overall, it was a grand outline of how the Australian Government and people should move confidently forward into the 21st century. It clearly suggested a re-jigging of Australia's relationship with the world powers. MacMillan had produced a litany of examples of how Australian had jumped from one imperial bed into another – namely Great Britain and then the United States. The country's survival was always dependent upon the power and grace of another country. 'Whose turn would it be next to provide the umbrella of safety for this country, China, Japan or Indonesia?' MacMillan prophetically warned.

The solution to this problem or so MacMillan thought was total independence and neutrality, and this could only be guaranteed by the creation of unique weapons and an equally unparalleled power system. As much as nuclear weapons and nuclear power were abhorrent to MacMillan, this was the only way he envisaged Australia casting off the shackles that kept the country slavishly tied to other nations. MacMillan had utilised his atomic testing experience and decades of extensive research to develop a low yield, nuclear hyper-weapon capability that could be controlled with radio wave buffering. The military would be able to register a thermo-nuclear weapon on a target, albeit land or sea based and surround this target with an electronic shielding cone. The development of an advanced solar power system would then be harnessed to destroy the dangerous radiation in the cone via incineration. There would be minimal damage to the environment and the prevention of long-lasting nuclear devastation, like Hiroshima, Nagasaki, or Chernobyl.

Unlike other nations who possessed a nuclear weapons capability as a 'first strike' measure or retaliatory apparatus, MacMillan's system was highly selective, produced minimal environmental damage and the radio wave buffering could also be used to shield Australian cities and targets from nuclear destruction. This system completely changed the leader board in the arms race and made most other nuclear weapons redundant. In a similar vein, it would provide for Australia the 'Strategic Defence Initiative' or 'Star Wars' type program that President Reagan, in the 1980s, had touted for the United States.

The second part of MacMillan's grand scheme was to utilise nuclear and solar power as Australia's long-term power options. MacMillan thought it ridiculous to rely on a single power system. Solar power, on its own is unreliable and costly. It may work as a stand-alone system on an outback farm but cannot cope with city life, manufacturing, and population growth. Besides, the system has its own built-in redundancy and a reliance upon foreign manufacturers. In a similar vein to computers, solar power technology and batteries must be updated continuously - which is an expensive waste of power and resources. This initiative would also eliminate the need to use coal in a domestic and foreign sense. The nation would be able to meet all its power needs without contributing to global warming and, therefore, assist in not destroying the planet. Brian said that he had heard whispers about this defence option twenty years ago when he first went to Intelligence Corps, but most analysts thought it was the stuff of 'Dr. Who.' He said, 'obviously the Government took this seriously and wanted MacMillan out of the picture. But how did he end up dead in a bunker in the goldfields?'

Nathan's cell phone 'tinged' again, and he listened intently to the caller. Brian looked across at Nathan who was nodding his head in agreement to what was being said on the phone. Nathan commented, 'you sure you can pull this off, if needed?' You will only need to be on standby for tonight and tomorrow. Mate, I owe you a big one, thanks. And on that, he hung up. He had intentionally kept the phone call brief as he was convinced now that Ma Baker and her crew were using a multitude of electronic resources to track them down. Little did he know their stay had been paid on Brian's *Mastercard* and Madison Baker had accessed Gus's records.

He told Brian that the call had been from David Jameson, an old RAAF veteran that he had known for over fifteen years. They had met at a dining in night when by coincidence they had joined a priory of the *Scottish Knight Templars* in Melbourne. They were both looking for something novel to occupy their time and thought this would be good for a laugh. There were those in this organisation who took it extremely seriously, but Nathan and David thought it would be a suitable place to meet 'interesting' people and to dine out once a year in their finery. David was a *real Australian character*. He had a lot of history in the military, and was an avid adventurer, like Nathan. He was ten years older that Nathan, but you wouldn't think so because he was so active and young in spirit. David had joined the RAAF in the early sixties to be a pilot and had served in Vietnam in 1965. He took an extended leave from the air force but failed to mention

he had offered his services to the Israeli Air Force and was involved in the *6 Day War* in 1967. He shot down five Jordanian Hawker Hunters over the Golan Heights with his Mirage III. He toured Vietnam again with the RAAF flying the sturdy F4 Phantom fighter/bomber. Like many air force pilots, he went commercial after the war, but that life also became humdrum so he quit and flew anything he could in Rhodesia during the 'bush war' until the country became Zimbabwe in 1980. He stayed in Africa, flying for various anti-poaching organisations, UN relief missions, tourist operators and for ranchers and farmers. He had been with a South African girl for ten years, but the lifestyle became less and less attractive to someone who wanted to settle down and have a family. He always thought it ironic how the appealing things that attract people to one another invariably becomes the catalyst, the wedge, which destroys the union. His girl had thought it so romantic cradling the arm of the famed fighter ace, bush pilot, and Aussie larrikin down the streets of Joburg, but the novelty wore off when the long, lonely nights began to roll into weeks of desolation. So, after one plane and relationship crash too many, David decided to return to Australia after 20 years in Africa.

Unfortunately, David started having severe migraines that prevented him from flying. He did try to teach flying for a while but that made the situation even more frustrating. It was like a cruel tease. Here was a man that was born to fly but could now only assist others to fulfil their dreams. David decided to stay with aviation but decided to build and repair gyroplanes. He had flown this type of craft all over Africa. They were simple to fly, easy to build and had become a boom for budding aviators, as they were affordable; he could test fly them on his property for fun. His experience and knowledge did not go to waste, and he made a good income out of the business. He manufactured the quirky aircraft in the massive sheds he had built on his bush property and would transport them in a small Isuzu truck to clients. The vehicle was of particular use as he could take the aircraft to potential buyers and demonstrate the aircraft's abilities. The clients would get to fly and most times this closed the deal. The business gave David the security he needed in his later years but like Nathan and so many of the people they knew, he was always up for that last adventure, that last thrill to hang his hat on...

Brian looked across to Nathan and said, 'so, what's the plan now?' 'I'm still waiting on some more emails and phone calls before I decide the next move,' said Nathan. *We need some more information on the people who are trying to kill us.* What are their strengths, weaknesses, routine, and intentions? Just like any other enemy, we have ever encountered. I'm trying to build some resources for us in the process. Just taking advantage of our military brotherhood, and all that.' 'What are your thoughts on the manuscript,' said Brian, 'a load of old toss, a scientist's 'wet dream' or do you think MacMillan had something real going on there?'

Nathan took a gulp of a freshly made coffee and outlined his opinion on what he thought of the manuscript and MacMillan's ideas. He also helped himself to one of Brian's chocolate digestive biscuits. It made sense to Nathan that Australia should cut the chord from these associations; relationships that started in friendship but invariably turned into an overlord dynamic. My God, how many wars had Australia fought in the name of empire or some strategic alliance? Damn, we had fought the Boers before Federation, two world wars, jungle wars, and wars in God-forsaken countries where most of the Australian public hadn't even heard of their names, like Somalia or Rwanda. The main legacy from all that were broken veterans and an enduring cost borne by the Federal Government and taxpayer. How many campaigns had ended in disaster – Vietnam, Iraq, Afghanistan? Had the nation's reputation been enhanced or are we seen in some international quarters as the bumbling sidekick to

Uncle Sam? And what is it they say about the definition of insanity - *doing the same thing over and over and expecting a different result?*' The idea of developing a defence capability that divorced the nation from international allegiances and their entanglements wasn't such a bad idea.

As far as alternative powers sources went, moving on from coal wasn't a bad concept either. Nathan wasn't exactly an eco-warrior, but he could see the merit in not relying on an outdated system as well as having a guaranteed backup operation. Hydro electricity hadn't brought the benefits it had promised and was costly to the public, especially since State Governments had sold off State utilities to private enterprise. An idea good in theory but private companies are out to make money, they aren't benevolent societies. They are in it to make a buck. All the Government did was shift what they saw as a burden to private operators and in the meantime, the public is still being screwed.

'Hey Brian,' he said in an inquisitive tone. 'Do you remember a guy called Ernie Bridge, a West Australian politician when he lived over in the West, back in the 1980s. 'The name is familiar,' said Brian. 'Yeah,' said Nathan, 'this guy was a politician who played guitar in parliament and had a great idea whereby the states would pump water from the Ord River up in the north of Western Australia. There is more water up there, around six times the capacity of Sydney Harbour, after the wet season rains. The states could run pipe down to W.A., South Australia and across to the other states and there would be enough water to use and create new and wonderful cities in the desert. Our version of Palm Springs or Las Vegas. Hydroelectricity for everyone! Great idea but all the politicians were concerned with was the cost.' 'Impossible to get an idea like that running today, at today's price the financial outlay would be astronomical,' said Brian. It was a sad indictment for a country so rich with natural wealth and blessed by an educated population that these projects could not get off the ground. Take the United States for instance, there was a need for power and during the Depression, the Hoover Dam was created. The Australian mindset cannot seem to get beyond a monetary figure and the scope of the project whereas the American psyche is more interested with outcomes and long-term benefits. 'You know,' said Nathan, 'Australian cinema could have been bigger than Hollywood. We were one of the first countries to make films, alongside the Lumiere Brothers but decided to distribute movies instead of making them, go figure?' Brian decided to provide his unique assessment of the situation. 'Mate, you know the way the country works. So long as the people or *"sheeple"* (as he commonly referred to them) are happy, the Government can do what they please.' He used the analogy of ancient Rome and how the citizenry had become nothing more than the 'mob' and the mob were easily pleased and kept compliant with the spectacle of the Gladiatorial games. As Brian questioned, 'What's the difference between ancient Rome and our society, nothing from where I stand. So long as the people, the mob, have their football, beer, and public holidays, they will do as they are told.' He further explained this was how State and Federal Government 'manufactured consent.' Give the people some 'feel good' green and gold flag waving moments from the Olympics, beef up the Melbourne Cup or get behind beating the Poms at cricket. The average *schlob* will go along with anything! Add to what Howard did by disarming the country and there you have it, presto, and an inert nation of obedient followers, all thinking that the Government is protecting them. He concluded by saying, *'Joseph Goebbels is alive and well and living in Australia.'* 'This is how you control the nation; this is how you promote multiculturalism; this is how you control the various States during a pandemic crisis!'

Brian was now on a roll, and he mentioned how the media was calculatingly implicit in the deception of the Australian public. Selective news stories and 'info-entertainment,' that created 'heroes' out of average

Australians just doing their job created a 'binary of difference' between those who were now the favoured social groups and those social cohorts not in favour anymore. In the past, this is how the nation coped with threats to a 'white Australia.' These threats go back to 'Kanaka labour' and a fear of the disintegration of Australia as a worker's paradise; the 'red scare' of the Communists or the enduring 'Yellow Peril' tale that would see Australia flooded with Asians. All you had to do was point the finger at someone and that person or group becomes the target. Now, in the inclusive wonderland that is Australia, you just leave out social groups you don't like anymore, you do not mention them, leave them out of social media, commercials, employment, or plots in movies. 'Shit,' said Brian, *this is how we ended up on the scrapheap. No country for old, white men.* Brian spoke of how the 'gender pendulum' had swung too far to the female side. In the name of supposed equality, women now occupied senior positions in the media, especially on the news programs.

His tone was getting more heated as he was getting worked up. 'You can't even find guys represented in commercials and if you do, *they look like idiots who have to be helped out by a woman or some metrosexual wearing a Goddamn man-bun.* The people that make shows like "Beauty and the Geek" should be fucking horsewhipped! All female activities are promoted on par or above those of men's and most industries, notably nursing, paramedics, teaching, hospitality, and customer service are dominated by females. Women being pushed into the trades also limit male employment opportunities. You wonder why it is harder for a guy to get a job in this country, especially as you get older?' Brian said cynically, 'But that's okay, women literally hold the purse strings and its their consumerism that drives the nation's economy. They are the ones that buy all the latest products and spend their hard-earned money. Guys like us hold onto our old crap and are not into gadgets. Not so patriotic if you look at it from an economic standpoint, is it?'

Brian started to get really wound up. He quickly lit another cigarette and ranted about how this quota mentality had ruined the effectiveness of the Police and the Military. He asserted how it now takes many mixed gender police crews to deal with a basic policing situation and how worse it was in today's military, especially morale and *esprit de corps*. We now have female infantry in our battalions. Most of these few women infanteers are on medical restrictions due to the severity and intensity of infantry training; one thing to pass a course but another to back it up, physically, day after day. Brian was venting and letting out many years of pent-up frustration, due to changes he had seen implemented, mostly in the last decade of his military service. It wasn't only his opinion but could be backed up by other male social commentators, and he trotted out names such as Canadian clinical psychologist, Jordan Peterson and referred to Marine Corps military studies on the combat effectiveness of male and female Marines. Terms like 'toxic masculinity' are used by feminists to push their political barrow and for 'white knight' sell-out males to negotiate a lap-dog position in this new socio-political climate. 'Okay,' he said. 'I'll finish, as I know you've heard it from me all before, but the Government and military hierarchy has destroyed the effectiveness of the Australian Defence Forces, *something Al Qaeda or ISIS could never do.* Regardless of all this, the stinking Government will still be calling on guys to fill in the ranks in the next major war. *I'd tell them to go and fuck themselves!'* And, on that emotional directive, he finished his lengthy tirade, lit up another cigarette, about turned and went inside his caravan as if the 'oracle' had spoken.

Over the last few days, Nathan had sent out many emails and texts to people he considered were rock-solid. People who were true to their word, a rare quality he thought existed these days. He was particularly hoping to hear from Garry Matthews, a friend he had completed some units with at university. Garry had majored in journalism and had an interest in history, like Nathan. They got on well because Garry was interested in all the amazing adventures Nathan had been in and said one day, he would like to author a book on the subject. Garry had started with the local tabloids but had gone 'free-lance,' which gave him more scope to work overseas on more interesting and bigger projects. Garry would be the guy most interested in the manuscript and the tragic history surrounding it. Nathan sat and wondered what his next move would be if Garry couldn't be contacted or couldn't help...

Chapter 13

BATTLE AT LAKE BOGA

The time of day had taken a backseat to the reading and analysing of the manuscript and the convoluted discussion with Brian. It was suddenly late afternoon, bordering on dusk; mostly white clouds traversed the sky with bright rays occasionally peering through their thick and slow-moving formations. It looked like some activity had picked up at the lake. Nathan could see some caravans arriving on the lake's far side and, because of the wind, someone had dug out a parasail and was traversing up and down along the beachfront. Out the corner of his eye, he could make out four tandem surf skis motoring at some pace towards their position. He sat and looked at the waterborne chariots for a few seconds more, expecting them to turn, but the realisation hit home, he yelled out to Brian in a loud but calm voice, 'Mate, we've got visitors, *and not the friendly type either.*'

Brian exited his caravan armed with a .303 Lee Enfield rifle; a slight modification was the six-power rifle scope. Nathan had gone to *Special Forces* and Brian had become a sniper with recon platoon in the battalion. He quickly sighted the weapon from atop of his caravan and reported *weapons were being carried* by those preparing to assault them; the surf skis carried two men, with the passenger carrying some type of assault weapon. Brian took a sight picture of a target and as he let off his first round - a bullet struck him

in the upper thigh, almost knocking him off the top of the caravan. *'Fuck, I'm hit'*, he cried out. A co-ordinated assault was in process. An assault team was attempting to make their way through the scrubby saltbush on the other side of the caravan. They saw Brian above his caravan with his rifle and decided to initiate. 'At this rate,' contact Nathan thought, 'we're fucked on both sides.' Brian had applied a tourniquet to his thigh using his shemagh and re-commenced firing at the surf ski attackers. One of the watercrafts was hit immediately and sank. The remaining craft chose to pick up their comrades and resume the assault. For a bolt-action rifle, Brian was putting down a serious barrage of fire.

Another watercraft was hit and this time it was the fuel tank. The craft and water erupted into *a geyser of flame and water.* This left only two surf skis and they decided to go into a circling safety pattern on the lake, out of Brian's deadly range. As soon as the firing had commenced, Nathan had quickly repositioned Brian's vehicle to face his immediate threat in the bushes and turned the high beams on; he also went for Brian's 870 *Remington* shotgun and ammunition bag that was always kept under his bed. It was starting to get dark, and it began to drizzle. The thick scrubby terrain had made the team assaulting Brian and Nathan select small 'animal runs' to act as a path guiding them forward. These guys had gotten lazy and decided to follow one another instead of attacking in a broad, extended line. The bright lights of the car also made their vision and progress difficult, as did the rain. Nathan let fire with the shotgun and hit two attackers, front on, as they emerged out of the scrub. *'Fucking amateurs,'* he thought as he quickly scanned 180 degrees from left to right, looking for more targets, and reloaded, all at the same time.

Brian was busy firing, keeping the assault craft at bay, which were driving wildly in an attempt not to be hit. On Nathan's side, the weapons fire had died down to intermittent firing as the assaulters couldn't really see anything to shoot from at ground level and they would not be able to until they had emerged from the bush. Without notice, a black Doberman sprang out of the thick foliage and went for Nathan, who instinctively moved to one side when he saw a sizeable black mass making for him. *The pump action was knocked from his hands* and the powerful animal slid past Nathan on the wet ground, re-gathered its footing, turned, rapidly leapt into the air - *and attacked*. At the precise moment, Nathan held out his arm for the dog to latch on to, to protect his throat. He then lowered his right knee towards the ground and thrust his right hand and sturdy *K Bar* combat knife into the animal's muscled stomach - *he thrust madly, maybe ten times or more.*

The dog fell and lay writhing for a few seconds, squealed, collapsed, and lay motionless, its bloodied stomach and intestines spilling all over the damp surface, steam rising from its carcass. 'Geez, now they're sending attack dogs at us, thought Nathan and he yelled out to Brian with some brevity, 'mate, are you okay, *this is getting fucking serious.*' With that, he hit the speed dial on his phone. The phone call connected, and he screamed a codeword into the device and received a verification from the voice at the other end. He thought to himself, 'I hope the cavalry gets here on time...'

The firing had become static for around the last 15 minutes, giving the assaulters in the scrubby bush time to re-charge their 'courage cells' and crawl precariously forward in the soil that was now becoming slippery mud. Nathan had recovered the shotgun and fired a salvo of shots at the attackers, and they all chose to hit the ground, choosing to fire wildly, in the faint hope their bullets would somehow find Brian or Nathan. It was Brian *who was at most risk*. He had stayed on the rooftop of the caravan, which made him vulnerable to the assaulters on land and on the lake. The wound to his thigh meant he could only engage targets on the lake, so he could not really assist Nathan. Suddenly, out of nowhere, a deafening *'Whooooom'* filled their eardrums, and, without any warning, a small seaplane flew perilously close overheard, the two powerful engines blanketing any noise on land and water. The pilot had his head out of the cockpit window, attempting to ascertain the tactical situation and a safe place to touch down, on the lake. He decided to circle around and bring the *Viking Twin Otter* in as close to the caravan as possible.

On seeing this, the assaulters on the water got cocky and ventured too close. Brian fired twice and the threat from the lake was no more. The 'Otter' came in low from the north and glided on to a lake that was as flat and stable as the top of a billiard table. Spray gushed upward and outward from the plane's floats and the pilot kept the speed up on the water until he was on the other side of the caravan and Brian's vehicle - affording him a great deal of cover from fire.

On seeing this development, Nathan screamed to Brian, *'get ready to move,* I'll cover you and then I'll make a dash for the plane.' As painful as he knew it was going to be, Brian rolled over and re-positioned himself so that he could fire at the land assaulters and had the advantage of an elevated position, even though he was dangerously exposed. 'Okay,' said Brian, in a great deal of pain, 'but you move first and then cover me.' Nathan thought, 'well as long as someone gets going, we must get out of here before the assault team get their second wind and make one final charge.' The danger will come when we are in the *Otter* taxing away, and he murmured to himself, somewhat worried - *'they'll be all over us like seagulls on a chip.'* Nathan made a sprint to the seaplane.

The pilot was gunning the motors hard as well as firing the odd burst from a small machine pistol into the scrub. The assaulters were now inching their way forward in the brown slush towards Brian's caravan - edging ever closer. Nathan turned around and gave the thumbs up to Brian, who shook his head, a sad look of resignation adorning his face. He uttered to himself, defiantly, *'I'm not running anymore, especially from these fucks.'*

Brian turned around and let off three quick shots towards the assaulters on land. He then picked up the trigger detonating mechanism, or 'clacker,' which was connected to thick, black electrical wires leading into the caravan from its small skylight. He viciously depressed the top plate of the device a split second before a bullet found its mark - right between his eyes! Before Brian could even crumple back, the caravan erupted, with the landside of the caravan showering the scrubby bush with razor-sharp fragments and copious splashes of burning fuel. The noise temporarily deafened Nathan and the pilot, and the large mushroom shape of fire and smoke was seen all the way across to the other side of the lake. Some time ago, and probably during one of his anti-conspiracy periods, Brian had created an improvised claymore mine out of one side of his caravan.

The claymore mine was developed to engage massed attacks, as experienced by Diggers during the *Korean War*, when thousands of Chinese soldiers would attack as a screaming, firing, human wave. The mine fired 700-quarter inch cylindrical balls and was highly effective. In the case of Brian's anti-personnel weapon, all the badges, knick-knacks and metal paraphernalia that had harmlessly adorned the caravan's outer walls were in fact designed to be deadly shrapnel. Behind this wall of shrapnel, a narrow, false wall had concealed thin wine casks filled with a mixture of gasoline and dishwashing liquid; essentially, improvised napalm. The thick, backing wall inside the caravan had been reinforced to ensure all the explosive force was directed away from the caravan, towards an 'enemy.' An improvised detonator system made the weapon complete and highly potent. When Nathan had viewed the look of resignation on Brian's face, he had gestured the pilot to move twenty metres away, as a precautionary measure, not sure about what was about to happen.

Now, Brian's 4x4 vehicle had caught fire and its propane tank exploded, sending black toxic plumes spiralling into the air, venting more fire, and flickering embers into the brush. The aluminium caravan had rapidly burnt down to the wheel arches and now lay gutted and smouldering. The caravan's intense fire had easily caught on in the scrubby bush, which was now raging, as it became nightfall. Assaulters not killed by the improvised anti-personal device beat a hasty retreat, running from the flames, grabbing some of their fallen comrades in the process. In this lull, there was nothing more to do than take off. The pilot nosed the plane into the wind and powered-up the engines. A slight bucking sensation on the water followed as the powerful aircraft accelerated and then, seconds later, the plane was airborne. David turned to

Nathan in the co-pilots seat, 'Sorry about your mate. That was a gutsy move back there, real hero stuff.' In a quiet reply, Nathan said, 'yeah, sure was' as he gripped the manuscript tightly, and with that they flew in silence. David turned the controls slowly to the right and the plane made a wide banking turn on its way to a destination known only to the two men... ✒

Chapter 14

THE 'CALL'

'*Another mate lost,*' Nathan thought. The relationship may have been fractured but they were still old friends with a lot of history between them. The pain cut deep. The plane had flown for 10 or 15 minutes on what later turned out to be a crystal-clear night. Nathan had lost track of time as he wrestled with all the dramas of the last few days. He thought this would have been a simple adventure, checking out some old bunker and a disruption in his normal, boring routine. He never envisaged the loss of two old comrades, a trail of destruction and a resumption of old behaviours that some would think bordered on the psychotic. As far as Brian went, he knew he was always looking for a way out, a 'blaze of glory' was Brian's form, to the end, especially if it was a sacrifice for a colleague or a half-decent cause. Well, Brian got his wish...

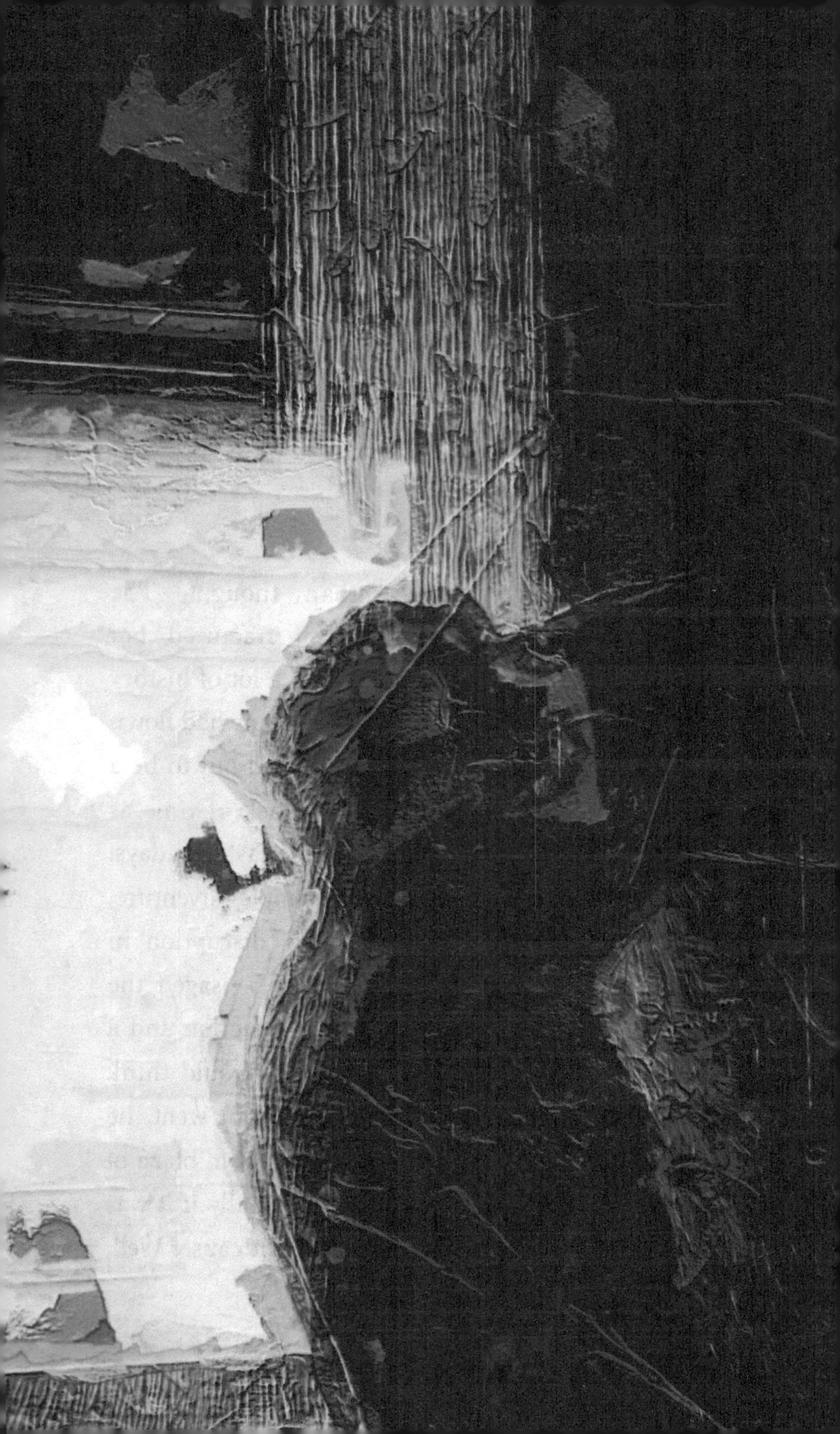

The plane touched down on the small lake by a bush cabin, effortlessly; David could probably fly better drunk than some sober, or so Nathan thought. The property belonged to a member of David's pilot fraternity, and they frequently shared aircraft. Nathan helped David to secure the plan and they walked to where David's *Jeep Grand Cherokee* was parked. They drove quickly but safely during the evening to David's property, in silence. Both men knew the toll this adventure had taken. After 10 minutes, they arrived. It was how Nathan had last seen it a year or so ago: well, laid out, meticulously maintained but with an African design and 'feel' about it. The animal heads on the internal walls and outside wicker furniture were the giveaway. Nathan quietly said, 'Man, I need to take a shower and have a look at my arm, where that damn dog bit me.' 'No worries' said David. 'You know where the bathroom is, and you can sleep in your old room. I think you still have clothes there?' Nathan sort of staggered to the bathroom, closed the door and ran the shower. The steaming hot water felt great, even medicinal as it enveloped him and he thought, half-seriously, 'if this hot water could only wash away my sins?' He took the usual, hasty army type shower, not the 30-minute extravaganza that his wife would normally have done, because he was mindful of the scarcity of water on rural properties. His arm was okay, only a few small puncture marks and bruising from

'Cujo,' the dead attack dog. Nathan's heavy field jacket had withstood the worst of the assault. A splash of *Betadine*, and all would be good. As he came out of the bathroom, David announced that hot food was on the table, an ice bucket, and a bottle of *Jack Daniels*.

The first shot of the whiskey didn't hit the sides as Nathan poured another round for the two men. Sizzle steak and vegetables was the board of fare and David wasn't a bad cook. Most guys who've been in the military or have lived on the go are quite adept at cooking; another urban myth that guys can't adequately feed themselves. Nathan tucked into the well-cooked steak as if he hadn't had a decent meal in a long while and besides, it always tasted better when someone else cooked. They ate without saying too much and re-filled their drinks, as necessary. David told Nathan to take the last steak and when the meal was done, they sat in the sitting room finishing off another drink. Nathan spoke with some emotion, '*Mate, if you hadn't arrived when you did, I would've been toast*, literally. Brian always had an exit-strategy and in the firefight at the lake, opportunity presented one for him. He was never going to make 'old bones.' David was sincere, 'think nothing of it. I know you've got my back, brother.' They drank a toast to Brian and sat quietly for a while. For the most part, that's all guys had to say. No long, drawn out 'I love youse' or crying on a shoulder or getting 'silly' and blubbery drunk, professing eternal homage. They poured another drink, with David saying this would be his last and then off to bed. It was then that Nathan's phone rang.

He looked at its face and it stated: 'No Caller ID.' Normally, he wouldn't answer these calls as it was the usual tele-marketing waffle or some Nigerian scam artist attempting to gain his personal information. He never gave out his phone number, only to trusted friends. And it was late at night. 'Yes,' was all he said, very quietly. 'Is this Nathan Phillips, former *Special Forces* soldier, scholar and adventurer,' came next, in a woman's voice. Nathan had a feeling he knew who this was and had been expecting a call for some time. There was no point in a masquerade. Cheerfully, he replied, 'Hello Madison, how are you? Bit late in the evening for a call, isn't it? Please forgive me if I slur my words. I've had a great meal and a few drinks, and I feel light-headed. Just about ready to go ni-nights, how about you?' The voice was calm and polite as the female voice responded. 'How perceptive of you Nathan, I've been literally dying to chat to you. Just been to a BBQ this evening. By the way, I saw an old friend of yours there, not as jovial as you, perhaps. We didn't find Ghent to be very talkative either; I don't know what you said to him.' She was trying to goad him, get under his skin and see how he would react. Madison went on, 'Good to hear you're looking after yourself. Hate to see any harm come to you. I'd like to have a natter with you in person, if that's possible. A trifle matter about an old dead body, a manuscript and such like. I can guarantee your safety, if that's an issue. 'Don't worry about all that's happened over the last few days, all water under the bridge as far as I'm concerned. You've lost a few, I've lost a few, so I figure we're about even. Don't you think?' 'Well Madison,' said Nathan curtly, 'I don't really see it that way.' He knew she was dragging out the time so her tech people could get a fix on his location. Nathan then said, 'Call me at 10 tomorrow morning and we'll arrange something, ciao', and on that he hung up. David had come back from the kitchen and said, 'who was that?' Nathan quickly replied, 'no time to discuss, pack what you need. We need to get going in two minutes. I'll update you in the car.' David was back before Nathan knew it. Both men were used to travelling light and tonight would be lighter. The two men leapt into the *Jeep*, and it roared into life and headed down the highway. David asked, 'where to?' south, towards Melbourne, was the response. 'I think I'm going to need some more backup,' said Nathan. David agreed with a strong nod of his head and looked at Nathan with a reassuring smile. Nathan was hatching a plan but still hadn't figured out all the moves yet...

Chapter 15

TAKING
A BREATH...

At any other time, all the death and destruction of the last few days would've been an ongoing news story and the tabloids would have had a mighty field day. It wasn't in Madison Baker's interest to bring too much attention to herself, her thugs, and subsequently, to her employer. She had been working overtime to sanitise the situation, feeding the media snippets of disinformation, and telling the Police hierarchy what they needed to know. *They all went along for the ride...*

It is amazing what people will believe when the truth is skilfully manufactured for them and sounds half-feasible. The public is so easily manipulated, she thought with some disdain. The daily newsreader

would announce the following headlines: 'an ongoing biker turf war was the cause of the commotion in Melbourne. A compressor had exploded in a street that was being repaired by a road gang. Over-zealous kangaroo shooters up at Lake Boga had accidentally hit a caravan's propane tanks, resulting in the death of a poor, old grey nomad. A crop-dusting floatplane had to take an emergency landing on a lake up near the Murray River, engine issues involved extremely loud backfiring.'

If the story is repeated frequently enough and with conviction across the many facets of the media, it goes from being a simple story or an urban myth to God's own truth. It is all a bit like when you have watched some tedious commercial for the umpteenth time. You have deduced the commercial's main theme, such as selling soap powder, but you haven't properly interrogated the subject, what they are really selling or saying. However, when you spend those extra few seconds interpreting their meaning, it comes as a surprise that the 'soap powder' is no longer the main theme but the product is all about re-wearing old clothes and bringing them back to life with this powder - not just the act of washing and cleaning clothes. A slight distinction but an important nuance, nonetheless. This is how Government works; a slight tweak of the truth here and a manoeuvring of the truth there. Statistics are fudged, consultants, at taxpayer's expense, are brought in to validate a position and the media, which has long forgotten the credo of real investigative journalism, pontificates the integrity of the story. Why do you think a Minister is flanked by members of his portfolio at news conferences? It is designed to lend more credence to the Minister's psychobabble that has been carefully constructed for public consumption. It is not because he or she is their best friend, or he or she is telling the truth. It is a preferred image *of honesty and solidarity* they wish to portray. Nathan remembered one of Winston Churchill's old adages, 'lies, damn lies and statistics' and thought, 'as true now as ever.'

Nathan and David had driven on the speed limit for an hour before they pulled into a trucker's stop and ordered coffee. It was around three in the morning. They would wait there for an hour or so before driving the remaining short distance to Melbourne. In the meantime, he would tap out some more texts to people, especially Paul Burton as he needed some help with equipment and Paul was the man. If Paul couldn't get it, he knew a guy, who knew a guy who could. As well, they didn't want to announce their arrival too early. There are so many 'security' and 'safety' cameras concentrated in Melbourne and he knew that facial imaging recognition or the *Jeep's* registration and description would run up a number of red flags that would be picked up by Ms Baker and her deadly associates. This is why they had driven to Lake Boga. Sure, they were identified and found but it gave them time. A lot more time than if they had been in the city. Nathan remembered again what Brian used to say, 'It's hard to hit a moving target.' Nathan had arranged to meet Paul not far from Café Sicilio after his call with Baker. Cops say criminals always return to the scene of a crime, but not always. Nathan thought they wouldn't expect him to frequent the same area, which he knew so well. Besides, it was always a heavily concentrated area with workers, students from Melbourne University, tourists, and locals, which meant there would be a lesser chance of gunplay. As well, the nooks, crannies and general 'rabbit warren' design of the suburb made it easier to evade capture and disappear.

The *Jeep* entered the dingy outskirts of Melbourne on daybreak, and they proceeded south down Sydney Road. Milk and bread delivery vendors were dropping off their goods to the various milk bars and early opening supermarkets. Night cleaners were finishing off their tasks, ready to start their next cleaning job or eager to go home and get some well-earned sleep. The only other activity came from the open 24-hour *McDonalds* restaurants they passed or the occasional jogger getting in an early morning run. The idea was to keep a low profile until Nathan had his ten am call with Baker, then go and see Paul. After that, they would head off back to the country areas of Victoria, which both men knew so well. In the meantime, they would find a safe spot to park and take turns having a nap until it was time to move. A quiet street adjacent to Princes Park would suit their purposes.

At precisely 9:30, David gave Nathan a tug of his jacket to wake him up. Nathan shook his head and said, 'I was only resting my eyes, honest' and they both had a laugh at his silly comment. The *Jeep's* engine was fired up and they moved forward towards Carlton. There was plenty of time so no need to speed or do anything that would bring attention to themselves. Most of the morning peak hour traffic had dispersed and their journey was routine. As they entered the suburb of Carlton, David indicated he needed to get some gas as the gauge was getting low and it was a good precaution.

They pulled into a twenty-four-hour service station and Nathan said he would get out and fill the tank. Across the street, an Italian man in his thirties, with jet-black hair and matching clothes, was taking great interest in Nathan and the vehicle, jotting down its make and registration. Unbeknown to Nathan, *a picture was taken of the two men on the Italian's mobile phone,* and he made a quick call, speaking fervently, but only in Italian. Nathan went inside the service station and paid for the gas. Both men nodded at each and started off again, this time to find a suitable car-parking spot for their rendezvous with Paul.

They had just turned into a side street where they would park and meet Paul. *'Bam!'* – suddenly, their vehicle was ferociously hit side on by a large metal bull bar connected to an old but sturdy *Ford* tow truck. The vehicle hit the driver's side with such force that David was slumped against the wheel, unconscious - his scalp bleeding profusely. Nathan was stunned, as his head had smashed against the *Jeep's* side pillar. He was trying to regain his senses, but he felt like the world had de-accelerated into slow motion. In vehicle terms, this was like being *'king hit.'* Just as he was trying to regain his consciousness, a short, stocky man opened Nathan's door and two other men dragged him out. Nathan could only make out blurs instead of individuals. Instinctively, he threw a short-left jab at the closest man but before he could throw another punch, a black leather 'billy club' came swiftly down upon his head and that was Nathan's last act of defiance. A black veil of darkness slowly descended over his eyes. The men threw Nathan's slumped form into a second vehicle, a delivery van and it sped from the area. By this time, some people had arrived and were milling about while other citizens and by passers attempted to assist David who was still unconscious. An ambulance had been called, *its sirens wailing louder* as it approached.

Nathan gradually opened his groggy eyes; he shook his head even more slowly and tried to stand. This was impossible, as he had been rope-tied, by his feet, chest and hands to a sturdy wooden chair that must have been made of oak or some other type of dense, hard wood. He looked around and could see he was in the middle of an old smelly garage on dirty concrete flooring; he could also tell by the greyish tools that hung on the grubby walls, the oil dispensers, drip-trays, sawdust, vehicle hoist and the aroma associated with such an occupation. Light was discharging to only 30 percent of the room by a single light bulb in the middle of the ceiling. The remainder of the room was in complete darkness. From the shadows he heard an old Italian man speak, 'I know what a Sicilian necktie is, *but I think you will be wearing one, very soon*'. The man walked little by little out of the shadows, with his small terrier dog. The 'penny dropped', and Nathan just shook his head slightly from side to side. 'Damn, he thought, when it rains, *it does chuffing pour!*' The three younger men involved in the 'smash and grab' earlier stood behind but flanked the old man. 'But first, you owe me for the inconvenience you put me and my Benito through'.

The Italian had lived in the inner-city area all his life since arriving in Australia from Naples, after the war. He had acquired property, made money, and gained respect. He loan-sharked money to other Italians at exorbitant rates and had created his own vicious crew that dealt with all opposition. He had retired some twenty years ago, not long after the death of his angelic wife. The sons by his side ran the family businesses now. His comment acted as a cue for one of the men to step forward and to strike Nathan's jaw with a sickening force. As the man's powerful arm swung, it exposed a handgun in a shoulder holster. The man punched Nathan a few more times to the head and then stepped back. Blood was starting to drip from several small facial wounds, *his nose and his face were getting puffy.* Nathan spat out some blood from the inside cuts to his mouth. Round two. Another man stepped forward and was just about to strike Nathan when the cell phone in his trouser pocket went off. Nathan remarked, 'Don't worry, I'll get that later', to which the old man replied, '*for you, there won't be any later, you fungool*'.

The same son strode forward again to throw a bevy of punches but was interrupted as the garage's metal back door was thrown wide open and crashed with a resonating ring against the back-brick wall. Paul and Phil both speedily entered carrying 9mm *Glocks* with silencers aimed across the room at the men. Nathan shouted - '*they've got guns*', to which Paul nonchalantly replied, 'thanks, makes my conscience easier'. On that quip, Paul, and Phil, emptied their magazines into the four men, who screamed and gasped as their lives were being extinguished. Phil walked over and shot the old Italian in the head, and his whimpering dog, which was emitting a low, howling noise, to complete the reckoning. Paul ran over to Nathan and cut his bindings with a small *Gerber* folding pocketknife, that he always carried. Nathan's muscles were stiff and bruised and he was still groggy from the car crash and the beating, but he put his right hand on Paul's shoulder and just nodded his head in appreciation. '*How did you know where to find me*', Nathan said. 'As luck would have it', said Paul, 'I turned around the corner and saw the whole show these guys put on. I gave Phil a ring as I tailed them to this business, which was only five minutes away'.

Phil said it was time they left, but Nathan still had some unfinished business. He quickly looked around and fished out a jerry can of petrol from behind a bench and started sloshing the fuel all over the garage and on the four corpses. 'We don't want our DNA ending up with the cops, do we, and any finger being pointed at us?', as he emptied the high-octane fuel on some oily rags. The other two men stood guard outside as Nathan torched the rags, which, in turn, ignited spilt fuel all around the premises. Initially, this would look like a tragic fire until the forensics confirmed homicide. *More time for Nathan.* By the time the blaze had taken hold of the building the men were well on their way from the crime scene. 'The area was just about due for another mob hit', Paul remarked. 'Don't worry, there will be plenty of suspects and the cops will have their hands full for some time'. 'And don't fret about David', said Phil. 'I rang the Royal Melbourne Hospital and they said he only had cuts and abrasions and a minor concussion. They'll be keeping him in for a day or so', Nathan was relieved to hear that. With two deaths already weighing heavily, he did not want another friend's death on his conscience.

Within a minute or two of leaving the burning garage, Nathan's phone rang again, and he knew it was Ms. Baker, but he was not in the mood for a chat and wasn't ready to tell her what she wanted to hear. He ignored the call. Nathan stated the obvious, 'I think I need a drink'. The men drove fast to a lane that was 5 minutes from Phil's night club and left the car. The short walk and fresh air did Nathan a lot of good. His head began to clear, and he could start to think again. He did not dwell on the beating and was already looking at the many tasks that lay ahead. Ironically, Nathan would never dwell on the physical beatings he took but could always feel the residual damage that he sustained form the mental beatings from personal relationships. The three men negotiated the stairs to Phil's nightclub, which was deserted during the day. Phil produced a smallish chrome ice bucket, hand towels for Nathan's wounds and plonked a bottle of *Southern Comfort* and shot glasses down on the table.

Paul remarked to Nathan, 'you don't look too bad, you take a beating pretty well'. It was Paul's turn to take the piss out of his mate. Nathan could not laugh because it hurt, but he put on his serious face and said, '*if it wasn't for you two, I'd probably be residing in a forty-four-gallon drum right now, so, again, brothers, thanks!*' As it turned out, he was not all that badly hurt. The small cuts and bruises would heal, the ice would certainly arrest any major swelling and he had not lost any teeth. 'Thank God for that', he was so relieved. Nathan loathed going to the dentist. He would tense up, clamp up and the dentist could not do a thing. He had to take *Valium* on prescription at his last dental appointment. Later he had thought. 'I can freefall from a plane on oxygen at 20,000 feet without a worry in a world, but a specialist exploring in my mouth with a small metal tool freaks me out'. The men got stuck into the bottle and it was not long before Phil went and fetched a jug of beer and some bar snacks.

Paul started talking, 'alright, down to business'. He outlined how he had made discreet inquiries to all his contacts and was happy to report MacMillan had once been married and his wife had given him a daughter. His chaotic behaviour did not only worry the university faculty but terrified his wife. She decided to leave him, go back to her maiden name and take the child somewhere safe. Apparently, MacMillan was so obsessed he did not bother to locate them. As it turned out, the mother passed away only last year but the daughter is now living near Ballarat. Her name is Lauren Gale. *'Well, we need to find her and pretty damn quick,* 'cause if Baker locates her then she is for the chop', said Nathan with a determined voice. Paul replied by informing the group he had a lot of contacts in the Ballarat area, and they were working on a positive lead as they spoke. However, they all knew one guy in Ballarat that they could rely on and decided he would be their first point of contact. The main fact was the girl did live in the area. They were all hoping

Lauren Gale would be able to shed some light on her father, the manuscript and how he ended up dead in an underground bunker.

The men were just finishing their snacks and had stopped drinking when Nathan's phone rang. He knew who this was and had a feeling of dread, like when you have not responded to your wife's calls, and you know you're in for a stern ticking off. *'I've been trying to call you for the last few hours'*, said Baker, in a mildly angry tone. 'Well,' said Nathan, 'I was indisposed for a while there but I'm good now'. 'What is it you want', he replied casually. Baker's tone eased and she replied, 'You know what it is I want, Nathan. Give me the manuscript and I'll leave you and your little rascals alone, no hard feelings'. Nathan replied in a cynical tone, 'Well, Madison, I sort of don't believe what you're saying and wouldn't expect by-gones to be by-gones if I was in your position. Failure doesn't really look good on the resume'. He went on, 'So, I'm going to have to reject your offer and take my chances, which to be honest, I think I've done alright so far'. Baker chose to remind him, aggressively, 'I don't like rejection Nathan, especially from some old has-been, no offence intended, but I'll do whatever is necessary, and you know that'. Nathan replied with an implied instruction, *'you do what you have to Madison...'* and on those words he hung up.

The boys had heard the conversation. They knew that Baker and her crew were *'heavy hitters'*. They had not been recruited from the local boy scout troop and wouldn't give up easily. There had been losses on both sides, and it was virtually becoming a battle between 'old school' vets versus 'new school' expendables. Nathan's phone rang again, and he angrily commented, *'For fuck sakes,* who is this now?' He took the call. It was Garry Matthews, Nathan's old alumni friend. 'So sorry', said Garry, 'I've been overseas the last three weeks on a story in Mogadishu about pirating and then in Nigeria covering internet scammers. I have only just got back. How are you mate, what's been happening?' Besides welcoming Garry, Nathan spent the next 5 minutes giving him a general outline of what had been occurring since the bunker had been discovered by David. Nathan was now doing his talking on the move, as they did not want to be sitting ducks in the nightclub if Ms. Baker and her team rolled in. They were on their way to Ballarat in Paul's *Mercedes C230 Kompressor* and would be there in just over 90 minutes. 'Look', said Garry, 'leave this with me and I'll make some ultra-discreet inquiries. My editor has been waiting for years to latch onto a story like this. I will get things happening here and meet you at Melbourne Airport, when I can get away. By then you may have found the wayward daughter and I can interview her, what do you think?' 'My thoughts exactly', said Nathan. 'I can be contacted anytime. Great to hear from you old mate, take care, bye'.

The powerful Kompressor drove effortlessly at high speed on the Western Freeway, west towards Ballarat. The three men tried to relax but the stakes were getting higher all the time. Nathan surveyed life outside the car, taking particular notice of vehicles driving too close to them; parked vans on the sides of the road, with bystanders talking on their phones; objects in the sky, particularly small flying objects he couldn't make out and especially any road works they encountered. This sort of detail to attention had kept him alive in Iraq on the road convoys from Baghdad to FOBs and the para-military training academy he worked at. The military training and brainwashing never leaves you. It resides just under the intellectual and psychological surface. The higher you go and the harder you train the less chance you have of shaking this intrinsic behaviour, which at times feels like a curse. He could not help it if he always locked the door every time he stepped into his cabin, even though it was out in the boondocks. He could not help sleeping with a *Gerber* machete under his bed, a handgun in a draw, or noting implements in his cabin that could be used as weapons. He could not help always selecting the 'gunfighter' seat in a *McDonald's* restaurant, knowing the 'threat' could only come at him one-way. He would run scenarios in his mind wherever he went - and people *think the 'Jason Bourne' persona is only a fictional construct!* Nathan never liked crowds, especially its mentality to panic and turn a dire situation into a dangerous one. He always said that if he had been on the *Titanic*, he would have got off the ship early using a door as a raft and would've sailed back to the chuffing iceberg! This type of prolonged conditioning turns a person into a Jekyll and Hyde character, where there is always a conflict of interest and an endless battle between personalities. Nathan thought this is what it must be like to be schizophrenic.

The men were only thirty short minutes from Ballarat when a blue and red flashing light, followed by a siren, fired into life around 30 metres to the rear of their vehicle. The motorbike police officer quickly accelerated to a position level with the driver and signalled he wanted the car to pull over. Nathan did a complete 360-degree scan and then took out his *Browning* from his grab bag and placed it under his Premier League baseball cap. The vehicle was now stationary, and the cop walked slowly towards the driver. *'Driver's License, please',* came from the officer. Paul quickly produced his licence whilst Phil and Nathan just looked straight ahead. 'You were driving nearly ten kilometres over the limit and failed to indicate when you changed lanes, 2 kilometres back', said the officer. *'Do you have a reason for this?'* Paul replied courteously, 'I thought I had indicated back there and the trouble with this car is I'm still getting used to it. I have only had it a short while and it gets away from me sometimes. I'm terribly sorry, officer'. Paul then played his ace card, 'how long have you had the *BMW*? When I was with the motorbike squad, we rode the *Honda Boldor 750 CBR*. They wouldn't hold a candle to your bike'. The officer asked Paul if he had been in 'the job', at what time and did he know 'so and so' and such like. The officer's demeanour changed from a stern bureaucrat to a guy you could easily like. He bent down and peeked at Nathan and Phil inside the car. 'Damn, what happened to your friend, he looks like he's been in a fight with Connor McGregor!' Paul played it cool and said, 'no, silly bugger fell down some outside stairs, concrete and paving, blood everywhere, but he bounces well, and it could've been worse'. The Officer put away his black duty book and suggested Paul take it a bit more slowly and carefully with his driving. He did an about turn, walked away, mounted his bike, and rode off at speed on his shiny German motorbike. Nathan placed the *Browning* in the grab bag. On seeing this move, Paul spoke in an agitated tone, *'are you fucking serious, would you have shot that copper?'* Nathan paused and looked directly at Paul, *'I will do whatever it takes to ensure the safety of my friends and myself'*. After losing two close friends in a matter of days, Nathan was not taking any chances and would do whatever was necessary. The air was thick with tension but now was not the time to argue or to be annoyed. Paul started the car. It was only a short drive to someone who may provide the answers they needed...

Chapter 16

LONG, LOST FAMILY

They were on their way to locate Lauren Gale but would meet Graham Thomassen in Ballarat first and would arrive at his residence in 10 minutes. The boys had kept a tight security vigil during their drive. They had not seen a car or motorbike anywhere near them since the highway patrol officer had pulled them over. Among other things, Graham had also worked in security a long time, and this is where he met Nathan and Paul. As well, Graham was a 'Justice of the Peace' and was heavily involved with militaria and firearms. He knew a lot of people, particularly in the Ballarat area and this extensive knowledge would lead Nathan to Ms. Gale. The striking thing about Graham was his size. Graham was of Viking heritage and could have easily played 'Thor' instead of

Chris Hemsworth or 'the Mountain' in *Game of Thrones*. He was tall, with a muscular body builder's frame and sported a long white hair and thick Santa Claus beard. Most people were instantly intimidated *by his colossal size* but once you knew him you soon found out he was an *articulate gentleman and gentle giant*. Graham rarely had to resort to violence - as his size was persuasive enough.

The *Kompressor* arrived at the weatherboard house, which was situated in a quiet street away from main traffic. Graham was standing out front. Phil slid across to the right and Graham got in. All the men knew each other and exchanged pleasantries before Nathan looked at Graham and said, 'I hope you've got something?' Graham explained that the girl and her mother had lived together in the small township of Creswick, which was about 15 minutes to the northeast from their current location. The mother had bought a nursery business nearly twenty years ago and ran this, pretty much up until her death.

The town has a bit of a reputation as being a bit of a 'hippy town', due to its proximity to the hot water springs in the nearby towns and its reputation as an *Avant Garde* community. Apparently, the famed Australian artist Norman Lindsay and his family resided there for many years. 'So, the town is full of fucking greenies?' said Phil, which drew a long, disapproving look from all the other men. Graham continued by saying the quaint town is built around forest management and there are only three main roads in an out of the place. The forest area is so substantial in growth and expansive it acts like a dark green shroud around the township, extending for tens of kilometres. The forest area also has a reputation for housing drug crops. The drug operators are 'middle-of-the-road players' who make a particularly good living out of their marijuana crops, which eventually finds its way to Melbourne. The local cops are bought off and everyone walks away happy.

The sleek *Kompressor* entered Creswick, which, like many country towns in the area, had thrived during the Gold Rush era but took on a different role these days. These quaint, leafy townships were now popular haunts for a day out in the country for city folk or a place where *petit bourgeois* types could quaff local wines whilst professing an esoteric knowledge of some useless subject. Paul followed Graham's instructions and it was not long before they were at the 'Creswick Nursery', which was located close to St. George's Lake, a popular reservoir and swimming hole. Nathan thought it best that Graham and Phil stay in the car as the sight of four men, especially Graham was likely to scare off anyone. The sign on the door said 'welcome' and a bell rang as the door closed behind them. An attractive, young blond girl in her late twenties appeared from back room, walked to the counter, and asked in a natural, friendly way, 'can I help you?' Her hazel eyes, which strikingly contrasted with her fair hair, made Nathan pause before he spoke. 'Hello Miss, my Name is Nathan, and this is my friend Paul, we've come to talk to you about your father'.

On hearing the word 'father,' the girl looked momentarily stunned but soon spoke excitedly, 'Do you have any information on my father, is there something I need to know?' The girl inquired if the two men were from the Police or a Government agency, to which they replied, 'no'. They said they had come across some vital information concerning Lauren's father and intimated that other interested 'parties' would approach her, but they had located her first. Nathan left out the recent deaths, the trail of destruction and the possibility of a repeat of these dangerous scenarios in the near future. It was evident that Lauren wanted, and more to the point, *needed* any news or insights regarding her father. Her Mother had only started speaking of him near her death and had largely kept him a 'blank canvas' for most of Lauren's life. All she knew was that he was a bright man. She had made some inquiries in the past, but these led to many closed avenues. It was obvious Lauren was a clever girl. Regardless of what little information there was, she had thought her father must have been working on something particularly important.

Lauren ushered the men to the room behind the front desk. They could sit down, and she would make everyone coffee and then they would talk some more. 'Standard NATO', replied Nathan and he went into the brief story surrounding the coffee formula and its name. The girl felt at ease with the two men and could sense they were here to help, not harm. Nathan told Lauren to brace herself as some of what he would tell her was confronting. He explained how and where her father was located but did not know where his remains were now. The other interested parties were characterised in such a way that Lauren knew they worked for the Government in some capacity and were not 'nice' people. Nathan then produced the manuscript from his grab bag and provided a succinct outline of its contents. Lauren looked at the raggedy cover, the dog-eared pages, but most importantly, the handwritten scrawly narrative that was in her father's unique handwriting. She began to sob. This was the only physical link she had to a man she never really knew. At this point, it was of no concern what the pages offered up to her. It was *the frail human connection between Father and Daughter* in the written word.

Nathan waited for a minute or two for Lauren to regain her composure and said, 'so as you can see, your life is in peril, and we would like to guarantee your safety'. He went on to affirm, 'there are people out there who probably think you know more than what you do, and these people don't convince easily'. Lauren questioned, *So what is in this for you?* 'Absolutely nothing', said Nathan. 'Not even a brass razoo'. Nathan explained to her reassuringly that he and his compatriots had served their community and nation in various capacities. At some time in their lives, they were either military, police or had worked in the legal system. They had all sworn various oaths; oaths to defend or to uphold the right or for peace and prosperity. Just because they no longer served did not mean the oaths they made no longer existed. Just because these men were older did not mean they could not fulfil their obligation. These were men of honour, a rare quality in today's society - *they could not be bought or sold.*

Lauren could clearly see men of integrity by delving into the trustworthy eyes of Nathan and Paul and was convinced of their sincerity. She said, 'okay, what you want me to do?' The plan was simple. Lauren would go to the safety of the crude, back cabin at the tail end of his block and be guarded there, twenty-four hours a day by resolute men who would be heavily armed. With the *Cossacks* and extra colleagues brought in by Nathan, they would have plenty of professionals and 'muscle' on the ground to cover the security situation. Garry Matthews would interview her, dissect the manuscript and the whole story would appear in the media. She would not be away for weeks or anything like that. Lauren said this would not be a problem as the business was run on a roster system and she was due some leave.

As Lauren lived at the nursery, she went into her small bedroom and commenced packing some of her belongings and keepsakes. Nathan and Paul discussed navigation from there and logistical issues such as food, water, and bedding. Lauren packed fast and within ten minutes they were all walking out from the back room. At the same time, the shop door opened, the bell rang, and two young men moved towards the counter, dragging, and scuffing their feet on the floor. They were locals and dressed in tradie trousers, dirty work boots and local football club hoodies. The lead man looked at Lauren, Nathan and Paul and then directed his aggressive questioning at Lauren, *'where are you going?'* Lauren sheepishly explained she was going on a week's holiday with some old friends. *'Well, this is news to me',* said Tyler, as he was starting to become agitated. *'I would have thought a girl would tell her boyfriend if she was going off on a holiday on her own?'* The man was dark in complexion with a mullet hairstyle and had a sombre, unattractive nature as well. Being a local, he had a reputation around town and was not averse to picking pubs fights in the area. Most people avoided him. He was a carpenter by trade but had become a big player in the local drug market. His 'bad boy' demeanour endeared him to the local girls. He had pursued Lauren because not only was she attractive but also, he could obtain the plant nutrients required for the cultivation of his drug crop without raising any suspicion.

'It's time we were off', said Paul. Before Paul had barely finished speaking, Tyler interrupted, *'no-ones talking to you, old man'.* Paul fired back, *'yeah, you'll be fucking no-one if you speak to me like that again'.* On that comment, Tyler leapt at Paul, who moved to his left side, thrust a right palm strike to the nose and a left knuckle punch to the right temple. Tyler collapsed on the floor, a bleeding, dazed mess. Tyler's mate had moved quickly forward to involve himself in the fracas, but Nathan applied a *Ranger* chokehold on his Adam's apple, rendering him ineffective. The man tried to move but Nathan looked at him and simply said, 'just don't...' The tension was broken when Lauren spoke first and said that they should leave, now. All three appeared from the shop as Lauren's girlfriend appeared to takeover the business. Phil and Graham had been leaning against the *Kompressor* and saw what had transpired inside. Phil said to Nathan and Paul casually, 'we knew you had it covered'. The seating was re-arranged so Graham sat in the front passenger seat, and everyone could fit in the back. The rear wheels spat out gravel and grey dust as the vehicle headed off to Nathan's block.

Tyler was fuming as he and his mate staggered outside. 'Those arseholes are dead, I tell you, *fucking dead!*' Tyler's seething continued for a few minutes more and all his mate could do was nod in silent agreement. He dare not saying anything to incur Tyler's rage. Already a plan was formulated in Tyler's mind. He would gather his drug crew and follow the tracking app that he had connected to Lauren's phone some time ago. But first, he needed to quell his nosebleed and change his bloodied shirt. Lauren alerted Nathan and his friends of Tyler's activities and his predilection of being the 'big man' in the area. She stressed to Nathan, 'he won't take this lying down, so you need to be on your guard. He nearly killed a rival drug runner last year. He is a real psycho'. Nathan assured her, 'don't worry, we've handled bigger nut-jobs than this character'. The men looked at each other in the car without blinking an eyelid and the car gathered pace. 🖋

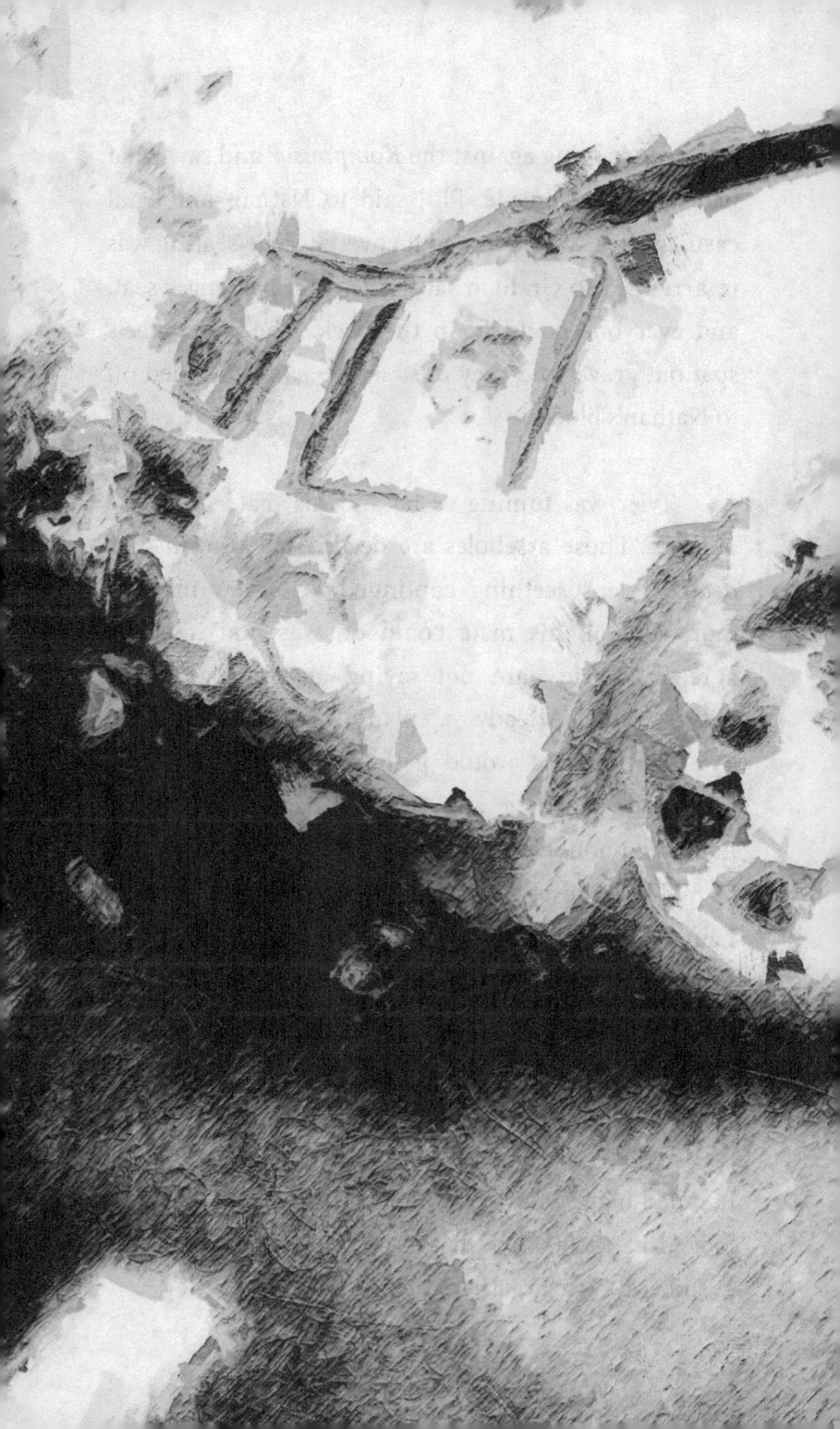

Chapter 17

THE *AGENCY*

T he shiny black *Ford Everest* pulled up to the Government building, which looked like any other State or Federal Building or politician for that matter, grey, dour, and slightly imposing. The car had stopped in a 'handicap zone', a parking officer rushed forward to remonstrate with the driver but thought more of it once the black tinted window descended and he saw the 'no argue with' occupants inside. Madison Baker left the vehicle and walked briskly and confidently into the foyer of the Government building as if she owned it. Her heels struck the marbled floor in rapid, noisy succession, as if to announce to anyone present this busy woman was on a mission. She entered the elevator and reviewed in her mind what she would say to the *Director*. The door opened at the relevant floor. Baker faced a door with the letter one on it and she went into what became the anteroom to the *Director's* office. Positioned against the left wall were three uncomfortable looking metal chairs. The secretary's table faced the door. Baker sat in the middle seat and looked straight ahead. Ten minutes later, the secretary announced, 'the *Director* will see you now'.

Baker walked a few paces to the black door on the right side of the room and entered. The *Director* was reading a thick document in front of him and, without looking up, said, 'take a seat'. The man behind the imposing mahogany desk was in his fifties and looked a lot like Alec Baldwin, but weighing ten kilos less, and with dark greying hair. He wore a tailored crisp black suit with a cream business shirt and red tie. He read for a further minute, put the document down on the desk and then gazed at Baker for ten seconds before he spoke. 'Okay, where are we with this operation', he said. He already knew the answer. Madison Baker began, 'We have recovered the prime subject's body and that is now at the *Agency's* underground storage facility at Uluru. Subject Ghent passed on the manuscript to a third party and then chose to take his life. He has been disposed of. A fire has disposed of his dwellings and any other traces. The third party was tracked to a remote area of the state. He has since eluded our efforts to capture him and retrieve the manuscript. We are investigating friends, acquaintances, possible locations, and all other leads'. Baker paused. The *Director* spoke in a rhetorical tone, *'this third party seems to be giving you a lot of trouble, hasn't he?'* Baker, feeling fractious by the *Director's* comments, shot back instantly, 'Nothing to worry about, minor glitch really. Some old hack from *Special Forces* and some of his lame buddies. We've yet to play hardball, but don't worry, I have the resources and the situation will be resolved'. The *Director* rose out of his chair, walked around, and stood in front of the seated Baker. The purpose of this intimidatory display of power was to remind Baker of where she was in the pecking order of the organisation and the seriousness of the situation. 'I put you in charge of this file because you always get the job done, *do not let me down on this one,* Madison'.

The *Director* then spent some time to educate and remind Baker of her mission's importance. The whole balance of this nation resides on the maintenance of the status quo, historically, financially, and politically. It has been such since the First Fleet arrived in Botany Bay. The contents of the manuscript and or a resurrection of the life and times of Prof. Hamish MacMillan will only threaten the stability of that paradigm. It will alert the population to the notion that there was a chance when Australia could have asserted itself monumentally in the world. When the Government had an opportunity for Australia to rely upon itself totally for defence and could meet all its power needs. The 'Australian

Dream' could have been universally realised as everyone would get a slice of the pie. It is one thing to promise a utopia but another thing to deliver on it. There would have been an end to the 'haves and have nots'. *'Do I need to remind you of who comprises this status quo?'* The *Director* then went further into his professorial mode. He cited how the country was and has always been run by important, self-interest groups. *'Gangs'*, he colloquially referred to them. *The NSW Rum Corps* was the first gang to grab power when it displaced Governor Bligh and others have been admitted over the generations to the select club. There are the political gangs of the major parties who have run the nation since Federation. Remember the political attack on that upstart Hanson when she was attempting to cut in on their territory? Then there is the various Church Gangs who do not wield as much power as before but still get a tax-free gift and still wield incredible influence. We also have the Grammar School Gang that utilises their network to maintain their elite social status. Further to this, is the Police Gang, the Military Officer Corps, Public Service and Union gangs that wield the muscle power. It is in the interest of all these elite gangs to keep the masses conned and to maintain their influence.

The purpose of this is simple – stability, domestically and internationally. If the country acts as the 'grey man' on these two fronts then the gangs do not have to work too hard for their money, medals, titles, status, or survivability. There is no fear of a Russian Revolution or political extremism like the type we see in the United States or ultra-extremism in other parts of the world. In these countries, assassinations are always a possibility and political overthrow a probability. *The Gangs do not want this.* Make no mistake, Australia is not the egalitarian paradise it makes itself out to be. There is no egalitarianism when you only get justice if you can afford a Queen's Council in the courts. There is no democracy when the political system is mostly geared to those who have been to a prestigious university, connected to the Trades Union movement, and an election comes around three or four years. Notice the clampdown when members of the public chose to speak out in defence of their freedoms during the pandemic? Some people would argue the nation is a utopia, a capitalist paradise but for the bulk of the population, *they are nothing more than cash cows to be milked dry or cannon fodder to be used as grist in the mill of war.* The bulk of the population think they have it good, but they are only one-step up from the indigenous people. You do not get an argument from immigrants. To them, Australia really is a workers' paradise. That is only because they come from larger corrupt nations that are poor or violent, like Afghanistan and its new Taliban regime. They see opportunities in Australia that no one sees in the sub-stratum of employment. They are the true silent minority, and you will get no argument from them. The *Director* finished his lecture and said flatly to Baker, 'I want this matter resolved as soon as possible. Do whatever it takes. *Do you understand?*' Baker nodded her head and took this as a dismissal. She quickly stood up and walked out.

The *Director* took the bottom file and placed it on top of the one he had been reading. The heading announced: *Madison Baker*. He decided to review and re-familiarise himself with the woman he had entrusted such an extremely important operation. If he had to select another agent, he would opt for a slightly different personality. He took his time and read through the columns outlining Baker's fundamental achievements and history. *Education*: Degrees in Political Science, Terrorism and Cyber-Crime. Master's degree in Middle Eastern languages and religion. *Work history*: A brief stint as an Army Officer in the Reserve – Intelligence Corps; Police Officer, Investigator and Police Negotiator. Transferred to the Federal Police and now the *Agency. Hobbies*: Fitness Training, firearms, motorsports, and shoes. *Psychological Evaluation*: Highly intelligent. Tends to be ruthless in the pursuit of her goals. Loner. Extremely career driven. *Relationships*: Nil. *Comments*: Work colleagues saw her laughing at the scene in the 'John Wick' movie when the cute, small dog was killed. The *Director* placed the file down and thought, 'well, the ball is in her court now'. He buzzed his secretary and she answered, 'yes Sir'. 'Please get me the complete file on Marcus Hayden, would you?' He had chosen Baker's replacement in the event the matter extended longer than the deadline he had set. *'Damn it'*, he thought, he would instruct Hayden to freelance the operation and be ready to step in at a moment's notice. It was time to work on other pressing matters, but he thought he would first break for lunch. 🖋

Chapter 18

TIME
FOR
REVENGE

The Italian restaurant was unusually quiet for this time of the day, except for the dozen European men who sat at one long wooden table towards the back. The man, who had taken the photo of Nathan outside the service station with the dark hair and dark clothing, was speaking in coarse Italian to the group. He was becoming increasingly agitated at some of the other quieter men at the table. *'They killed my uncle, your uncle, our friend and provider, his sons and our cousins. These bastards must pay for this!'* A look of acquiescence came over the faces of the men who had been holding out. The angry man spoke again, *'I want to know who these people are, where they live, what they drive and what they do'.* He looked across at Vito, 'make inquiries at the hospital where the ambulance took the driver of the *Jeep. Make this guy priority number one'.* He told the men to ready themselves, to get their weapons, and to be available for a phone call at anytime, day or night. The meeting broke up and the dozen men went on their way. Vito climbed into his *Alfa Romeo Giulietta* and headed towards the nearby hospital.

The hospital was only 10 minutes away and Vito found an easy parking bay. He walked into the building and headed for reception. He asked on what ward was David Jameson located. Before the female receptionist could ask the reason why, he flashed a Victoria Police Detective's badge. The reply was instant, 'ward eight, room 12'. Vito travelled in the lift to the appropriate ward, located the ward nurse and produced his 'credentials' once more. He was given directions to David's room. David was fidgeting in a hospital chair and holding the bag of sundries provided by the hospital. He was waiting on some test results and hoping to be discharged soon. Vito walked into the room, much to David's surprise, as he was expecting the Head Nurse. He remained seated as Vito introduced himself as Detective D'urso of the Melbourne Criminal Investigation Branch (CIB), flashed his 'badge' and said he was investigating David's recent road accident. David thought this seemed odd that a detective would investigate a simple road incident, usually the prerogative of the general duty cops, but he decided against asking a few of his own questions. Vito asked, 'and who was travelling with you at the time of the incident? I would like his name and address, please'. David knew that things were not kosher. For a start, he had never known the police, especially a Detective to say 'please' and was surprised the 'Detective' did not ask any pertinent questions about the crash but went straight to Nathan's identity and address. As a precautionary measure, Nathan had rung David as soon as he was able and informed him of all that had transpired after the car accident.

Alarm bells started to ring in David's mind. David went along with Vito's ruse and gave him Nathan's name and an address. However, it was the block next to Nathan's property. He specifically mentioned it was only used as a weekender and around Christmas time. No one would be living there now. To all other questions, David said either he did not know or made up a convincing story. He did comment Nathan would be at the block in a week's time. Vito appeared satisfied, left a blank card with David, if he remembered anything else, thanked him and walked out.

Vito was on the ground floor and walking out to his car. He took out his phone and relayed the conversation he just had to uncle 'Mario', the angry Italian with the dark hair and shady clothing. Up in Ward 8, room 12, David was on his phone to Nathan conveying all he had offered to Vito. Nathan responded, 'Thanks David, couldn't have handled it better. Mark Simmons will be there shortly to pick you up and bring you out to the back of the block. Again, old mate, well done and I'll see you soon'. The Head Nurse suddenly appeared and told David he was free to go. He picked up his plastic bag and caught the lift down. He was tired of sitting around so he thought he would stand out front and wait for his ride...

Chapter 19

KEEPING INVISIBLE

The men and Lauren had driven to 'Caroline's Coffee Caravan' as it was handier to get something to eat before they went to Nathan's cabin. He would send someone on a shopping errand for rations and bits and pieces later. Lauren was introduced to Caroline. The two women talked while lunch was being prepared. The men gathered at one of the benches and Nathan informed them of what had just occurred at the hospital and what David had told the bogus detective. It was easy to derive a conclusion. Family, friends, and associates of the men killed in the garage were now readying themselves for retribution against Nathan and his cohort. Phil made the comment, 'So now we have a government hit squad, Carlton gangsters and possibly red neck

drug runners on our tails, all itching to put big round holes in us. *Who next, Illinois Nazis?'* All the men laughed loudly at the 'Blues Brothers' reference. The hilarity was certainly not a display of nervous bravado from the men. They were not fearfully concerned about the odds or who they would be confronting. Each man had faced greater foes in their lifetime and had experienced a dozen hopeless and dire situations from their military, police, or security service. But here they were, sitting around a bench, at a food caravan in the Central Goldfields of Victoria and having a joke.

Nathan had a glimmer in his eye as he began to speak, 'you know what, we can make this work to our advantage, and, if it goes our way against this enemy, we can all walk away from this'. Nathan made the point that time was of the essence, and they needed to prepare before all the warring factions converged on the block. The key he said was to get 'the enemy' all here at the same time. He specifically labelled the opposition as enemy to pigeonhole all the likely combatants. That way Nathan's men would not view the people coming to try to kill them as a fictional 'Moulder or Scully', 'Uncle Vinnie' or some 'good ole boys'. They were the enemy, simple. These were people to be dispensed with, *terminated with extreme prejudice*, as the CIA would say.

Caroline and Lauren walked over to the bench with the drinks and meals and people began eating. Caro sat next to Nath. 'You were right when you said those spooks would pull up in their SUV. They hadn't a clue where they were going as there are so many new roads and tracks in this area'. She was concerned for Nathan's safety when she made her next comment. 'A moody looking woman got out of a black *Ford* and came over and bought a *Diet Coke*. Be careful of her Nathan, *she has bitch written all over her*'. Nathan said not to worry, because he 'had her number'. He had seen people like her, male and female, over the years and the one constant element about such individuals was they always thought they were superior to anyone else. Arrogance was a poor substitute for ability. It also acted as a liability.

Nathan's plan now was to use the vast spy network Madison had at her disposal against her. Graham would travel to Albury, up on the Victorian/New South Wales border and use Nathan's credit card. Phil would borrow Nathan's cell phone and travel to the southwest coast of the State, somewhere like Warrnambool and make some calls to a variety of businesses and supermarket chains in the district. Paul would borrow Nathan's '67 *Fastback* and drive the *Mustang* around Melbourne. The idea was to send conflicting messages as to Nathan's whereabouts. In the meantime, Nathan would use Caro's spare phone to make his preparations. Later in the week, either on Saturday or Sunday, they would all re-convene at the back end of the bush block.

Having eaten their meals hurriedly, as the men had always done in the military, it was time to carry out their instructions. Nathan and his friends would first secret Lauren to the crude cabin at the end of his property. He would then guarantee her safety until Mad Dog and his *Cossack* lads arrived to commence their security duties. Caro said her goodbyes to the men, kissed Nathan and waved as they drove the ten minutes to the block. On Nathan's instruction, Paul left the main road that would lead to Nathan's main cabin and took a gravel side road to the left. This track went in a huge horseshoe shape leading away from the property for five kilometres but came back around to the right and joined an unused track and fire trail at the eastern side of what Nathan considered as the rear end of his block. The complete eastern end of the property bordered on an animal wildlife corridor that ran North/South. The dirt track was adjacent to the corridor and the fire trail was to the east of the dirt track. This passageway extended for five hundred metres on Nathan's block and for kilometres beyond that.

Nathan thought it prudent that he and Phil

reconnoitre the back cabin before settling Lauren in. The two men had to patrol westerly through the thick animal corridor until they hit Nathan's fence line. The scrub was two metres high in some places. Dense brush clung to the men's clothes, and they had to pick off the clinging vegetation. A native vine meandered through the thicket that also made movement difficult. On Nathan's side of the fence, the bush was not as thick but still provided some concealment. The two men negotiated the fence, one at a time, and moved in awfully slow bounds until they were two metres from the crude shack. As the hut was on the downward slope of the block, it was hard to view from Nathan's main cabin that was 250 metres higher up on the slope. As well, Nathan had planted a few rows of dense shrubs and trees leading down to the shack and around it. You would not know it was there unless you stumbled upon it. Nathan had utilised this ploy when he wanted to go 'missing' for a few days or just wanted to avoid people. The men paused because they could hear something or someone rummaging in the enclosed patio era of the dwelling. Both men produced their handguns and walked slowly forward, weapons in both hands and eyes over the sights. Suddenly, a small dark grey wallaby bounded out to the left and headed uphill and away from Nathan and Phil, its speed increasing as it gathered distance. The two men lowered their weapons and took a long look at each other. Nathan went into the patio era, which was about three metres wide and five metres in length and checked it for any signs of human intrusion or intervention.

The patio was well constructed from old and cheap recycled materials and was half of Nathan's 'house of pain'. A small metal chimney and open brick fireplace was situated in the middle of the room and butted against a brick wall that faced outwards. The patio was adorned with foreign flags, photos, regimental plaques, and militaria, which were souvenirs of his many travels. There were also exercise weight balls, a punching bag, free weights, rower, and a running machine. The main room that adjoined the patio was a sturdy wooden cabin with a white, high-pitched ceiling, pine panelling along the walls and several large colourful rugs were scattered on the wooden floor. A sliding door separated the two living spaces. The cabin doubled as Nathan's music room but could easily accommodate a double mattress, which Nathan always had leaning against a wall.

Nathan gave Phil, who was still outside, a reassuring nod and he went back and fetched Lauren and the other men. Lauren emerged through the bush and took a long-stunned look at the shack. To say that she was shocked and disappointed was an understatement. Her normally smiling countenance disappeared; any joy had galloped away from her face. Lauren resembled an extremely disappointed child that had opened a Christmas present expecting a *Barbie Doll* only to find a pair of socks. In spite of this, Nathan said with some pride, 'welcome to my crap shack!' He went on to reassure Lauren her stay was only temporary, a week or so at the most and it was very cosy in the music room. 'There aren't any bugs, rats or snakes', Nathan assured her, and he said they would bring to her any food that she desired. Her safety and well-being was their number one priority. Nathan whistled and Graham and Paul joined them. 'Fuck', said Paul, 'I forgot how basic this shack was', trying to be diplomatic. Graham had never seen the shack and just looked in wonderment. He muttered quietly to himself, 'talk about "bleak house"'. The adjoining toilet was a 'long drop', in the ground. Basically, a hole that was dug 6 metres or so deep by an auger. A makeshift toilet was placed over the hole and the whole setup was encased in a portable shower tent. The latrine was crude, but effective.

Another benefit of the 'crap shack' was that it was only three hundred metres away from a series of mine shafts, tunnels and mullock hills that existed on the eastern side of the fire trail. The area was known as 'Kong Deng'. The Chinese miners had made substantial finds in this mining area during the gold rushes, and some had become very wealthy. Kong Deng was the Chinaman that had discovered the gold and prosperity and he was lauded by the Chinese Government for his efforts. Many a dead Chinaman went back to the homeland for burial concealing gold in their corpse. Nathan had thoroughly explored all the shafts and tunnels as part of his interest in abseiling and caving; he knew the area like the back of his hand and had navigated around the area to keep his navigation skills sharp. This is where he would lead Baker's crew, the Italians, and the drug runners to their doom, but there was a lot of work and planning to do before this could happen. As Nathan was getting Lauren comfortable, they could hear motorbikes and a vehicle approaching on the gravel road to their east. Nathan looked in that direction and said, 'Phil, do me a favour and guide everyone to the shack, thanks'.

Phil re-emerged in ten minutes with Mad Dog and six heavily armed, tattooed and mean looking bikers, all carrying bulging dive bags laden with ammunition and a variety of explosives. Another vehicle had joined the procession and David and Mark also appeared. Nathan rushed forward to greet and hug the men, especially David. Being a lot older than everyone else, Nathan's concern was greater. There was a general frivolity as old acquaintances were renewed - but all the men knew they had been brought here for a specific purpose. Once all were present, Nathan told they group that he would be outlining his plan in twenty minutes. In the meantime, the bikes and vehicles needed to be concealed. Paul and Graham would guard Lauren until Nathan had his briefing and the bikers established their own security roster.

Soon all the immediate tasks were complete, and everyone was waiting in the patio area of Nathan's crap shack, finding a place to sit among the gym equipment. Nathan looked around at the group assembled and the room fell silent. Nathan sketched how the key to success was to have all the opposing forces meet here on the following Saturday, which happened to be the anniversary of 'Victory over Japan' in *World War Two* or 'VJ Day'. How prophetic was that Nathan thought, 'victory over a cruel and insidious enemy?' Already, Nathan had made plans to give the opposition the run around as to his whereabouts by having Graham, Phil and Paul travel around the state spreading false trails. Nathan stated that he was the prime figure all these groups were looking for. When the time was right, and Baker's frustration was peaking, the trail would wind back to the Central Goldfields. Baker and company would act like hounds chasing the fox until the fox decided to appear and make his last stand. The logic was basic. With any animal pushed into a corner, they act in two ways: they either cower or *come out fighting*. It would look like Nathan was trying to find refuge, back in an area he knew well, when in fact he would become highly dangerous. He knew these people would be obsessed with his destruction, but their arrogance and fanaticism would work in his favour. The opposition would not expect to find the *Cossacks* or Nathan's growing crew of highly skilled veterans lying in wait. Nathan would brief everyone on their roles and tasks as the time drew near; for the meantime, the security of Lauren was paramount.

Nathan walked around the patio, taking it in turns, to thank all those present and to see if any assistance was needed. Paul, Graham and Phil were getting ready to head off and acquire their separate vehicles to commence their tasks. Paul would grab the *Mustang Fastback* in the shipping container up at the main cabin and Graham would drive Phil to Ballarat. The *Kompressor* would ferry Phil around the bottom end of Victoria. Graham would head north in his own car. The bikers had posted a six-man team to guard Lauren and had placed sentries in key areas to function as early warning and to be on the lookout for drones. Mad Dog had picked his best men and Nathan knew this just by the way the bikers conducted themselves. Nathan approached his loyal and trusted friends and said, 'Guys, thanks so much for this, I owe you all, big time', and with that verbal gratitude he shook every man's hand. He asked, in fact, he pleaded they did not take any unnecessary risks. The men would routinely report in every two hours. He further asked that they not sacrifice themselves if compromised. 'If I don't hear from anyone, at the arranged time, I will take it that you have been captured by one of these parties, most probably Baker and her gang. *Don't be a hero*. Hold out if you can but tell them where I am'. He assured them that he would still have time to be ready for the coming battle. These were his best friends, and he was putting them in harm's way, but each man knew they would have done the same for each other. The men headed off to their assigned tasks and Nathan's thoughts and prayers went with them. He stopped and paused for a moment to take a mental note of the situation. Lauren was being heavily protected – *check*! The 'which way did he go' ruse would be started in a couple of hours – *check*! He would borrow the biker van concealed near 'Kong Deng' and go fetch Garry Matthews, who would be arriving at Melbourne Airport in three hours - *check*! ✒

Chapter 20

A NEW PLAYER...

Marcus Hayden had just finished his lengthy phone call with the *Director*. The conversation had gone for nearly an hour and the dialogue was one way, straight down from the top. The *Director* had made it very explicit concerning the outcome of Madison Baker's current operation. He did not want any trails, electronic, paper or otherwise to lead back to him and the *Agency*. Full stop. In the event the operation was going 'off the rail's', Hayden was to have *carte blanche* concerning resources, people and the overall conduct of the operation. He would step in and right any wrongs. Hayden knew he was being brought in as a backup. This was what he was always good for – 'taking out the trash, when the garbage collector had failed to do so'. He was still finishing his lunch at the Brunswick café that mostly catered for Vegans and 'health food nuts'. The décor was a mixture of old chairs, tables, and the tunes played ranged form

indie house music to Edith Piaf. The décor was a bit grubby in places, 'a decent clean up wouldn't hurt this joint', Marcus thought, but the food was wholesome and inexpensive. It was also a discrete venue where he managed to get a lot of his planning done. People came and went but no one looked out of place, they were all there for the food, the vibe, and the hubbub.

With his hunger sated, Marcus walked to the counter, paid for his lunch, and sauntered out on to the main street. It was post lunchtime, so most people were back in their offices or doing whatever it was they do. Marcus was around six feet 2 in the old terminology and possessed a lean, athletic frame. His age was around thirty, but he easily looked five years younger, especially as his jet-black hair had not shown any signs of grey. His hairstyle was in the old, short crew cut fashion and he was wearing a navy-blue Huntington jacket and tan coloured chinos residing over his cheery red Doc Marten boots. He did not look like your average Government intelligence operative but that was the purpose. He would drive over the Westgate Bridge back to his apartment at Newport, access all computer files concerning the operation, and peruse these documents for the rest of the day. He needed to identify and be acquainted with all the players in this game, friendly and otherwise. He needed to familiarise himself with likely scenarios and the possibility of any abstract situations. Marcus's car was parked in a cobbled side street. He chose his own vehicle than the Government issue car. He knew there was the propensity for damage and wear and tear, but he would take style, reliability, and personal knowledge of the one vehicle than free mileage any day, which wasn't an issue on his salary.

Marcus drove a maroon, 3.8 litre, 1967 Jaguar Mk II that was in pristine condition. He adored the vehicle's aggressive styling, its solidness and how it effortlessly clung to the road. Marcus believed in 'driving' vehicles and not just moving metal boxes from **A** to **B**. He took great delight every time he sat in the leather upholstery behind the car's wooden steering wheel and cherished his beautiful ride. As he approached the car, he could see a young scruffy looking man, in his early twenties, leaning against the rear passenger side of the glistening *Jag*. The young man was babbling to a couple of friends, and they all looked they had bought their attire, on reduced sale, from a *St. Vincent de Paul's* opportunity shop. One of the men standing on the curb was smoking a bong made from a protein shake maker but they all looked around when they saw Marcus approaching. Marcus stopped, took a stern look at the man resting against his prized machine and gestured with his thumb that the man should get off his car. Out of glazed eyes, the man responded with a whining plea, *'don't hassle me man,* I'm not hurting anyone, and besides, *I've got a mental disability'.* To which Marcus replied in a loud, assertive voice, *'you'll have a fucking disability if you don't get off my car!'*

The aggressive tone and words stimulated the drug affected young man to advance on Marcus, but that was such a big mistake. A quick move to the right side by Marcus and a straight right punch to the left side of the young man's neck dropped the man to the pavement in an instant. Such a dedicated strike involves the carotid artery and blood flow to the brain - a pause in blood circulation generally results in rapid unconsciousness. Too hard a strike can cause massive swelling, negative blood flow resulting in a lack of oxygen to the brain and death. The other two men stood slack jawed and taken back by what had just transpired, uncertain of what to do. Marcus was losing patience and decided to motivate them, *'so, instead of standing around looking drugged out, fucked out, sucked out and waiting for a handout, pick up your loser mate and fuck off before I get really aggressive'.* The two frightened and indecisive men took this as a command and they roughly grabbed their stunned friend under his arms, beating a fast pace down the cobbled and graffiti covered street. Marcus Hayden was a 'hard man', not to be trifled with. He did not like fools or people wasting his time, and he was certainly not afraid to tell people so.

The *Jag* started on the second turn of the ignition and moved along the grotty back streets until he turned right onto the busy main road back into the main city of Melbourne. Within five minutes, the maroon classic was heading over the busy West Gate Bridge. Flashing speed signs on the bridge indicated eighty kms but the traffic was always that intense no one was about to drive faster than 60. Ten minutes later, Marcus was in his apartment. Five minutes more, Marcus was sitting down with a coffee, his laptop on the table in front of him, perusing files and making notes as he went. The apartment was very utilitarian with a dark sofa, diminutive dining table, chairs, and a small cabinet, which supported a flat screen TV. Not that Marcus watched a lot of television. The walls were painted antique white, not that Marcus was very much interested. There was a studio kitchen in one corner and a bedroom trailed off to the right of the dining/family area. In Marcus's case, 'family area' was oxymoronic as he had never been in a committed relationship with anyone in his life and certainly could not entertain the idea of a family. His parents had divorced when he was a teenager and he had joined the Army to try and find an institution that could provide some structure and stability in his life. His military career was short lived but eventful. From boot camp, he became an infantryman, joined the airborne battalion, and went on deployments to East Timor and Iraq. He was considered 'officer material' but just as his military career was blooming, he took discharge and joined ASIO and then the *Agency*. Like Madison, he had diligently applied himself and worked his way up the spy/security totem. He was resolute in his attitude to stopping terrorist threats in Australia and did not believe in deploying troops to lost causes in the Middle East. Unlike Madison, he generally worked alone and didn't have to sleep with anyone to get things done. He only knew Madison in a professional sense but didn't like her methods, even though she got results. Too many times did she leave a trail of destruction for other people to clean up - her method was always to go too hard, lacking the finesse needed at crucial times in this line of dangerous work.

He sat intently looking at the computer files before him, feet up and resting on the coffee table. He saw Nathan's name and his *Special Forces* pedigree and had a slight recollection he had either met this man or heard of him from another time - he made a mental note not to underestimate this man as Madison had. He did not recognise the names of Nathan's friends: Paul, Phil or Danny and was bemused with the connection to the *Cossacks Motorcycle Club*. He was surprised at the connection to the *Cossacks* and made a mental note their involvement could pose serious trouble. He also saw the latest intelligence reports that depicted Nathan all over the state, at once, and thought, *'how clever'*. So far, he knew Madison and her team were only playing catch-up. Madison was so driven in her methods and personality. It made her one dimensional - chase and catch her quarry, like a cat with a mouse, but Nathan and his 'boys' were always one-step ahead. Also, it was pointless heading to Nathan's cabin as Nathan would be too smart to be sitting there, waiting to be a target.

Marcus decided to look at Nathan's bank records and identify any consistencies that would provide a clue to a behaviour pattern or a contact that had yet to be determined. We all must live and pay to survive in this world. It also said a lot about who we are, what we do and what our priorities are. After ten minutes, Marcus had not seen too much out of the ordinary, so far. Petrol always paid for on the *Mastercard*. Grocery items procured at a variety of supermarkets and outlets. The odd purchase here and there, such as athletic shoes or *Mustang* wiper blades on *E Bay*. Marcus was interested and thought, 'owner of a *Mustang*, not bad... another classic car enthusiast. Obviously, the man has some taste and qualities. What the bank records did show was that Nathan had not subscribed to any loyalty plans or shopping behaviour that dictated patterns of where, when and what time he shopped. And then, the obvious leapt off the screen and hit him – *'Caroline's Coffee Caravan!'* He knew Nathan's block was only 10 minutes away from this eatery, and his bank records illustrated he frequented the diner nearly every other day, sometimes as much as five days a week. This would be good starting point for his investigation as well as getting a feel for Nathan's territory. It was less than two hours by road. The drive would present a fantastic opportunity to motor the Mk II in the country.

He decided to shower and change his clothes. Marcus would also re-fuel the vehicle before he left Melbourne's outskirts. By the time he left, it was 1:30 in the afternoon and the weather forecast was for clear skies, light winds. The maroon *Jag* devoured the highway, and the big British car hummed and ran better as the drove wore on. It was not long before he could see Caroline's signage on the road ahead. The time was 3:10. A few customers were being served chicken wings and fries and took their seat at one of the sturdy wooden benches. Marcus exited the *Jag* and casually walked over to Caroline, who was behind the counter in the caravan. In an upbeat voice, he asked, 'what would the chef recommend?' Caroline had seen the *Jag* roll into the car park but was terribly busy and didn't really take all that notice. Initially, she thought the classic car probably belonged to an old geezer. Now that Marcus was standing before her, she was suddenly intrigued. There was something about this man, besides his rugged, handsome looks.

Marcus was wearing a pale-yellow Fred Perry polo shirt, 501 Levis and black Doc Marten shoes. Well, she thought, *'this man certainly has his own style*, even if it is a bit out of date'. The classic clothes complimented his build, but his persona gave off a vibe that announced that Marcus had 'an old soul' and could have fitted in easily back in the 1960s. It wouldn't have been out of place to see Marcus riding a Lambretta down on the promenade by Brighton beach with the other Mods. 'Well,' said Caroline, 'anything I create is worthy, not bragging but I'm a pretty good cook'. 'Pretty good to look at too, I might add', said Marcus. 'I bet you say that to all the girls', Caroline shot back at him. To which Marcus seriously replied, 'Not really, I don't talk to women a lot'. This comment intrigued Caroline even more and they started casually chatting about the usual things – work, family, travel, and personal aspirations. They spoke unbroken for the next hour, except when Caroline served him a cheeseburger and a *Coke*. It was starting to get late and nearly closing time. Caroline suggested she would like to continue to chat, and she gave him her phone number. Marcus said he felt the same way and said he would ring her the next day. He could see she was excited at the prospect by the fluttering of her beautiful hazel eyes, the constant flicking of her bouncy hair and flashing smiles. Interestingly enough, Marcus found Caroline easy to talk to and thought her innocently charming with a profound sense of humour. Prising information out of her would be easier than he thought and enjoyable with it. He said goodbye to his 'new friend' and drove back to Melbourne in the *Jag*. Caroline followed the sight of his sexy car until it disappeared from view. She felt happy to have met Marcus. It had been so long since she had met a 'nice' guy and she was already hoping things would progress. Too many 'bad boys' had crossed her doorstep in the past. With a slight spring in her step, Caroline cleaned and closed the coffee caravan for the evening. It would be Friday tomorrow and then the weekend, already she was making plans to have a friend work the business for the weekend, just in case Marcus wanted to meet and do something. Caroline knew that she was getting ahead of herself. However, the probability of finding a decent man on a road junction in the central Goldfields was not hard but near on impossible. She had more chance of finding an *old, big, fat, gold nugget.*

Marcus arrived back at his apartment block near 11pm. After going for a long drive for the remainder of the afternoon and early evening, he had stopped briefly for some basic groceries, like bread and eggs and some beers. As he walked into his apartment, he felt quite chuffed at how the day went and his meeting and connection with Caroline. He would phone her the next day, not too early but in the afternoon. As the saying goes, *'treat 'em mean and keep them keen',* because he sensed Caroline would be sweating on his call. He would suggest they go for lunch somewhere, possibly Ballarat as there is a nice upmarket restaurant situated by the lake. Just fancy enough to be impressive and Caroline would see this as being a romantic gesture. It would inspire her imagination, stimulate her romantic inclinations, and draw her closer to Marcus. It would also have the effect of loosening her tongue. No need to use Rohypnol or Ketamine, he mused. As Bryan Ferry once crooned, 'love is the drug'. He would find out what he needed by layering on the charm. His mind wandered a little and he thought about Caroline's pretty smile and easy manner and wondered if in another lifetime, they would make a wholesome couple. His concentration only waned for a few seconds and then he went back to business. He opened a mid-strength beer, flopped down on his sofa, and started reading the 'operation log' that updated him to what Madison had been up to. This was normally reserved only for the *Director's* attention, but he was given absolute clearance. It seems that Madison and her team were following Nathan's bait - they were still off on a wild goose chase all over the state. Again, Nathan's boys had kept ahead of the wolf pack. In the morning, he would re-visit the files, looking for other angles of investigation but he was confident he could get all his information from Caroline. He would have an hour-long physical workout, where he practised his *Krav Maga* techniques and then prepare for an early dinner in Ballarat. The wall clock said midnight, so Marcus hit the light switch and went to bed.

After rising at six, Marcus managed to complete all his chores and research well before lunch and decide to polish and detail the *Jag*. This was not only for his benefit as he loved to see his pride and joy so clean and shiny, but to impress Caroline. At one in the afternoon, he rang Caroline. Immediately, he apologised for the late call and made some flimsy excuse about work, some bogus file, and an impatient boss. Caroline said she completely understood and said there was nothing for him to apologise. He could sense the excitement in her voice because of her speech inflexions and she seemed to hang on every word he said. Marcus expressed regret again for ringing so late but suggested they have an early dinner at the lake restaurant that is if she was not too busy? His treat. He thought, be a 'gentleman' and considerate of others and their lives and activities. At least this was his facade. Caroline couldn't say 'yes' quick enough. Marcus suggested he would pick her up at her place, a good opportunity to recon her house and area and they would have a nice dinner. They chatted for five minutes more and then Marcus said he had to go but was excited to see her again and to go out together. After he hung up, he thought to himself, 'Marcus, you are one suave bastard' and he let out a small chuckle to compliment his inflated opinion of himself. He prepared his clothes for dinner, showered again, and put on his best *Paco Rabanne* aftershave. Before he knew it, it was time to drive to Ballarat and the restaurant.

Chapter 21

GAME CHANGER

Caroline was waiting excitedly out the front of her small but quaint country cottage as the *Jag* pulled up. Marcus leapt out and lightly skipped up the few steps to her front door. To say she was eager was an understatement. Caroline had been ready for hours. After Marcus' call, she had decided to give her house a thorough clean from top to bottom and then embark on a personal beauty program. Toilets were thoroughly scrubbed, kitchen spotlessly cleaned, bed linen changed, and the place dusted and hoovered throughout. Eyebrows were plucked, legs shaved, hair dyed, and unsightly follicles attacked with the *Veet* hair removal cream. A long moisturising bath followed. *'Who knows, the guy might want to come in later',* she thought, and slightly hoped.

The house was made immaculate on the inside but was a bit untidy in its outside appearance. Caroline was quick to point out to Marcus she was not much of a gardener and her business took up so much of her time for household chores. Marcus complimented her on her brightly attractive floral dress and said that the dazzling colours matched her beautiful hazel eyes. She blushed and thanked him for the admiring compliment. The sun was shining gloriously, and, in her mind, things could not be better. Caroline had not felt this special for a long time. Work was always hard and sometimes a drudge and, at times, she wondered why she bothered, but today she felt and looked as radiant as the late afternoon sun they were strolling through. He opened the car door for her, and they set off for the restaurant.

The drive from Caroline's cottage took around twenty-five minutes to reach their destination at the lake, which is at the northern part of Ballarat. Parking was easy, especially when compared with Melbourne and they entered the restaurant as a young, attractive couple. This cute image was not lost on Marcus. At their table, Marcus pulled the chair out for Caroline and they both sat down and ordered. A waiter produced a menu a minute or so later and they sat, in silence, deciding what to eat. 'I'll have the roast lamb', said Caroline. Marcus said enthusiastically, 'that's just what

I was thinking'. Marcus liked lamb but not all that much but here was another small opportunity to make Caroline feel they had so much in common. For most people, it is the little things in common that build and maintains relationships. People connect as a result of a similar likeness for food, a choice of pets, cat or dog or support for a football team. These are the day-to-day themes that carry a relationship. Morales, values, religion, and political affiliation tend to be the deal breakers, the core to a person's character and beliefs and the highly divisive elements that may impede a relationship gelling in the first place.

Marcus complimented Caroline on her pretty dress once more and went on to say how much he admired her for being a successful, small business owner. *'I wouldn't have the courage to embark on such a project'*, he said in a self-deprecating way and Caroline agreed it was a constant risk and always hard work. 'And what is it you do for a living?' asked Caroline. Here was now a terrific opportunity to make Caroline feel even more exalted. The key to lying and being believed is not to deviate too much from the truth. Marcus said that he worked for the Government but all he engaged in was statistics and boring stuff like that. He added, 'The best I'm hoping for is a decent superannuation pension one day for years of faithful service. *I've yet to find my passion, my true calling'.*

With that comment, Caroline paused and looked at him sweetly as if he were a lost puppy. She felt sorry for Marcus, which is what he wanted, and asked how he came into possession of such a beautiful car, on a public servant's salary. He sorts of half expected this question to come up. 'Well,' he said, 'the car had belonged to my father, but he passed away some years ago. I maintain it as a tribute to him'. His explanation touched her heart. Caroline did not know what to say but thought he was the most decent man she had met in years. The various courses came and went, and they had a very animated and stimulating conversation all evening, punctuated by a great deal of laughing and banter. Marcus had briefly asked about her friends and so forth but didn't pry too much so as not to cause any suspicion. He thought, *all will be revealed, at the right time*. Much to Marcus' surprise, he had really enjoyed Caroline's company and repartee this evening. They had a real connection. It had been one of the best dates he had been on in a long while - not that he went on many dates.

As it turned out, they were the last couple to leave the restaurant and they both commented on how the evening had flown. The *Jag* cruised back to Caroline's house in the still countryside. A slight moon was peeking through the woods and the whole evening felt magical. Caroline felt inebriated but it was not anything she had drunk. She was starting to fall for Marcus and began noticing the little things she liked and found interesting about him, like his smile, sense of humour, manners, and decency. She thought, *'his physique wasn't bad to look at, either'*. The *Jag* gently pulled up to the gravel drive by the house and stopped. Both adults stared at each other, deciding who would be the first to speak. Caroline uttered, *'I'm dying for a coffee,* would you like to come in and join me?' Marcus' response was immediate and precise, *'I'd love to'*. He knew where this old cliché was probably heading, and he followed Caroline the few steps to her front door. Although this was all part of his ruse to solicit information, a part of him wanted her so badly. She turned around to see where he was in the faint moonlight, and he gave her a full kiss on her beautiful, soft mouth. The kiss lingered for an eternity and they both revelled in its sensuality and intimacy. Caroline was still fumbling for the house keys at the same time and attempting to open the front door.

Finally, the door was flung wide open, and the couple emerged through the entrance as 'one', in a tight, lover's embrace. The couple were headed for the couch, which was across the room - stumbling and fumbling for buttons and zippers to undress one another. All the while, the kissing, caressing, and exploring did not cease - belts were unfastened, and shoes flung randomly aside. The switch on a nearby table lamp was grappled with and hurriedly flicked on; Caroline paused, looked adoringly at Marcus, and said softly, *'Lover, I think the bedroom will be more comfortable'*. They rose as one, half-dressed and Marcus picked her up in his strong arms and carried her effortlessly into the bedroom. The room was bathed in half-light with the moonlight providing a backdrop to the fabric padded bed headboard that was positioned against the windowsill. Marcus carefully and, ever so gently, placed Caroline on the soft bed and lay by her side, stroking her hair and kissing her silky neck and sweet lips. Caroline felt blissfully paralysed by his attention and intent to afford her so much pleasure. She had not been loved in such away for a long time and wilfully slipped out of her remaining clothes. *Caroline would give herself to him completely, this night.* Marcus followed her cue and removed his remaining garments, without stopping his kissing or caressing of her bare form. By now, Marcus was aching to have her. Bedding was flung aside so they could consummate their physical union and inner desires and now, dappled rays of moonlight lay across their writhing naked and moaning bodies. It was not cold in the room but becoming fresh, but neither did Caroline or Marcus notice the dropping temperature. What they both knew was that, although extremely late in the evening, they had a long, irresistible night ahead...

It was nearly ten in the morning when Caroline awoke from her deep slumber. The sun's piercing rays and shadows were projecting across her bed and her room in abstract angles. She could feel the warmth, as she had not opened her eyes yet. A few birds were twittering, noisily outside but she was oblivious to any ruckus as she was still savouring her night with Marcus. Caroline thought lovingly about some of the romantically wild and beautiful moments they had, and a cheeky, mischievous smile appeared across her pink lips. She slid her warm arm under the doona across to where Marcus was sleeping, but that side of the bed was stone cold, and *he was not there.* Her eyes flashed wide open and darted to where he had been sleeping and a feeling of dread and loss rapidly descended upon her. She wondered if she was waking up alone, as she had done so many times before. Afraid and somewhat hesitant, she called out loudly, *'Marcus... Marcus!'.* At that instant, Marcus rounded the corner and walked into the room, resplendent in her long blue fleece nightgown, arms laden with a burdened breakfast tray festooned with juice, coffee, cereal, toast, and scrambled eggs. 'Good morning, baby', he chirped and placed the tray down on the bed, besides his new, sexy lover. He leaned over and gave her a long, powerful kiss. 'Well,' said Caroline, 'How lucky can a country girl get, dinner, romance, great sex and breakfast in bed?' The couple kissed passionately a few times more and Caroline then sat up in her bed, with a few pillows behind her, propping her up. At this precise moment, life was perfect.

Caroline did not want to burst her 'happy bubble' by asking awkward theoretical questions about them, concerning what was going to happen now or what was in their future. She thought, *now is not the time to get ahead of myself*. In the past, she had been labelled 'clingy' and 'demanding' when asking men such questions. This time she would just enjoy the journey and see where it took her. They ate their breakfast together, in bed, and chatted and kissed and looked, tenderly at one another between slices of buttered toast and mouthfuls of crunchy cereal. Caroline coyly asked if Marcus had anything to do during the day and would he mind spending the Sunday with her. He said that would be fine, his words were, *I would love to* and he stated he couldn't think of anywhere else he would want to be, but he would have to drive back to Melbourne later in the evening or early in the morning as he had an early start with work. Of course, most of this was a lie. In his role with the *Agency*, Marcus could come and go as he pleased but, as much as he was fond of Caroline, he truly did not want to get her hopes up and hurt her. His own feelings towards her were now in conflict and he mentally chided himself about keeping to the mission. He felt joyful and confident in

her company and enjoyed their conversations, which, most times, invariably led to giggles and laughter. He had never experienced such emotions and sensuality with anyone else. Marcus had girlfriends in the past, but they felt more like acquaintances than someone he would want to be with, day in and day out. As far as their lovemaking went, they were in fine tune with each other's emotional wants and physical needs. For Marcus, it wasn't a task, or a job requirement to make sweet love to Caroline, as he had done so on other occasions with women. They had shared a beautiful, loving, and seductive experience together. He felt privileged to have made love to such a magnificent soul. Still, Marcus had a job to do...

The young lovers spent most of the afternoon lying in bed together. The TV was on in the background, with some old movie that had been played a million times before; Marcus had gone back and forth to the kitchen making copious cups of tea and cooking toast, which they consumed, in between bouts of cuddling and kissing. All the while, he was gaining her confidence but was suffering from guilt pains because of the way he felt about Caroline. Now was the time to ask some pertinent questions before he changed his mind. Marcus snuggled up to Caro, who had a velvety, grey velour blanket draped around her because she was still naked. He decided to blurt out. 'How do you get on with friends' way out here and working on your own in the caravan? You must get very lonely'. Caroline said that like most girls, they have a phone network, and she keeps in contact that way. 'But, besides the public, don't you get lonely not seeing a good friend, occasionally?' 'I know you have your regulars, but they don't really count as close friends'. He went on to say how it must be difficult to know anyone due to the location of her caravan and her isolation to properties in the area. Caroline said that she didn't mind being on her own, now that she had her beautiful Marcus. He paused and kissed her for that lovely sentiment. 'But you must have a good buddy out here, *especially when I'm not around?*' he said. 'Well,' said Caroline, 'I know a guy who is more than a friend. A big brother, in fact. We go way back; many years and he is always popping in to see how I am and lives not far from the caravan site'.

Caroline spoke of how Nathan had taken her abseiling for fun and country drives in his *Mustang Fastback*. He had many tough ex-military friends coming and going from the cabin on his block. Some of these mates were ex-Special Forces whilst others had been in the police force. Caroline hadn't seen him for a few days now, she supposed he was on a job or off with some of his mates. However, she knew he would come by soon. He always did. She knew one of his close friends had recently died, so this may account for his absence. Caroline would pop by the cabin and feed *Moochee* the cat, every other day. The cabin had a cat flap, and the old cat came and went as it pleased. Caroline had innocently offered a great deal of information about Nathan and his friends. She would die inside, right there, if she knew she was betraying a confidant and Marcus was just playing her. Whilst Caroline had offered some information, she hadn't really told Marcus anymore than what he already knew. The important thing was, she had not divulged any information concerning Lauren or what she knew about MacMillan or Ghent.

As far as Marcus was concerned, all this information was important as it confirmed that Nathan was still in contact with many of his army buddies, knew people in the police and was a hard man to track down. He had solid friends, was smart and tough and hardly ever slipped up. A difficult adversary, Marcus thought. He already knew this, but Caroline had provided intimate verification. Deep inside, he was incredibly pleased Caroline had not told him anything that compromised her coveted friendship with Nathan. He leaned over to her slowly and roughly ripped back the soft fleece blanket that protected her gorgeous naked body. She looked back at him with a surprised look but, before she could utter a syllable, his taught muscular frame lay on her supple form, *and he was kissing her with a passion she had never experienced.*

The couple had made love, intermittingly through out the long warm afternoon. Marcus could not remember when he was so happy to be in the company of someone, and it was not just the fantastic sex. Caroline was napping blissfully and soundly making love all afternoon tends to tire a person. Marcus was gently caressing Caroline's hair as she slept on his chest, but he also stared up at the ceiling. He had mixed feelings. On the one hand, he was a highly paid Government official who was entrusted with maintaining the rule of law, as the Government saw fit. On the other hand, his life had been mostly vacant since he left the Army, so many years before. Frequently, he conducted tasks for the *Agency* that he was not fond of and, repeatedly, he acted in vicious and hurtful ways that he plainly did not like. The *Agency*, with its 'Black Ops' culture, sophisticated equipment and operations had been so seductive at the beginning, but the lustre had been fading for some time and the novelty of it all had nearly worn off. Besides, he was weary of being a loner. Marcus did not want to end up like his parents, harbouring the bitterness he saw in them or other people who were single and unattached. His mother had whispered to him when he was still a boy that the time would come when he connected with another human being like no other, a special and unique person who he could see spending the rest of his life with. With Caroline, his mother's prophecy was realised, and the time now was to act. He decided he would not go back to Melbourne later in the evening. This is where he wanted to be, in the loving warmth of Caroline. The difficult part was how he was going to sever the chord to the *Agency*...

Chapter 22

GOOD OLD BOYS & OLD ITALIANS

I t had taken some time for Tyler to recover from his altercation from Paul. After the initial assault, he had experienced delayed concussion and was ferried, by his friend, to the Ballarat Base Hospital. The story went that he had been kicking a footy and mucking about with some mates and was injured in the process. The nurse said he would be released in a day or so. Paul had been easy on him. Outside of a bloodied shirt and a dent to his pride, the only residual effect was a throbbing headache. As he sat up in the clean white hospital bed, Tyler furiously outlined what he wanted his mate, Brendan, to do. 'Mate, go and get all the boys and tell *them I want them ready to fire up when I give the go ahead.* Tell them to bring their shotguns and as much ammo as they can carry. We are going to sort out these friends of Lauren and *fix her up as well.*' He was starting to become really worked up and seethed about how they needed to do this. It would be a show of strength to outsiders, especially these smart-arse city types. They would not be pushed around by anyone. Any weakness now would be an invitation by his competitors to muscle their way into his operation. He thought by eliminating Lauren, Paul, and the boys, he would also remove any threat from his local competitors; he would be killing two birds with the one stone. Tyler couldn't be more wrong...

After receiving his instructions, Brendan raced off from the hospital to contact Tyler's drug crew and to make preparations. The crew comprised of around 15 men, all local guys in their early twenties. Each man had their own job in the operation. Some men cultivated the crop, others distributed the weed, whilst some functioned as security. Other men saw to the cultivation and distribution of the drug. The men had resorted to the drug trade as it was an opportunity to earn easy money. Outside of a few men with trade skills, most of the crew had little education or zero inclination to work hard for a living. To use the common vernacular, *'they ain't the sharpest tools in the shed.'* Jobs were scarce in the country unless you wanted to work real hard and there were plenty of those jobs about, on farms and in construction. The only thing going for them was their allegiance - mostly out of fear, to Tyler. The crew had, in the past, had a few minor run-ins with other local drug dealers, but Tyler's instruction was taking them all to another dangerous level. The men collected what weapons and ammunition they had, fuel, vehicles, and anything else they thought would be of assistance in the coming fight. It would not before long before they realised how they were so much out of their depth...

Meanwhile, in Carlton, Mario was still organising his crew for their assault on Nathan and his friends. He was having difficulty putting a team togethers as most of his crew worked in their own businesses and needed time to find replacements. Some of his associates were also getting a 'bit long in the tooth' to be gangsters and were only involved as a result of Mario's insistent cajoling. It wasn't as simple as he thought it would be. Nevertheless, weapons had been stockpiled, suitable vehicles selected; mostly vans and these people movers were fuelled and ready to go. Mario had enlisted Vito to gather more intelligence on Nathan, but the only information forthcoming had come from David at the hospital. He thought this would be the right time to reach out to his cousin who was a Senior Inspector with Victoria Police for information but even that was a slim hope. He knew he couldn't keep his crew together for more than a week or two before it all fell apart, *so time was of the essence.*

Chapter 23

THE INTERVIEW

Garry was patiently waiting at the designated pick-up point, with a single green canvas duffle bag, which looked shabby and weary from many overseas assignments. A small black worn computer bag hung lightly over his left shoulder. This was at the ground level pick up point, at the main car park on the other side of the road, opposite the domestic departure entrance at Tullamarine airport. Garry looked like your typical tourist, what with his scruffy cargo trousers, loose fitting T-shirt, two-day beard, *Nike* runners and minimal luggage. He had the sort of worn and tired appearance that suggested he had always just arrived and *forever belonged to somewhere else.* Garry had been working as a free-lance journalist around the world's hotspots for so long that he virtually lived out of a bag or two, but he could hit the ground running anywhere his boss sent him and wouldn't leave until he had his story. Nathan pulled up and gave Garry a

toot with the van's horn. It had been a few years since they had last met, face to face, and he wasn't sure if they could recognise each other. But they did. Garry jumped into the van. Both men smiled, shook hands and Nathan drove around to the northern outer side of the airport, which would take him back to the bush block on a meandering route via Sunbury.

There was a slight pregnant pause for a minute or two as neither man really knew what to say to get the conversation going. Nathan decided to start with the usual, 'how was your flight,' to which Garry replied, 'fine but it's getting like flying in a sardine can these days, too many big people into too many small seats.' This seemed to relax the men and they began talking about the situation at hand. Garry asked what Lauren was like. He needed to ascertain her credibility, which was critical to the story's validity. Was Lauren intelligent, overly emotional or a 'space cadet'? Did she use drugs or had mental health issues? What was her relationship and history with her father like, if any, and was there any information that could be of use from the deceased Mother, such as records or photographs? Nathan said that they really hadn't had much time to ascertain the answers to most of those questions and was hoping Garry's journalistic skills would bear fruit. Their sole purpose at this time had been personal protection. As Nathan emphasised, 'we need to get this story out there to not only offer the country *a possible new way forward, a new direction* for this *bloody country,* but to *save the lives of a lot of people* who were at the mercy of Madison Baker and her cronies.' Garry nodded in agreement and said, 'definitely, the only way to keep everyone safe is to have this on all forms of the media and to create such a stink. The Government can go into damage control and deny as much as they like but when they are bombarded with questions and accusations of murder, secret weapons, and a massive cover-up, you will be the real heroes in this. With any luck, the Opposition Government will demand a Royal Commission.' Nathan told Garry that he would pop in and see his friend Caroline at her coffee caravan and to make sure things were fine with her. He said that he saw her as a kid sister and was always looking out for her. Nathan arrived at Caroline's eatery from a different route. After following the main road from Sunbury back to the central Goldfields, he opted to choose a variety of bush roads; sometimes doubling back to make sure he wasn't being followed.

The van slowly pulled up 20 metres from Caroline's coffee van. Both men got out and ambled over to the van. Caroline, who was busy battering some fish fillets, stopped, and looked up. 'Hey Caro, how are you doing?' said Nathan. 'This is my friend, Garry. He'll be helping us with Lauren.' 'Hi Garry,' replied

Caro cheerfully, 'is there anything I can get you both?' 'A couple of coffees would be fine, and I'll have a caramel slice,' said Nathan. Garry sat as a silent passenger in the following conversation between Nathan and Caroline. Nathan asked how life was treating her and how her business was fairing. Caroline replied with simple adjectives but was more interested in telling Nathan about her new, dreamy boy friend. 'Good on you,' said Nathan excitedly, 'tell me more about this guy?' Caroline went into great detail to describe his features, manners, and his slightly *bohemian* wardrobe.

The last thing she mentioned about Marcus was his swanky car. Like most men, Nathan wasn't too interested about Marcus' physical looks and features or his wardrobe; the car did interest him, and he thought, 'ah, a *Jag*, classic car and a man after my own heart.' Nathan then asked Caroline what Marcus did for a living as he was concerned whether this Marcus guy was self-sufficient or a moocher. Caroline said that he worked for the Government in statistics, or something mundane like that. She wasn't very sure. But he did ask many unusual questions. 'Okay,' thought Nathan, 'Government guy who asks questions.' Nathan asked another seemingly innocent question, 'Caroline, where did you meet Mr. Wonderful?' Caroline stated how he had just turned up at her 'Coffee Caravan' and they just started talking. 'Oh, that seems nice and fortuitous,' replied Nathan, but the warning hairs on the back of his neck were slightly prickled. Again, Nathan made an innocent inquiry, *What sort of things does he ask about?*' 'Oh, nothing too heavy, just things like do I have a lot of friends, and do I know people who own properties close to my 'coffee caravan.' He also asked about the sorts of people who pass through my business, do I get a lot of ex-military guys through here or did I know any?' Caroline had innocently furnished Marcus with basic information about Nathan and some of his military colleagues. Caroline was proud to know Nathan and what he had accomplished in his life. She had always thought he had a resume and life experience like no other. Caroline stated that Marcus had said he had spent six years in the military when he was a younger man. 'I think he was in the infantry?' she stated. On the face of it, it all seemed innocent. However, to an inquiring, intelligent and suspicious mind such as Nathan's, there seemed to be too many factors that could be a coincidence. He hoped for Caroline's sake that this was all so innocent, but he couldn't take the chance. He made a mental note to contact Paul to see if can find out anything on 'Marcus Hayden.'

Nathan continued conversing with Caroline until they finished their beverages, and his delicious caramel slice, but only decided to engage in simple chit-chat and to divert the attention away from the new boyfriend. The business, weather, rainfall, and the coming football finals were all covered. Nathan rose from the bench seat and gave Caroline another peck on her cheek and cheerfully said goodbye and wished that things continued to go well with her new beau, Marcus. He didn't like it but deep down he had his suspicions. Garry said it was a pleasure to meet Caroline, thanked her for the great barista coffee and decided to pay for their snack. Both men walked away at the same time, saying their goodbyes to Caroline, and jumped into the van. 'Beep, beep,' went the horn as the men sped off to the 'crap shack' at the back of his block, via the long and convoluted route on the back roads.

Nathan drove fast, he always did. The isolated dirt back road coughed up vast plumes of chalky gravel dust as they hurtled down its solitary length; Garry was slightly scared with the vehicle's speed and grabbed the side rail on the van's front passenger pillar. They were within 200 metres of their arrival point before they were directly adjacent to the 'crap shack' when a beat up, dark grey Nissan Patrol 4x4 emerged forcefully on to the road from a fire cutting that was concealed at a right angle. Besides the driver, two heavily armed and tattooed bikers leapt out of the vehicle brandishing a pump action shotgun and two Russian assault rifles. Nathan's vehicle slid slightly sideways to a stop on the dirt road and the bikers rushed over, in menacing fashion, to the vehicle. Straightaway they identified Nathan and gave him the thumbs up sign and the vehicle travelled towards the extra 200 metres where they were escorted by more armed bikers to a small bush car park off the dirt road. Nathan's arrival had already been radioed by handheld radios to Mad Dog, who was overseeing the operation from the crap shack. The car park was 50 metres on the eastern fire trail side of the road but led into a lush thicket that had been additionally camouflaged from the road and overhead from prying drones and helicopters. A lot of thickets had developed all along the road due to back burning and previous bushfires. Both men alighted from the van and were escorted to the other side of the road and to the 'crap shack' by a single armed and aggressive looking biker.

On arriving, Nathan said to Garry, 'welcome to the *Casa del Phillips*!' Garry stood in dumb silence as he looked at the bleak, crude shack for a few seconds and astonishingly announced, 'my God, people don't live in that hovel, do they? Damn, I sort of expect one of the Beverley Hill Billies to live in a shack like that. Where's Jed Clampett?' Nathan looked a tad offended by this statement and said, *'awwww, why does everyone say that?'* Mad Dog came out, strode over to Nathan, and gave him the standard biker's hug and casually commented, 'How's it going brother, all good here.' Nathan happily introduced Garry to the biker, and they firmly shook hands. Garry had seen a lot of violent places and brutal men in his time, but he was taken back by the commitment coming from the members of the *Cossacks*. Nathan had informed Garry of the laneway shoot out near Phil's building and the subsequent ambush where a number of club members and Danny had been slain by Baker's crew. He could identify the anger in the men's eyes and their irrevocable resolve to put things right with their club. 'How's Lauren going,' asked Nathan. Mad Dog spent a few minutes advising Nathan of the current situation since they had taken on security duties.

Lauren had been fed well and was sleeping okay but she was getting bored with her environment and was starting to fret because of the situation she now found herself. He was clearly relieved that Nathan and Garry had arrived as it would change the daily momentum that had become tedious - a few new faces and someone else to talk to would be liberating for her, socially and spiritually. Nathan knew Garry's interview with Lauren would be a cathartic experience for her on so many levels.

All three men walked in the shack to find Lauren sitting in a patio chair, reading a book on modern gardening techniques. Nathan said *'hi'* to Lauren and introduced a smiling and cheerful Garry, who asked her when she thought it would be a good time for an interview. Lauren spoke excitedly and said, *'whenever you like.'* Garry suggested that they get a coffee, make themselves comfortable and re-convene in ten minutes. Nathan busily tapped out a text to Paul concerning Marcus Hayden. A Sony micro recorder was placed on the table and a small video camera was situated on a tripod in such a position that it could film the interview and interviewee. Nathan said he would help out as required. Mad Dog decided to wait outside. Garry asked if Lauren was comfortable, to which she nodded. He then began the interview with the usual perquisites, such as: *what is your name, date of birth, where do you live and what do you do for a living?* With those mandatory details completed, he began the interview in earnest. Garry asked Lauren what her earliest recollections of her father were, if she had any. She replied that she had never known her father but only knew him from what her mother had offered her in the last year of her life. Her mother had relented somewhat in her stubborn stance and had informed Lauren of her father's academic background and the reasons why her mother had left him and had remained estranged. Lauren said that her mother did not know if or when her father had died but had her suspicions when the child maintenance payments ceased, only a few years after Lauren was born. Her Mother had gone to a variety of Government welfare agencies to question this but was always given the run-around, to the point she no longer bothered pursuing the matter. There was a marked age difference between Lauren and her parents, and she had been born when her mother was in her early forties; very often did people think Lauren was a grandchild and not a daughter.

Garry politely asked Lauren if she could remember anything else that her mother had told her about her father. Lauren apologetically replied that was all she knew, and her own research had not furnished very much information. The interview had only been going for less than ten minutes and Garry was disappointed to say the least. He was just about ready to turn the recording equipment off when Lauren announced, *'but I do have some photographs of my father.'* This comment perked up Garry and he asked if she could place them on the table. Nathan was visibly interested as well and moved slightly forward but out of camera range. Lauren produced an array of photographs, many of which were in black and white and laid them out in a playing card deck sequence on the table. Hamish MacMillan had sent these reminders to his wife. He was reaching out to her in an attempt to re-connect but his wife either had missed the point or just didn't care any more. Tragically, an opportunity lost for any sort of reconciliation. Both men perused the old images. Nathan instantly identified two identifiable pictures of the professor conducting experiments in the laboratory bunker. Other pictures denoted various scientific field trips that looked like they had been taken somewhere in Australia's 'Red Centre.' There were photos of men standing around vehicles, collecting rock samples, or taking measurements with various types of equipment, Geiger counters and that sort of instrument. Then, all of a sudden, *one picture stood out amongst the others... This was the diamond in the rough! The Mother lode!* On the glazed glass tabletop lay a slightly crumpled, sepia photograph of smiling men standing in a group photo. In front of the men, on a simple wooden frame, lay a thermo-nuclear device, roughly the size of a 200 litre olive drum. Scrawled on the bomb in chalk, was the name *Lauren*. Garry flipped the photo, desperately hoping to locate information on the back. He was in luck. In cursive script was the information: 'Woomera, Tower XV, 1998'. The men didn't say anything but each one knew what the other man was thinking. Lauren hadn't realised the significance of the photograph she had received as a young girl and had kept the photographs stored away until Nathan and his friends crossed her doorstep. MacMillan had invented his 'bomb' and here was the photographic proof, not just some pipe dream. The area where the bomb had been evaluated was also identified. This was a starting point, a watershed for further investigation and search for the truth! Garry turned off the recording equipment. 'Well,' said Nathan, *'this changes everything.'* 'That's for sure,' said Garry. 'I know this all happened some time ago, but if we can locate the bomb or some credible information surrounding the weapon, we can validate MacMillan's theories and the Government link.

The men discussed the only way this was going to happen was to travel to Woomera and investigate the site in the photograph. So far as the men knew, nuclear weapons had not been tested at this site. It had been primarily used as a rocket-launching site and provided assistance for the Americans during the Apollo space missions, via the use of the tracking equipment that was there. Nevertheless, there must be some radiation still present, even if a buffering system was employed to prevent nuclear fallout. This would be confirmed by a Geiger counter, and they could take some small soil samples as well as filming the investigation. The trouble was this evidence was all on Government land that spanned for hundreds of kilometres and was protected by private security! Lauren appeared disinterested in all this talk of secrets, Government, and the search for the truth. She felt that she was as far from any knowledge of her Father as she had ever been. Lauren excused herself and went into the cabin to rest on the camp bed. Outside, the two men continued to talk, knowing they needed to get this information soon before Madison Baker *could alter the truth or erase the trail.* Nathan went outside the patio and located David, who was doing his turn to stand watch. The men chatted for ten minutes, and the conversation was ended with Nathan giving David a mighty congratulatory slap on the back. Nathan spoke to Mad Dog and a muscled biker came and relieved David of his duty. David picked up his phone and made a brief call, said goodbye to Nathan and exited through the green wildlife corridor to the east, and to the dirt track, where he was going to be driven back to his property in southern NSW. The wheels had been set in motion for a mighty trip to central Australia...

Chapter 24

THE DEAD CENTRE

David arrived at his picturesque rural property early the next morning, around five am. It was still dark, but the glistening sunrise was emerging slowly from shadowy hills in the east. He thanked the driver a couple of times and walked down to his home from the gate at the top of the paddock. The wooden plaque on the gate announced '*Heiligdom*,' Afrikaans for '*sanctuary.*' Not much had been said in the long drive home, as the gruff biker driving the van wasn't the chatting type. David decided early that he would sleep during the journey. He would need to be rested and thinking straight as he had a lot of serious

work to do later that morning. David thought he would first eat a hearty breakfast of waffles and eggs, consume a 'bucket' of coffee to keep him awake for the interim and then start his preparations. A nap was the plan and his reward for the afternoon.

After an enjoyable meal, he walked out briskly into the cool of the yard and jumped into his trusty truck. The *Isuzu* chugged into life slowly, with black diesel exhaust fumes clouding the air. David carefully positioned the large vehicle in front of the huge, wheeled transport that contained his personal gyrocopter. The truck reversed until it was level with the automatic trailer hitch on the container. One gentler nudge and the hitch engaged the tow bar of the truck with a resounding '*clunk.*' David stepped down from the truck, connected the thick trailer chains and attached the electric cable that worked the brake lights and indicators. Back in the truck's cabin, David assessed the brakes and indicators and could see, using his mirrors that they all worked. The last thing he wanted *was an over-zealous cop pulling him over for faulty taillights!* The container was always ready to go. However, David liked to check and re-check, it was in his DNA from his service life and the nature of flying aircraft. Frequently, David would get calls to showcase his gyrocopter, which he named '*Cerberus,*' to potential buyers looking for a similar aircraft. As a result,

Cerberus was always fuelled, additional fuel and water cans were in the container, along with tools, spare parts, cooking equipment and clothes. David's trips would frequently last a day or two, so he needed to be self-sufficient. The plan at this stage was to re-connect with Nathan and Garry somewhere over the border in South Australia. After a discussion of the forthcoming activities, the men would drive to a suitable remote location to unload *Cerberus* and prepare her for flight. The aircraft did not require your traditional bitumen airstrip. It could be launched from any flat surface, such as a saltpan. Being a short take off aircraft, *Cerberus* only required a couple of hundred metres.

David's aircraft was loosely based on the *Xenon XL* model and could easily accommodate three people. This had been the demand for potential buyers, especially rural purchasers who needed plenty of capacity for passengers and all types of equipment. The vehicle was light to handle. The aircraft could be pushed slowly out of the container, attached to a safety belay rope by one person and retracted by the electric winch back into the container. After demounting the aircraft onto the blue stone, hard standing in the yard, David commenced to do his many checks. Like any aircraft David had ever flown, he methodically went about *Cerberus* checking its external frame, struts, prop, gyro prop, wheels and outside attachments for serviceability and any sort of damage and wear and tear. He was meticulous to the point that the three undercarriage tyres' air pressure was exact and correct. The engine and its compartment were then inspected from top to bottom and included all fluid levels, hoses, couplings, wiring and fuel system. David paid particular attention to the rotor head that was connected to the autogyro prop. A ballistic recovery system (BRS parachute) had been installed on this new model. Upon a rotor head failure or breakage, the parachute canopy would be propelled out from the side of the aircraft, deploy, right itself along the aircraft's bulkhead and ensure a safe landing. This innovation has been used in standard aircraft for some time and was a Godsend to those pilots who fly the gyrocopter, as this aircraft completely depends on auto-gyration of the large propeller if the engine fails. There is no glide element with gyroplanes. No gyro prop and the craft will fall like a brick to earth.

The last vital area to be examined was the cockpit and the internal elements of the aircraft that included gauges, internal safety equipment, radio, manuals, and flight logbooks. When all the checks had been complete and David was satisfied his aircraft was ready to go, he turned on the ignition and fired the engine to run the main drive propeller. He sat and listened intently to the engine as well as inspecting the gauges.

No flat spot noises in the exhaust or any warning signs via the gauge needles. *Cerberus* was purring like a kitten. David killed the engine and went inside to make another strong coffee whilst the engine cooled down. In five minutes, he returned with a mug of coffee and a fruit bagel. He walked very slowly around the aircraft, inspecting the fuselage, again, and taking mental notes as he sipped his coffee and downed the snack.

In ten minutes, *Cerberus* had been carefully winched back into its large metal container, secured with tied-down straps, and pronounced ready to go. Three hours later after his nap, David packed a small bag with toiletries, phone charger, *Gatorade* and some other odds and sods he thought he would require on this trip. One minute later, the Isuzu was pulling out from the property's main gate and making its way to the highway, as indicated on the cabin's internal GPS. A long drive was ahead but this would be punctuated by a number of rest and fuel stops. Although David was probably the oldest member of Nathan's band of 'rascals,' as Madison had called them, he was giddy with excitement as any schoolboy would be on his first big adventure...

Meanwhile, Nathan and Garry were preparing for their trip with the same sort of precision and detail. Firstly, a small but accurate Geiger counter needed to be acquired and other specialised scientific measuring instruments. Garry also required some long-range camera lenses and a lens that could be used in a darkly lit environment, such as a dark cave or poorly lit warehouse. He would also take his standard recording equipment. Nathan would ring Phil to source and ferry the equipment before the end of the day and would also request three sophisticated handheld radios complete with auto scrambling, which would conceal their radio communications.

Nathan was putting his kit together too. He was lucky he stored most of his vital pieces in his 'war bag' at the back cabin. Like most old soldiers, Nathan had kept his army trunk when he left the military, and, like most old soldiers, he kept a number of items in his trunk that were for his '*eyes only*.' As this would be a covert but highly dangerous task, Nathan thought he would take no chances. This mission had to be spot on as they would not have any second chances. He placed a well-used olive-green Army echelon bag to one side and started placing select items into this carry all. A couple of smoke grenades and flares wouldn't go astray, he thought as well as a small pair of binoculars. His 5.56 calibre Ruger Mini 14 with folding stock was placed into the bag, along with a webbing chest vest that contained 10 rifle magazines, all containing 30 rounds of ammunition. He had a belt rig already setup that was a heavy leather belt with a holster for the *Browning*, plastic scabbard for the *K Bar* and a large utility pouch, where he would keep such necessary things as a torch, batteries, black balaclava, and compass, pace counter, cable ties, nomex gloves, night vision scope and writing implements. A small patrol pack would be included for some rations and water and for carrying bigger items - as always, he would bring his trusty 'grab bag.' He would dust off an old green pair of overalls and place in a black pair of Magnum jungle patrol boots. A lightweight camouflage net, a roll of hessian and a small roll of chicken wire would be taken and carried in the patrol pack. Most of their investigating would be conducted at dusk or dawn and Nathan thought this equipment should see them through their task. It also gave them the option to stay until they had collected what they came for. Once Nathan was satisfied with his kit choices, he thought it was time to eat, have a brew and consult a road map for their impending journey.

Garry had finished his preparations and was taking it easy but thinking of the task ahead. The men began to casually chat about other things besides the task ahead. In a way, it was good for the men to talk about life in general and to relax for a bit. A depressingly long drive lay ahead but an excellent opportunity to blow this story wide open. After thirty minutes,

Nathan said he would take a nap in one of the camp recliners he had in the patio. Garry decided to read a book on his *Kindle*. In the background, Mad Dog's boys continued their patrols and were as prepared as ever. It was time to rest and relax. 'Sleep when you can, eat when you can and drink when you can' had been a habit forced upon him by old soldiers when he had been a newbie. This simple dogma had served him well over the years. He wriggled a bit until he was comfortable in the recliner, placed his camouflage baseball cap down, over his eyes and started deep breathing, as if he was going into mediation. Nathan's pulse slowly descended, his mind relaxed and he effortlessly fell asleep.

Chapter 25

THE HUNT FOR SECRETS

It was late in the afternoon, probably around 4, when Phil appeared with the requested stores. Nathan had managed to get some quality sleep in, and Garry had fallen soundly asleep in his chair, commencing to snore and snort like a pig. *It was a wonder Nathan hadn't woken up!* In spite of the noise, both had slept for a good couple of hours. The men would need their reserves as it was a gruelling 12-hour drive to Woomera from the back block cabin. They would call David once they were on the road and nominate a rendezvous somewhere over the South Australian border, most probably at a roadhouse where David was re-fuelling and taking a break. The men would discuss their plans for the infiltration of the Woomera rocket range and training area. Nathan already had a loose plan in his mind. A more detailed plan and set of orders would be presented to the group prior to their incursion. After securing a viable desert site for the aircraft to launch, the operation would be conducted in three phases. Phase one was the infiltration of the Woomera rocket range by gyrocopter. Phase two would be the investigation of 'Tower XV' and its surrounds. Phase three would be extraction by aircraft back to an alternate landing site. David would move his operation somewhere else in case his initial launching site had been compromised. He would observe the new site and be prepared to move again if the total security of his site was breached.

Each phase would be broken into sub elements. As far as phases one and three went, that was the prerogative of David and his expertise. He would know where to land and where to extract Nathan and Garry. If he failed, Nathan and Garry would need to evade base security and escape from the base security if their position was compromised. This would be dangerous on foot and the chance of success without capture a remote probability. The execution of the operation and its mission to recover important data and deliver this information to the media was crucial to David's ability as a pilot. Nathan was certain David's lifelong experience and unflinching tenacity would not let them down.

It was around five pm by the time all the new equipment had been checked and all their equipment surveyed once more. Garry gave Nathan the thumbs up as he was rearing to go. The men said their farewells to Phil, Lauren and Mad Dog and walked through the bush corridor east to the waiting bikers and the late model *Ford* transit van. One of Mad Dog's biker lieutenants handed over the keys to Nathan and the knowledge that he had personally prepared the vehicle; tyres pumped up, oil checked and topped up, fuel inserted and a spare fuel jerry in the back. Even the windshield had been cleaned! Nathan thanked the man for his diligence and jumped into the vehicle. Once inside, he turned and looked at Garry for a second, started the engine and they drove to the sound of the GPS telling them when and where to turn. It would be five or six hours before they caught up with David. There would be plenty of time to discuss the operation and to consider the overall strategy; a stratagem that was being carefully formulated to protect Nathan and his friends.

Nathan switched on the lights as it was starting to get dark. At this stage, *his main worry was hitting a kangaroo* on a country road, so he slowed down to around 85 kilometres per hour. It would not be until nearly midnight when the dark blue transit would cross the Victorian/South Australian border. Nathan didn't mind driving, especially at night as he was used to long drives. He had been posted to Townsville, before he went to the Regiment and had driven the long distance back and forth to Sydney to see his parents on leave around 7 times. Like most arduous things in life, you must pace yourself and break the 'journey' into manageable chunks. He would drive for a few hours and let Garry take over, who was now taking a nap. A call to David would be made and then he would have a sleep. Nathan tried not to let his mind wander as it only takes a second for a kangaroo or wombat to stumble out on the road. He never drove with the air-conditioning on but preferred a cold circulatory breeze to blast from the vehicle's heating and cooling system. A big part of Nathan was excited to be on the road and travelling to a destination that may bring closure to this whole episode. Another part of Nathan was concerned that they would return from this operation. He knew from experience, that sometimes, all the best planning and preparation in the world made, not one iota of difference. He had known men, in and out of the army, great operators in fact, who were killed because of two factors: *bad luck and fuck up*. Sometimes, being in the wrong place at the wrong time or a weapons malfunction at a critical point in time is enough to get oneself killed. Sometimes, a personal mistake, intelligence inaccuracy or operational blunder by a colleague will result in tragedy.

Nathan circulated in a world where *'bad luck'* and *'fuck up'* was forever present. Without doubt, it was a major risk going to Woomera and investigating an old and abandoned tower to ascertain if a nuclear device had ever been there. They would have to navigate around the security forces that patrol the area. Security had been upgraded since the protests at the detention centre in the early 2000s. And there were also local police elements. In their favour was the remoteness of the area and time it would take for security and police to bring in reinforcements. However, Nathan trusted his skills and the competency of those he called friends. He was relying on the simple and incontrovertible fact they had all been better trained than the people they would be facing...

Nathan had been sleeping soundly for nearly two hours when his phone rang. Much to his surprise, he woke with full cognisance of where he was and quickly answered the phone. He was too tired to cuss this time, as he usually does. David had jumped the gun and was wishing to know an estimated time of arrival for the transit to Renmark, just over the border. Nathan looked at Garry, as he wasn't certain of where he geographically was, but Garry had heard David's inquiry and simply stated, *'thirty minutes from Renmark.'* The information was relayed to David and the two men spoke for a minute or two on the phone; Nathan thought David sounded like he was tired and bit lonely and just wanted to talk. He had parked his truck and container adjacent to a large service station, on the road to the small township of Berri. The station catered for overnight truckers, and they would be able to re-fuel and get a bite to eat if they chose to. Nathan said that depending on how the men felt, they would push through to be just outside of Woomera by early morning. The men would sleep for most of the day, move to a suitable, secluded site, prepare the aircraft, and then stealthily insert into the range area later that evening. If the men were too tired, they would sleep at Renmark and travel to Woomera later that day. However, the plan was still to insert later that evening, regardless. Nathan passed on what was said in the conversation and the idea of sleeping at Renmark or pushing through, for another 6 hours. Garry wasn't fussed and said he felt okay. Nathan, closed his eyes, pulled down his cap and said, *'wake me when we get to Renmark.'*

Chapter 26

NEARLY THERE...

A slight nudge from Garry and Nathan knew they were entering the historic South Australian town on the Murray River. For Nathan, it felt like he had just closed his heavy eyes, as he was starting to feel the debilitating effects of residual tiredness from this whole affair. The streets were completely deserted, apart from the odd cat crossing the road at a gallop, whilst the very dazzling yellow lights and silence on the wide highway presented a surreal feeling to their entrance. Garry followed the highway signs leading to the small township of Berri. Within a minute, they could see David's white truck and steely grey container parked by the side of the road. Parking the transit in front of the *Isuzu*, Nathan and Garry wearily left their vehicle and unhurriedly walked back to David in his cab. David was napping and unaware of the two men approaching. Nathan wandered up to the driver's side the vehicle, aggressively tapped on the driver's window and loudly announced in a stern voice, *'sorry, but no vagrants allowed in town.'* David sprang upright, rigid in his seat, expecting the directive to have come from the local constabulary. Of course, it was Nathan playing the fool, again. 'How are you feeling,' Nathan inquired, and David said he was better rested after the short nap. David was introduced to Garry, as they had never met before, and it was decided they would cross the road to the 24-hour service station together, eat, have a few brews, and generally discuss the plan for their entry to the Woomera rocket range.

The restaurant attendant, a plain and slightly obese countrywoman in her fifties, looked pleased to see three paying customers at this un-Godly hour as it would keep her busy and kill some of the time remaining on her night shift. She smiled at the men. Nathan and his friends selected an exceptionally large table by the wall that faced out on to their vehicles. The wall was fabricated from large pane windows, a common design with these type of service stations. To the attendant, these guys were just planning or re-planning their road trip. Coffees and English Breakfasts were ordered, all round. David had been tasked with the route in and route out for the mission. He had spent considerable time on *Google Earth* inspecting a substantial portion of the rugged terrain that involved 'Tower XV' and had produced his own detailed colour maps of the area.

Two smaller scale maps were passed across the table to Nathan and Garry. The satellite pictures, taken over a few days, had indicated no human activity in that area. And there was nothing to suggest this hadn't been the case for some time. No fresh vehicle tracks or additions to Tower XV could be observed. The 'Sat' photos also included hazards and features on the ground, like internal and external fencing, bitumen and dirt roads, small hills, and any aerial hazards, such as overhead cables, any high features or radio towers.

From his study, he had selected several launching and landing sites and alternatives. These sites would be numbered alphabetically and known by each man. If things went badly, and Nathan and Garry were pursued, their survival would depend upon meeting at site, A, B or C for a quick extraction. David would only need to utter a letter on one of the hand-held radios and the men would head to the nominated site and vice versa. It was agreed that David would fly incredibly low and a few kilometres to the north of the tower, break left over the security fence and then touch down briefly at the designated landing site. David would then fly *Cerberus* low to the North again, break right and continue to head north until he landed at his selected landing site. The aircraft would be camouflaged, and David would wait on the 'crack code' to fly *Cerberus* to the pickup point. It would be extremely difficult for anyone monitoring a radar system to identify and locate David's gyrocopter. If they did happen to pick up a blip, it would appear as if an object had strayed into the range area and then reappeared kilometres away facing in a completely different direction. That is if they *picked up the blip in the first place!* The flight in and the later extraction would be planned for dusk and dawn, which would make any visual identification and visual distance recognition difficult. Nathan and Garry would trek to the tower area and conduct their investigation under the cover of darkness and early morning light. They would also have some time at dusk for more investigation, if necessary until they trekked to a designated extraction site.

The Federal Government, in its cost-cutting wisdom, had tendered out security at all its military bases and high-profile offices around the country. However, there is a façade created in this process, where bidding companies promise anything and everything, but the reality is it all boils down to the bucks. The case with most Government tenders is that the job goes to the lowest and least effective bidder. In the situation that Nathan and Garry were facing, the vast range area, which extends for tens of thousands of kilometres, would most likely be under the control of a night security crew that would be at least half the strength of its daytime counterpart, if not less. The security would be comprised of locals in need of a job close to home; some may have served in the military. If security were diligent, vehicle patrols might pass by them, but the general situation would involve one or two persons monitoring a control room. In the event of a crisis, their primary role would be to pass the problem up the chain for someone on a higher pay grade to make a decision. History would also be on the side of Nathan and Garry. Whilst security had been upgraded, nothing had occurred since the detention centre riots and the security would be complacent. Moreover, the wages in these sorts of jobs are abysmally pitiful, so Nathan and Garry would not be expecting to confront the 'A team.' As far as local police and reinforcements went, they were limited and confined to the township. The range area resides under Federal jurisdiction and police would need to be invited onto the range. Before they knew it, the meals and drinks arrived on a massive steel tray, which the attendant seemed to carry without the slightest inconvenience, in her right arm. It was decided by all to eat while everything was hot and continue with the plan's general outline, after ordering a second coffee.

The breakfasts had turned out to be exceptionally delicious and nourishing at this early time of the morning. Nathan had commented enthusiastically to the portly attendant that the meal was *on par with the ambrosia of Olympus'* and she went away as puffed up as a show bantam and as proud as any roadhouse short order cook could be! It was time to review the plan, once again. Nathan outlined that Garry would take the soil samples and be in charge of the investigation at the tower. Nathan would provide visual security and a radio vigil during the activity. The two friends would conceal themselves during the day and be ready to move to one of the extraction sites after dusk, all of which were only five minutes flight time for David. All David had to do was start the engine and fly to the designated rendezvous site. As far as any other contingencies went, they would stick to the extraction plan and only abort the mission if comprised on arrival or because of some unforseen event, such as snakebite or other major mishap. David would break daylight security, come, and retrieve them. If they were pursued outside of the range, they would make the hard calls at that time. Nathan did not want to contemplate having to destroy the aircraft or to resort to other aggressive methods, but he would do what was necessary to protect his friends. Nathan looked at each of the men. He asked if there were any questions or anything that needed mentioning. The plan was simple, but the rocket range was enormous, and the element of surprise was on their side. Nathan said, 'okay, if there isn't anything else, I suggest we finish our brews, re-fuel and get cracking to David's number one launching site.' The two friends didn't say a word, but Nathan could tell they didn't want to let him down and knew the lives of each man depended upon the other.

David and Garry went outside to get the vehicles and drive them to the fuel bowsers. Nathan picked up some drinks and snacks and paid the attendant, again thanking her for the sumptuous meal. When all the vehicles had been checked for water, tyre pressure and as fuelled up as they could be, they set off in a loose column, towards Port Augusta, with a spacing of two hundred metres. This would be their next fuel stop. They had a six hour plus journey, but this time, Nathan would take first shift on driving the truck, so that David could get as much rest as possible. His role in this operation was crucial, so he needed to be at his best. Nevertheless, it didn't take long before the men were in the groove of the long-distance drive. Once on cruise control, feet were positioned along the vehicle's internal firewall, where they could be most comfortable, and the seat had been snuggled deep and into the right angle and depth to provide maximum comfort to the derrière. Radio stations tend to fade in and out, so Nathan inserted a memory stick of beloved tunes into the *Isuzu's* entertainment system. David was oblivious to Nathan's movements as he was sleeping so soundly. The Eagles' 'Take it to the limit' softly ascended from the door speakers and Nathan was struck by how this familiar song encapsulated his life.

> *'You know I've always been a dreamer*
> *Spent my life running 'round*
> *And it's so hard to change*
> *Can't seem to settle down'*

The philosophical lyrics suited him to a tee. He had spent most of his life dreaming, running around, and found it hard to change and to settle down, especially as he grew older. He wanted to change, to be a better man, a peaceful man, a man who could reinvent himself, but this wasn't the course that life guided him on. Although he was only fifty years of age, he was coming to a point in his life where he wondered what was in store for him, that is if he managed to get himself out of this situation. He thought about how tired Ghent was at the end of his life and wondered how long would it be *before he felt that way?* For Nathan, Randy Meisner now soulfully sang the most poignant lyric of the song:

> *'So put me on a highway*
> *And show me a sign*
> *And take it to the limit*
> *One more time'*

Nathan thought, 'how many times have I taken it

to the limit?' Their current mission was a case in point. If nothing else, Nathan thought this would be a great song to be played at his funeral.

The crazy thing about long distance driving is that sometimes one part of the journey seems to go incredibly faster than the previous stanzas. The countryside had shifted from open rolling plains that were clearly designed for grazing, to thick, bushy, hilly areas that appeared impenetrable by foot or vehicle. Quaint sandstone brick houses featured in many of the towns that had once been vibrant communities but were now only an annoying slow thoroughfare for travellers on their way to some other place and not worthy of a visit, even a short one. All the while, the soil changed from darkest dirt, in places, to bright orange clay. This was especially the case at Port Augusta, where the vehicles re-fuelled and the men visited the rest rooms. More coffee was bought. The rich clay soil was juxtaposed with the deep blue water of the Spencer Gulf that led to the port and the rising green escarpment that was part of the Cultana military exercise range. One more leg of their journey to go. The vehicles set off, with David taking the lead in his truck. He knew where his preferred launching site would be, and they would be there in just under two hours. A cover story had already been concocted in the remote eventuality that they were pulled over by the police. The story was David was taking his aircraft to show a fellow aviator in Alice Springs, who was interested in purchasing the craft. Nathan and Garry were friends going along for the ride. David did have a friend in the 'Alice' who would corroborate their story. Although the men were tired, they knew this was the time to concentrate and to put on their *game faces.* Only two more hours of driving on a gun barrel straight public road, putting up with the stench of kangaroo roadkill that littered the highway and constantly wondering how on earth did the early pioneers and settlers put up with these harsh and unforgiving conditions... 🖎

Chapter 27

WOOMERA AIRLINES

The sleepy, dusty town of Woomera came and went as Nathan's procession continued to slowly edge its way north. Since leaving Port Augusta, the last car or truck they had seen was nearly an hour ago. They had driven past a few Aboriginal people walking along the road in Woomera, accompanied by a mangy black dog that looked very undernourished, but they didn't even rate a look. The town looked deserted. Funny, it *always appeared this way*. David's launch spot 'A' was another 10 kilometres to go. In just under ten minutes, the men pulled off the bitumen road, to the right, into what looked like a dry, clay riverbed. David climbed down from the cab and inspected the soil and could see, at first glance, that the bed was solid and compacted - the area hadn't had seen any decent rain

for over two years. The soil was sun baked hard and the riverbed was strewn with flat river rocks that had been smoothed by intermittent floodwaters for thousands of years. It wasn't sandy as some of the other riverbeds in the area. He gave the thumbs up to Nathan and Garry in the van and proceeded to steadily drive the truck and container two hundred metres. The riverbed was fifty metres at its widest point and spotted gum trees flourished along the banks in small clumps of three to four trees.

At around two hundred metres the vehicles were invisible from the road. At this point, a track led up from the riverbed to the left to exhibit a flat salt pan that parallel the road for three hundred metres. This would be the perfect launching point for *Cerberus*. The truck would surface from the creek bed and the gyrocopter would be removed from the container. The truck would re-position itself back in the creek bed for concealment prior to the launch. David would position a 'real time' security camera in one of the trees to provide security when he was in flight. It wouldn't be tidy to land and find the police waiting for them! But, for the moment, it would appear as if the vehicles had moved off the road and the men were simply camping. Nathan and Garry were impressed with the site selection and knew this would be textbook for their purposes. By this time, it was now early morning.

The morning desert coolness had dissipated, and the sun's warmth was starting to slowly build. Over a snack and brew, the men re-discussed what the general plan was for their infiltration, later that evening. All their equipment was re-checked, and David did what he could for his pre-flight inspection whilst *Cerberus* was still in its cage. Sunset would be just after 18:00 hours and the men would take off 30 minutes after that. It was now decided to try and sleep for the remainder of the day, with one man to stand guard for two and a half hours at a time. Nathan was extremely pleased with the way things had gone so far. They had considered all the main contingencies and the most likely 'actions on,' such as being discovered on infiltration and during their investigation of the tower. The rest they would *'play by ear.'* He was lying on an inflatable air mattress under one of the gum trees and had placed his desert shemagh loosely over his bush hat, to ward off the pesky flies that were starting to congregate around him. He probably wouldn't get much sleep; he never did before a mission. His mind would always be racing with various scenarios. However, he did feel content and relaxed because of the men he accompanied and was certain they would achieve what they had set out to do. Slowly, his thoughts slowed to nothingness, and he embraced the creeping slumber that was descending upon him.

David woke Nathan for the last watch. Nathan sprang to his feet and felt as if he had slept for ten or more hours – such was the depth of his nap and its remedial effects. He took a refreshing swig from his water bottle. David reported the area had been so quiet, he hadn't even seen a kangaroo or heard a car, in the distance, on the highway. Only the chirping birdlife made him feel that he wasn't the last creature on Earth. Nathan just nodded and David wandered off for his siesta. He checked his phone and there weren't any text messages. *Thank God*, for that, he thought. No dramas from anyone and no surprises, like Lauren being discovered in the back of the block cabin or the boys captured by Madison, as they led her on a 'magical mystery tour.' He could direct his focus to the task that was before them.

Nathan decided to make a coffee brew and to eat a decent meal, as his didn't know when his next meal would be. Baked beans were cooked on an open fire, and this was accompanied by a thickly buttered wholemeal roll. His gear was checked again, and he decided to dress and ready himself before he woke the other men, much later. Nathan produced his map and spent a great deal of time studying the terrain, potential 'hides' and escape routes and likely areas where security could descend down upon them. The amazingly clear satellite photos were an immense help and provided critical information that was lacking on his smaller map. Before he knew it, it was wake up time for David and Garry.

Surprisingly, all the men had slept so soundly that afternoon. The group prepared with a spring in their step and a determined purpose. Not much talking occurred as the men knew what to do and got on with the task, such as conducting a comms check with the handheld radios. *Cerberus* was driven to the start point of the salt pan and delicately released from its metal box. The remaining aircraft checks were completed, and the reliable truck driven back to the security of the riverbed. With all the vehicles secure, the men walked back up the track to the salt pan and took their positions inside the aircraft. The light was fading but David knew that by the time he had completed his final checks it *would only be a few minutes before taking off.* Nathan could feel sweat running down the back of his neck into his overalls, but this wasn't trepidation. The desert warmth was still keeping man and machinery warm, but it wouldn't be too long before the evening chill was upon them. 'Thank God it's a still night,' thought Nathan.

David looked at his watch, looked back to the left rear passenger seat and gave the nod to Nathan. Nathan replied with a single nod and the engine was started. The stout motor roared like one of those boats you would see flying upon the water across the Florida everglades, with the engine rearward. It was *terrifyingly powerful* but only gave off a flapping, wafting noise like a *dirty big fan*. It would also add to their concealment as the gyrocopter's engine did not mimic a plane or helicopter and most people had never encountered such a craft. As part of his preparations, David had placed glow sticks on the ground at regular intervals, either side, along the makeshift runway, particularly at the 300-metre threshold. Now, it was time to go. The accelerator was firmly depressed, the engine pitch grew louder, and the reliable aircraft began to roll, inch by inch, forward. David *gunned the engine,* and the men were sucked back into the seats by the acceleration. There was only the slight bump on the salt pan as the machine was propelled headlong into the night's darkness, by now with some intensity. At 75 knots per hour, David pulled hard back on the controls and *Cerberus catapulted into the air!* David looked either side of the cockpit and he could see the glow sticks fade as he effortlessly gained altitude. The aircraft banked slowly to the right but was heading north on its assigned bearing.

They had only been airborne a few minutes, when, *without an ounce of warning*, a black, feathery object, about half the size of a family refrigerator, appeared ten metres in front of *Cerberus*. David was surprised but he instinctively accelerated hard, guiding the aircraft upwards and banking it to the right with a dynamic turn. He didn't want to get hit head on, nor did he want the object to fly into the autogyro prop; worse case would be a collision on the port side. Better that than a cracked rotor head and the necessity to launch the ballistic recovery system parachute. Aircraft and object just missed, and it was only on its passing that David realised the black blob was an Australian Wedge Tailed Eagle, *and a big one at that!* It wasn't the first time a large a large bird had sunk a gyrocopter.

All the men sighed with relief, as David resumed his northerly course. In five minutes, *Cerberus* banked to the left and David indicated they would be in the range area in two minutes. Five minutes later, David could vaguely make out a dirt track that ran east to west and this is what would serve as his landing strip. Another 360-degree scan and the area looked clear. He gave the thumbs down sign to Nathan and descended. At 50 metres, he switched on the undercarriage search light that projected a powerful beam 45 degrees ahead of the aircraft. Almost at the same time, David reduced the engine's acceleration to only a few revolutions and *Cerberus* kicked into its auto gyration mode and softly descended until the wheels softly kissed the track. Time was of the essence now and the men had to exit quickly so that David could accelerate, take off and be on his way. Nathan and Garry rapidly exited via the side doors, ran five metres, and took a knee on the ground, both men looking out into the darkness of the range. They didn't expect company but carried out the drill, nonetheless. Dust was now billowing due to the engines rising acceleration and before they knew it, *Cerberus shot down the track.* A second or two later and David was mid-air and heading north again at full speed. David would fly north for five minutes and maintain a holding pattern in that area just in case the men required an early extraction. If communication silence was maintained for a further ten minutes, he would *zig zag* his way back to the salt pan for landing and wait by the craft for the remainder of the evening. *Cerberus* would be re-conditioned in its metal box during the day.

Garry sprinted over to Nathan, who had unslung his weapon and was looking to the south for any vehicle lights or traffic. His weapon instinctively followed his eye movement. The wind had started to get up, which would conceal any noise, but Nathan *was confident their insertion had not been detected.* They had a few kilometres to go until they arrived at the tower, and it was all on undulating, rocky ground, so the going would be slow and methodical. *Time to move off.*

Nathan took the lead and told Garry to stay in visual contact. It would be easy to get lost if the men didn't look out for one another. The wind was still up but no sign of lights or movement coming from the south. *So far, so good*. Nathan was taking his time and wasn't worried about when the men arrived at the tower. At any other time, it would be a short stroll but tonight every step would be slow and deliberate. The last thing he wanted was someone rolling an ankle.

In just over an hour the men had arrived at 'Tower XV.' The top part of the tower was seen thirty or forty metres in the faint desert night as it had been silhouetted against the glowing horizon, where the lights of Woomera provided faint illumination. In the dim light, *the tower had resembled a giant Meccano set,* with its huge girders and beams. However, the men had only seen a small portion of this metal construction. In Woomera's heyday, where rockets were fired and NASA spacecraft were monitored, the tower had functioned as a rocket launching platform. Once a rocket had been affixed to a firing podium, it had been pushed slowly by a diesel engine on a narrow-gauge railway track that led to a firing point adjacent to the tower, which was positioned in a re-entrant one hundred metres from ground level to the structure's highest point. The re-entrant looked like a vertical crease that had been cut into the escarpment and must have been fifty metres wide, *but this was all nature's handiwork.* In this fashion, any rocket would be protected from high winds by the escarpment and the intense blast from the rocket's engines would be absorbed by the rock or vent back down the valley. The men were now standing on the top of the escarpment and would have to cautiously snake their way down to valley floor that led to the firing point and the launch buildings. This is where the telling photograph had been taken of MacMillan, colleagues, and the nuclear bomb. It was difficult at night to traverse down the rock and shale that led down to the valley floor. The feet of both men would slip and fly forward on the torturous surface, leaving them resting on their backsides on the slope of the escarpment. However, this was a much better option than flying forward and somersaulting headfirst down the hill. Nathan showed Garry that by traversing downward, as a skier would on a mountain slope, he would have more control of where he was heading, and the descent would not be as taxing on his leg muscles.

By the time the men had reached the valley floor, it had taken them nearly as long as it did to reach the tower from their insertion point. The men walked forward to a clearer area and were in awe of the decaying metal leviathan resting in the re-entrant. The tower had been inactive there for many years and there was no sign of the powerful diesel engine that would push and cajole a rocket to the firing position structure. Nathan and Garry noticed that there were two thick concrete observation buildings to the left and right of the tower and these were both situated around seventy metres away. Both structures would have to be examined as they were identical to the building that was the backdrop in the photograph. They moved to the closest building, which was the one on the tower's left-hand side. Of course, neither man expected to waltz up and find a nuclear bomb sitting there, for the taking, but taking radiation readings, soil samples, verbal documentation and photographs would lend a great deal of credence to the old sepia photograph and MacMillan's manifesto. Whilst Garry moved forward to conduct his investigation, Nathan positioned himself back down the valley but well withing visual range of his compatriot. The soles on his boots were fairly flat and he tried to walk on rocky areas, so as not leave any sign. Nathan had asked Garry to limit his walking to a small area and to brush the sandy soil with a bushy tree branch to hide his footprints. It was an old technique, but it worked. He was looking for locations to construct a hide in the eventuality the investigation ran over time, as they would not be able to fly during daylight. All the while, Nathan was checking for movement or noise and monitoring the radio. The men would only come up on the radio if they had to. As they say, 'no *news is good news,'* so he wasn't worried that he had not heard from David. If he, had it would've been a 'crack code,' essentially a word that had a deliberate action connected to it and would only have meaning to the three men. It was approaching midnight and Garry was still conducting his examination of the first concrete observation building. At this rate, the second observation would not be investigated thoroughly until just before dawn. Nathan followed his footsteps back to where Garry was working and inquired, *'How's it going?'* Garry said that he was taking his time with the documentation because he knew they wouldn't be coming back. To be taken seriously with this story, the examination had to be clinically meticulous. Armed with this information, Nathan decided to construct a small camouflage hide for the two men in one of the preferred areas he had located. It was always going to be difficult at night, without the advantage of seeing the area in daylight, but he had no alternative. The men could rest in the concrete observation buildings during the day until they trekked to their extraction point later in the evening, but they needed a place to go if the situation was compromised.

Although the range was in one of the driest areas in Australia, rain did come and, at times, the rain was torrential. When this occurred, the 'red centre' was a different world. Animals and birdlife suddenly appeared, and the flora would materialise in a blaze of colour and a striking contrast to its dry desert surroundings. At the site of 'Tower XV,' water would come gushing down from the escarpment and continue along the valley floor. In the process, many rivulets were formed, and these small gullies snaked their way towards the south. Over time, small bushes grew out of these tiny creek beds and debris would be lodged by the flowing streams.

On selecting his site, Nathan first made sure the creek bed would easily accommodate the two men and their equipment. He then removed any rocks and placed these to one side. The hide was in and amongst other small gullies that rose and fell across the valley floor. He took off his patrol pack and carefully unrolled the bundle of chicken wire. The roll was tightly compressed but when unfolded was just over two metres in length and one and a half metres wide. Using the rocks and sticks that he could find, Nathan fastened the wire so that it would not easily move. He then placed a very thin and light layer of tan hessian over the chicken wire, which had been bent slightly upwards so that it was convex in shape all the way along its length. This way, the two men would be able to crawl under the wire and have a slight bit of room above them. The small desert camouflage net was then placed above the hessian, with some of it draping over the entrance. Sticks, leaves, branches, and spinifex foliage around and above the hide completed the deception. Nathan was quite proud of his work. At a distance, the hide would be completely invisible and would only be discovered if someone walked on it or dogs picked up their scent. The hide was also positioned so that anyone that came towards them would be facing the muzzle of Nathan's Ruger. Garry would be looking the opposite way, covering to the rear.

It would be warm during the day, but the hide offered enough shade, and they had enough water to sustain them. Once he was satisfied with the hide's construction, he backtracked from its entrance and took out a large freezer bag of what appeared to be small chocolate type pellets. He strategically placed these pellets leading away from the hide and heading back the opposite way down the valley. Once finished, he produced a small plastic container that contained an ochre powder substance. This he sprinkled near the pellets and anywhere he thought the men had wandered in their stay in and around the tower. *This was the backup plan.* By now it would only be another hour until the sun began to rise. Garry had moved to the second tower and had conducted the same thorough investigation as before. Nathan informed Garry of the hide and then resumed his security vigil, and patiently waited...

Chapter 28

TWO MEN & A DOG

The last half hour before daylight dragged so much that it was painful. Nathan was thinking about how they would probably sleep during most of the day and would certainly chat about the investigative work Garry did, in and around the concrete observation bunkers He was terribly interested to know about the Geiger readings and anything else he had found. Both men had taken an almighty risk by invading Commonwealth Land, but they knew it was essential for the truth to be told. As the sun was rising in the east, a slight haze was starting to form with it and extend to the horizon in the south. Nathan thought he was seeing things but noticed a constant billowing of red dust that looked like it was reaching up to the clouds and was too consistent to be a desert whirly whirly, or 'dust devils,' as sometimes known. The dust trailed off to one side and Nathan knew that was trouble en-route to their position. As luck would have it, Garry was just finishing and by Nathan's reckoning, they had thirty minutes - *forty at tops*, before a vehicle or vehicles arrived.

Nathan led Garry to the hide and assisted with placing in his equipment. He then went back down to the buildings and checked the inside of each structure and then started to sweep any footprints outside and checked the area for any other sign of their intrusion. More chocolate pellets and red powder was placed down, especially around where Garry had worked. After this, he started to walk away from the position until he came across a belt of large flat rocks and followed this formation, high and around until he came back upon the hide from the rear. He slid into the hide and crawled forward until his head was adjacent to Garry's feet. 'Pheww, said Nathan,' 'bout time you changed your socks, wouldn't you think?' They enjoyed a slight chuckle and waited to see what would be confronting them when the daylight finally took hold. The men chatted quietly in the cosy hide. It helped pass the time and dispense with any nervous tension. Nathan had a clear view down the valley for a good three hundred metres until the dirt track went off on a sharp tangent to the right, skirting around the diminishing rocky edge of the escarpment. Nathan decided not to use the binoculars. Although there is a tactical way to use the visual aid by cupping both hands over the lenses, he didn't want to take a chance with any glare. He could see the smoke clouds getting thicker and closer until a *Toyota* troop carrier rounded the escarpment's edge and headed straight for the observation bunkers. Only one vehicle came. Nathan looked intently at the vehicle in an attempt to gather the slightest clues of the capability of the men riding inside. The old and dusty carrier slowed down, and Nathan could see the men craning their necks in an attempt to scan the terrain. He also saw a K9 transporter that was attached to the rear of the carrier. He thought with a degree of trepidation - *'this is going to be close.'*

The vehicle had driven directly from range security and the two men who alighted from the vehicle looked like most of the scruffy types who worked in private security these days. One man was incredibly young and skinny, and the other man was well into his sixties and was morbidly obese. Nathan thought, *'ah, the Laurel and Hardy of private security.'* Both men were dressed in khaki uniforms, with sidearms and Nathan could see the big man had spilt most of his breakfast and coffee down the front of his uniform. The younger man looked cleaner and fresher, so it must be the morning shift. Already he had ascertained that the younger man would be the conscientious type and the older man was running down the clock to his pension. The men were talking loudly, and Nathan managed to pick up a reference to an alarm system that involved terrestrial sensors that could determine a security breach by animal or human based upon the unique signature and repetition of footprints or hooves. The security company had employed expensive drones, but these had been deemed too unreliable and were frequently lost out on the vast range or attacked by eagles. These sensors were at the furthest security key points, in the belief they could adequately cover the outer environs. A decision by the team leader at range headquarters was made to investigate the anomaly in the daylight. To Nathan, it sounded like the old security guy had seen enough and put down the security alarm to a glitch in the system. 'Well,' Nathan thought, 'you can't plan for everything - *like ground sensors that are top secret.*'

The young man was not budging. He told the older man that these checks were what they got paid for and he would let the dog out and have a quick patrol of the area. The older guy threw up his hands in resignation and rested his massive frame against the carrier's bull bar. Obviously, the man had been dragged away from his binge watching of a second-rate sitcom on *Netflix* or some mundane pursuit like that. A large German Shepherd was released from its carrier and instantly started sniffing the air and ground. The young security guy went to the closest observation bunker as the dog was pulling on its lead and taking him there. Nathan was convinced they wouldn't find any footprints, ground sign or clues as he had expertly sanitised the area. The dog paused, then bent forward and started chewing at something on the ground. The handler pulled the dog away and scolded the animal. The dog was taken over to the second observation bunker. Nathan thought, 'one down and one to go.' The man and dog team emerged and continued to patrol the area in a wide, investigative sweep. Suddenly, the dog's head rotated quickly around in a wild arc in the direction of the hide. Nathan could see the dog sniffing furiously. The powerful animal then started tugging on its lead and the handler let the dog have its way. The animal walked a few metres, stopped, started chewing at something on the ground and was pulled away, again, by its handler. The dog moved forward once more. This time, the animal moved within 50 metres of the hide. Nathan *disengaged the safety on the Ruger.* He wouldn't shoot the two men, only in self-defence but was certain he would probably have to eliminate the animal, that is, if they were discovered. The dog walked another two metres and decided to eat more chocolate looking pellets from the ground. This time, the dog started making a whimpering noise, all the while shaking its large head and pacing back and forward in an agitated gait. The handler pulled back on the lead, but the dog started sneezing and its nose began emitting a slobbery clear fluid.

The older guy was beside himself and thought the whole scene highly amusing. He couldn't resist commenting, 'so much for wonder dog, more like blunder dog' and he let out a long belly laugh. He went on to comment, *'this is what happens when the company buys canine rejects that fail obedience training.'* The younger man was apologetic for the dog's action and kept uttering it was something the dog had found and eaten from the ground. The dog's conniption had removed the focus from where Nathan and Garry were hiding. It was obvious the younger man had an affinity with the animal, but he had been showed up by the dog's antics and he was quick to secure the animal in its steel carrier. Sullenly, he walked back to the passenger seat and *slammed the door shut.* The old man was still laughing, more at the young man's infantile behaviour and he returned to his seat. The vehicle was started, turned in a wide arc and headed back from whence it came.

Nathan reported to Garry that they were in the clear and both men let out a long, deep sigh. Nathan had explained how close they had come to being discovered but his few tricks had done the job. Garry asked what had been sprinkled around the area and Nathan plainly said, 'Cat shit and cayenne pepper.' He had heard of the fascination and lure of cat shit with dogs by a vet on a lifestyle program. 'Apparently,' said Nathan, 'it's like Vegemite to dogs. He had employed this tactic on several occasions when on reconnaissance missions. It took a very well trained and determined dog not to eat the cat faeces. That was the game changer and this time they had been lucky. The security dog was of poor quality. In the dog's eating frenzy, it was easy to ingest some of the strong powder. As the men emerged from the hide, Garry said playfully, with affection, 'mate, you're not as stupid as you look, and I don't want to know how you came by all that cat shit!'

The men waited for a half hour to make sure the vehicle was well out of reach before they warily emerged from the hide, to swallow large gulps of fresh air and to stretch their cramped legs. This time, both men emerged wearing balaclavas, just in case the young security guy had planted any remote cameras. They didn't go to all this trouble to be identified. After a quick but thorough security sweep, Nathan considered the area safe for limited movement - he *didn't want to set off the sensors again.* He decided they would rest in the shade of the bunker in the heat of the day and only use the hide in the event of another security check. The heat was starting to climb intensely now and the last thing they needed was to dehydrate. Both men would take security watches until it was time to leave for the extraction site, later that evening. Nathan broke out some dry rations and the men ate and drank some water. Garry took the opportunity to inform Nathan of some of his findings, which were astonishing. The Geiger counter readings were consistent and sufficient enough to demonstrate that a powerful nuclear device had been constructed and most probably stored at the observation bunker on the left, for how long, that would need to be determined. A large degree of radiation was still present. The weapon and its mechanisms must have been here for some time for this to occur. The telling evidence that announced the presence of this device was found by Garry in the second observation bunker. It seemed this shelter had been used as a storage facility for components. Old and decrepit packing crates with labels and general scientific rubbish that still lay about, indicated the parts and equipment required to manufacture a nuclear bomb. The bunkers were large enough for such an operation and, coupled with the remoteness of the site, made it a perfect, secure area for construction.

Garry said he could build a serious news story on what he had found. There was now an abundance of scientific proof, and he would also use a number of acclaimed scientists he knew to verify his findings. It may not be as good as having the bomb or a story from someone who was involved but, as they say, 'if it walks like a duck, talks like a duck, then probably....' That is the irony of today's form of journalism, it doesn't have to be considered by the critical weight of forensic evidence. Just put the story out there and it will be believed via broad dissemination and mass public consumption. Maybe the long, lost story of Hamish MacMillan will flush out other scientists and work colleagues to add their stories to the compendium. Nathan was suitably impressed by Garry's work. But he knew that time was needed to tidy it up for public discourse. Garry's editor was behind him so there was only a matter of time before the story would be aired.

The afternoon was occupied by sleeping and being on watch. No noise, movement or dust signals had been seen for hours. For Nathan, it was an opportunity to rest as he knew the next phase of this saga would be taxing. Although in the shade, the heat was still stifling, which meant it took some time for the men to sleep, but they eventually did so and slept soundly. He would have the last watch before they hiked to their extraction point, and he needed the time to consult the map and mentally prepare for the night's activity. As it turned out, the rest of the day passed without incident; the darkness and quiet of the desert night was upon them before they knew it. Nathan had studied the map critically and had selected another one of David's extraction points. They would not dare go back to their initial insertion point. A salt pan to the northwest of their original landing site would be ideal. It was a few kilometres further from where they landed but only a bit more of a foot slog, and as it happened, Nathan felt like walking after being couped up all day. The plan was quickly discussed between the men, and they readied themselves for an arduous night trek. The hardest part was going back up the rocky and perilous escarpment. Again, there was no rush in climbing the escarpment and Nathan stopped frequently on the ascent so that they weren't fatigued by the time they reached the top. Slow and steady was the preferred action and the men reached the crest and the flat ground in just over an hour. Garry sat down on his pack for a moment, whilst Nathan moved forward ten metres to view the terrain and listen. Just because they had walked this route before didn't mean it was a safe passage!

After ten minutes, Nathan signalled to Garry that they were on the move. He took a quick bearing with his Garmin GPS and headed towards a point on the horizon; a star in the same direction keeping his navigation on track. It would be another 90 minutes before they would come across the salt pan. Once there, he would wait and observe that they hadn't been followed or there were any other security concerns. Once satisfied, he would send the 'crack code' on the secure handheld radio and then wait the nervous twenty minutes or so for David's arrival. If they were discovered, he would send the abort signal – '*foetus*,' and would attempt to lure the pursuers away from the area. The strategy would be to evade through the evening and to locate a site where a temporary hide would conceal their presence during the day. As far as other plans went, they would consider their options later.

In just under 90 minutes, Nathan could see the salt pan as it reflected in the pale moon light. The 'stomp' to the extraction point had been interrupted by brief rest and listening stops, just for insurance's sake. On these halts, Nathan used his monocular night vision device to sweep the terrain ahead. If needed, this device would help them to secure a site for a hide, if the situation deteriorated badly. The tired men sat in a small sandy gully that paralleled the salt pan and waited and listened. No noise. No movement. No distant lights flashing in any direction. With the handheld radio turned on and firmly in his grasp, Nathan squeezed the pressal switch and uttered the word '*demarcation*.' He waited for fifteen seconds and was about to repeat his message, when he heard the reply - '*Steiner*.' This meant that David had received the code word for 'come and get us' and at what extraction site. He confirmed this understanding with another one-word reply – '*Coburn*.' David would be soon powering up *Cerberus*. It was now time to do some work, quickly. Garry kept watch while Nathan paced out David's landing strip, placing glow sticks at the relevant distance intervals as well as the landing and overshoot thresholds. He also removed the odd branch and was jogging to get the landing strip ready.

He no sooner finished and sat down for a brief moment when he heard, oh so faintly in the distance, a *waft wafting* noise. David would be on them in a moment. As the noise grew louder, he took out his flashlight, aimed it at the approaching aircraft and punched out beams of light in morse code: - *dit dit dit, dit dah, dit dit dit*. The flashing spelt: *SAS*, which confirmed to David that it was Nathan on the ground, and they had not been compromised. David could clearly see the glow sticks and knew that Nathan had provided him with a safe landing and take-off zone. The engine slowed in its revs and the auto-gyration slowly brought the gyrocopter down to a soft landing on the salt deck. David motored the vehicle down to the take-off end, where the men were now waiting and once there and he was right to go, he signalled to the men to come aboard. Garry entered through the immediate door, whilst Nathan ran around to the entrance on the far side. No sooner had he sat down, strapped in, and looked up, did he see David giving the 'thumbs up.' A second later, *Cerberus's* engine roared and the aircraft took off as if it had been fired from a slingshot. A second more and the gyrocopter was airborne and rising. Once level and heading northeast, David turned his head and yelled above the engine noise, 'get all that you wanted?' Nathan just nodded his head solemnly and David turned and continued with piloting the craft. In five minutes, David performed an aggressive right turn to the east as well as dropping his altitude to fly as low as he could. Although there was a degree of moonlight, he had to be careful about the odd ghost gum that blended into the landscape. The agile craft then made another dynamic turn in an arc that had them on a bearing back to their vehicles.

Now, *Cerberus* scooted swiftly between twenty and fifty metres about the ground. In under ten minutes, David was approaching the salt pan where the men had commenced their adventure and he had decided the site was secure enough as there had been no movement in his area since yesterday. The faint glow sticks of the landing strip slowly became discernible as *Cerberus* was on its final approach to landing. *A quick turn into the wind,* de-acceleration of the engine and a fluttering of the autogyro prop and *Cerberus* was on the ground before they knew it. David made the operation look effortless. With excitement comes the rush of adrenalin and the men were fatigued; the unaccustomed heat adding to the tiredness. It was one of those times when men didn't need to say a word but just got on with the job. David's truck and carrier were driven to *Cerberus*. The engine was already cooling down as a result of the cold desert night air and David was going through his post-flight checks and re-conditioning drills. Garry was assisting with the process while Nathan kept security watch. Within twenty minutes, the gyrocopter was tucked away, and vehicles and men were back in the creek bed. Garry and David looked totally exhausted and would need to be in decent shape for their testing drive back to central Victoria.

Nathan announced he would take the first watch, followed by Garry and then David. He didn't say it, but David was a lot older and needed his rest as driving the truck and trailer was a damn site harder than driving the van. By this time, the men weren't talking at all, such was their tiredness. Garry threw out his swag roll onto the riverbed sand and collapsed on its mattress, blissfully snoring within minutes. David spent a little bit more time with his bed in the carrier and in a minute or so, his cabin light was extinguished.

Nathan was careful not to make noise but started a small fire, not so much for warmth but to give himself something to do and to keep awake. Within ten minutes, he was sitting comfortably on a log and drinking a hot and strong coffee. He was pleased for himself as the operation, so far, had been a complete success. Nathan was immensely proud of the men he had worked with and knew they could be relied upon in an instant; he couldn't say as much for most people he came across in the world today. He sipped on his hot brew and decided to check his mobile phone for messages. Not a lot of important messages but one text did stand out and it was from Paul Burton. The message read: 'Have interesting information on Hayden. Need to discuss this ASAP on your return. Everything else, good.' Nathan was concerned with the tone of the dispatch and the part about Hayden. He thought nothing could be done up where they were and he shouldn't sweat on the note, but he was more concerned for Caroline than himself or his colleagues. Nevertheless, it would all be sorted out after another long drive, and they would be back home soon. Nathan turned his attention to a number of bats that flew overhead and landed in trees by the creek bed. Loud snoring emanated from the camp, and he sat relaxed by a fire with his coffee. Tomorrow will be a long day...

It would be an early start in the morning. It always is. Nathan had decided to cut into Garry's security picquet and make sure he had slept soundly. He would sleep in the van as they drove and wanted to be fresh for when they returned home. A few critical things had to be done and he needed a fresh mind and body for the task. Again, not much was spoken at breakfast as the men could sense it was time not to *dilly dally* but to get on the road as soon as possible. They would rendezvous at the same places as they stopped at on the trip up, but these would be quick stops. After breakfast, the men quickly packed the vehicles and inspected their personal areas to ensure they had not left anything behind. A few moments later, David's vehicle turned in the wide creek bed and was rolling down the road before it had turned 8 am. Nathan drove the van and kept a two hundred metre spacing. A 16-hour drive was in front of them, and Nathan looked at Garry but neither man said a word. It was time to just suck it up and drive the long, gruelling distance back home.

Chapter 29

HOMEWARD
BOUND

The drive from central Australia was not as arduous or mundane as Nathan thought it would be. And it seemed to go a lot faster than he assumed. He considered how funny it was that the return trip always seems to feel shorter than the trip outward, which invariably feels tediously long. The men had driven long and hard all through the day and had earned their brief respites at roadhouses and roadside way stations for travellers. David had splintered off, just after they entered Victoria to take his route back to his property. All the goodbyes had been said earlier at the Renmark roadhouse, where Nathan had grasped David's hand and shook it with some fervour and hoped that this physical demonstration would not be lost on the older man. Yet, it was David who spoke first and very quietly, 'I know you appreciate all that I have done for you recently. It has been my pleasure to assist a dear and trusted friend, whom I have known for many years.' David continued, 'what you must know is the recent adventures, including my stay in hospital, have all helped to keep me feeling young. I have felt included and useful and, it is you, I need to thank.' He finished by saying, 'I am an old man now and I don't know how much more time I have left, but if I don't live another day, I can hold my head up and know that I have been trusted in the company of such fine men. *It is I who thank you.*' Nathan was flabbergasted and couldn't get out the words, even if he knew what to say! David's charitable words had engaged Nathan's emotions and he even felt as if he was starting to tear up. David had been an integral member of the group and the mission to Woomera could not have succeeded without his dedicated planning and incredible flying. Before Nathan could utter a syllable, David raised his voice and announced, 'well, I won't get home standing around here chin-wagging all day, so I must be off. Nathan, take care and we'll catch up down the track. Soon.' He turned, walked briskly over to the *Isuzu*, and was driving off before Nathan could blink. 'Well, how do you figure that,' thought Nathan. 'And I thought he was doing me a favour all the while.'

But now, Nathan's van was only 30 minutes away from the back block and they would soon be in familiar surroundings. Garry had resumed driving from Renmark, so Nathan could concentrate on what lay ahead and to come up with a number of scenarios. All of a sudden, Nathan's mobile phone rang. It was Paul Burton. He was asking how far they were away as well as wanting to tell Nathan what he had discovered about Marcus Hayden. In a way, Nathan was glad to get the information on the road, it sort of softened the blow of bad news. 'Hi Nathan,' good to hear from you. I hope things went well on your sabbatical in the sunny centre?' Nathan didn't want to comment too much on the phone but said that all had been achieved and he was glad to be on the way home. His ears picked up on what Paul told him next. 'Well,' he said, this Marcus Hayden fellow is another stooge who works for the *Agency*. This is reliable information I have sourced from a dependable mate who was recently on a small arms firing course with this guy. A solid operator by all accounts, who was Army Paras in a former life. It seems *we have a fox in the henhouse.*' Nathan paused for a second and then asked Paul to keep this information to himself and that he would personally deal with this, knowing full well how this knowledge would crush Caroline if she ever found out about it. Paul said that he had ten jobs to do and would meet up with Nathan and the boys out at the block in a day so.

The call ended and Nathan had a quick survey of the country landscape and knew he was about ten minutes away from the back block. He looked across at Garry, but he was concentrating on the road. It was obvious to Nathan that *he was juggling a number of challenging balls in the air,* Madison Baker and her *Agency* thugs, Carlton Mafia, and Creswick drug runners and now Marcus Hayden. He hadn't heard from Graham or Uncle Phil, who had been leading Madison on a merry chase all over the State. He was concerned with their safety but knew the boys were savvy enough to deal with any problems. He knew the key to resolving all these issues rested with timing....

The van had turned onto the north-south track that ran down to the back block of Nathan's property. Garry drove a lot slower on the gravel track as it had recently succumbed to a deluge of spring rain, and he could feel it was slippery under the van's wheels. A minute later, two armed bikers appeared from the bushes and flagged down the van. Once identified, Nathan and Garry were waved through, and they proceeded to the bush car parking site. The men were weary and slowly picked up their belongings and walked across the road back to Nathan's crap shack. Every movement seemed painful and took so much effort. The men looked at each other and laughed as they felt like they were walking like old men, stooped, and walking like men in their nineties. As they approached the shack, Mad Dog and Lauren trotted out to greet them. '*All hail the conquering heroes*' said Mad Dog. Lauren ran forward and hugged both men. It was great to see everyone, and Nathan took Mad Dog aside to get an update on the current situation. Things had been quiet all the time the men had been absent, and Mad Dog was disappointed they hadn't had the opportunity to take on Ma Baker's crew as he was itching for some retribution for his fallen comrades. Nathan assured him he would get his chance and to bide his time. Lauren came over to Nathan and said that the bikers had treated her like a queen, and she couldn't be safer. She asked how things went and Nathan said he would brief everyone after the men had something to eat and a few hours sleep. He had some important information to divulge and wanted everyone to know the current situation. Lauren said she was okay with that and ventured back into the cabin. Garry had moved some of the gym equipment aside in the cabin's patio area and had set up a couple of camp stretchers, adorned with cheap sleeping bags for the men to rack out on. Being completely relaxed by their return home, the men ate and slept as though they had been *awake for a week*.

Nathan woke from his sleep but still felt as though he was in a stupor. Garry was still sleeping soundly, and he left him alone. Garry looked like he was in a dead sleep and would be hard to wake, anyway. A glance at his *Casio G Shock* told him he had slept for four hours but he felt like it had been forty. He did feel refreshed, but he didn't look or feel like it. It was still early afternoon, and he had a lot to do before the day was out and he needed to get his skates on. He needed to contact Caroline as he wanted to meet with her and Marcus. He had promised a briefing on what had occurred in the 'red centre,' and he needed to outline what his plans were for the coming days. Nathan picked up his phone and rang Caroline. On the third ring, Caro answered, 'Hey Nath, how're you doing, haven't' heard from you for a while?' Nathan said he had been running around, doing this and that and wanted to catch up with his best female friend and meet her new boyfriend. Caroline was delighted with Nathan's suggestion and said she would love to cook for her 'two boys'. Nathan said to keep this as a surprise to Marcus as he wanted to make a big occasion of this and to bring a couple of friends to dinner, as well as some expensive champagne. Caroline said that evening would be perfect, and she would just tell Marcus that a few friends were coming over to dinner. Caroline let slip that Marcus was residing at her place on a casual basis and that he was normally waiting for her by the time she finished work. He could get dinner started and it would be ready later that evening. 'Fine,' said Nathan, 'I will see you tonight, around seven. Take care.' Nathan had already figured out what he was going to do with Marcus Hayden, and this was the least of his problems at the moment.

Chapter 30

LIES & REGRETS...

T he *Director* hadn't slept at all well since this MacMillan saga had raised its ugly head; he was using sleeping tablets again - *for the first time in years*. It had taken him many years, decades in fact, to put this all behind him and now, here it was, coming back to haunt him like one of Charles Dickens' ghosts from a *Christmas Carol*. He had even managed to forget about the location of the secret bunker in the central Goldfields. Now, *that grotto of lies and intrigue* had re-surfaced on his radar. The *Director* was twenty years younger back then, around Hayden's age, very self-assured and committed to building a career for himself in the *Agency*.

It was such a different time. The internet wasn't as sophisticated or meddling back then as it is now, and electronic social media was fairly non-existent. The job still involved a lot of solid detective work.

Crims, deviants, and political upstarts still had to be flushed out of their *rat holes* and a lot depended upon good investigation techniques, gut hunches, and whiny snitches. The media wasn't always fishing about, waiting for someone to slip up, like giving someone a backhander because they did or didn't deserve one. The nation's problems were low scale, and all the policing agencies were on top of the situation. Now, he thought, 'I only have to break wind in public, slip up on a phrase at a conference or look in the general direction of a pretty woman and people will line up to do a 'Harvey Weinstein' on me. He wasn't all that far off his retirement, but he didn't want to cut and run, *it wasn't in his nature.*

The *Director* still had a lot to do before he walked out his office for the last time. The paramount thing he was concerned with was selecting a suitable heir that would create as few waves as possible within the *Agency* and its operation. Unless someone else stood up at the *Agency*, the only two candidates were Madison Baker and Marcus Hayden. The *Director* shuddered at the thought of Baker getting the top job. 'Too ruthless,' he thought and wondered how she ever got to be the person she had become. He could imagine her torturing kittens as a child because how could someone be as pitiless as this young adult unless there wasn't a history of nastiness, or some grotesque skeleton hiding in her family closet. His attention then turned to Hayden, and he wasn't convinced he was right for the job either. Hayden was a superb field operator but just lacked something. At times, he came across as a man devoid of any emotion or empathy. It seemed obvious to the *Director* that whilst Baker was devoted to using her extended intelligence family to fulfil her wanton desires, Hayden was the exact opposite, choosing little or no members of the *Agency's* family to aid him in his duties. Damn, he thought, it was *so much easier back then*. You came from a military or police intelligence background, and you applied for the job, and you did the job. Now, it seems you must have some spiritual calling, like Madison to devote all your being to the task or conduct yourself like some 'lone wolf' like Hayden and lurk among the shadows. Again, the *Director* reminisced, 'it was oh so much easier back then.'

Against his better judgment, he decided to re-open the file on Hamish MacMillan and re-acquaint himself with all the sordid details. He thought with some dread, 'I don't think this is going to help me get any sleep, tonight?' The *Agency* had been tracking MacMillan for some time during the last few years of the twentieth century. But 'show me one ranting academic with crazy ideas and I'll show you twenty,' seemed to be the prevailing attitude at that time. The

Agency was more concerned with *pseudo intellectual wack jobs* affiliating themselves with Libyan extremists or neo-Nazi fanatics. MacMillan didn't fit into this category. He had some ideas that were 'out there' but had not aligned himself to any group or cause or seemed like the guy that could be persuaded to join a fringe group or cult. Still, this was a worry and the *Agency* thought they would bring him in to see what he had to say and what his ideas were and to decide what to do with him next. Subtlety was the key here. The best way to orchestrate this was to masquerade as a business keen on his ideas, a 'think tank,' or Government Department wanting his vast expertise and advice on this important subject. MacMillan was on the breaking ground for this type of technology. Gain the man's confidence with an opportunity too good to refuse, fluff up his ego pillow sufficiently and he will squawk like a parrot-celebrating sunrise. That was the plan with MacMillan, but it *didn't work out that way.* The secret bunker had been intended to function as a covert laboratory but ended up as the man's tomb. 'What in the hell went wrong?'

The *Director* started remembering some of the conversations that he had with the professor. MacMillan had been told that he would be working with the Department of Defence, in one of its boutique science and research divisions and would have unlimited access to resources and to anything he required to develop a prototype of the weapon and its buffering cone system. He was assured he would receive all the recognition and his country's gratitude. Government agents would take him to a purpose-built laboratory, such was the consideration for his theories. He would also be ferried to any testing facility he thought necessary to complete his work. MacMillan was drunk with pride and exaltation. Finally, people, especially those in high Government were taking him and his work seriously. All those years of study and struggle were bearing fruit and the country would revere him as its saviour from world domination and exploitation. But it turned out to be *a big, fat, lie.*

MacMillan was taken to the laboratory/bunker, where he developed and installed the solar system, the first part of his promise to produce dependable and efficient solar power. This would light the bunker until it was either turned off or destroyed. MacMillan toiled for months working on the advanced weapon system. He would be escorted by agents to obtain necessary equipment and to have 'days out,' so that he wouldn't get 'cabin fever.' All under the protective umbrella of the *Agency*. The location or the solitude didn't perturb MacMillan as the man was so driven in his quest for scientific excellence, and the trips to the Woomera bunkers had become a grand adventure. The *Director* had been supervising the security and day-to-day running of this operation, such as security and logistics and had come to know MacMillan. He knew about the broken family situation. He knew MacMillan didn't have many friends and he sort of felt sorry for him. The man had discarded everyone and everything else in his life on a giant scientific hunch.

Life is funnily complex, at times, thought the *Director*. So often, we toil to get to the finishing line, like an Olympic swimmer in a race. Sometimes, we sacrifice everything to get to that finishing line. However, the journey is the greater reward than the prize that lies waiting at the end of the race. In the case of MacMillan, it was better for the Government to 'play' him and have him develop the bomb and its accompanying technology and not use it than take the chance he will be taken up by a rogue element. They would at least have the prototype. MacMillan may have been an academic besotted with his scientific quest, but he was no fool. He soon realised that the Government assurances were false, and the promises were not forthcoming. The day trips became infrequent, and he ended up a prisoner of the bunker. In the end, the *Agency* did not know what to do with him. The realisation dawned on MacMillan that he had become a '*big fish, in a small fishbowl*' and his ideas would never be fully realised. He managed to secure the .22 pistol that had been used to shoot vermin with rat shot in the cavern, fabricate two proper bullets in his lab and take his own life and that of his pet. For the *Agency* and the *Director*, who was MacMillan's 'minder' at the time, there was nothing more for it than to dispose of the body and keep this all on the quiet. The *Director* was prepared to do anything for national security and the creation of a secret laboratory could be talked away but if it ever got out that he had orchestrated a fake drowning there would be hell to pay...

The *Director* decided to make himself a coffee and wandered into the kitchen off his luxurious St. Kilda Road apartment. Just then, his mobile phone rang. It was Marcus Hayden, so he connected. 'Hello Marcus, what can I do for you?' Marcus took a deep breath and responded, 'I have decided to resign, *with immediate effect*. You will find a signed email in your inbox.' The *Director* was quite surprised by this announcement and asked Marcus if he would reconsider, take leave and as much time off as he wanted. Marcus thanked the *Director*; he knew he would be offered a leave of absence, but it was time to move on. Marcus spoke with respect, 'Sir, I appreciate the opportunities you have afforded me and the trust you have shown in my ability. However, I have found a remarkable woman I would like to be with for the rest of my life. Maybe start a family, who knows? The time has come to commence another chapter in my life. I hope you can appreciate this.' The *Director* wished Marcus all the best in his new adventure. He had also been married, once upon a time. Now, divorced for many years, he was now only married to the job. With Marcus gone, the success or failure of the mission now sat firmly with Madison Baker. The *Director* ditched the coffee and poured himself a long glass of *Johnny Walker Red Label* -straight with no mixer. He had an inkling that things were only going to get worse...

Chapter 31

COMPLICATED RELATIONSHIPS

The rest of the day had been spent in diligent, but silent preparation and working out a plan and its subsequent orders that all could follow. As Nathan had learnt in the Army, you need to 'dumb' it down so even the platoon moron can get the gist of what is going to happen. That way, no mistakes, (well, only a few if you're lucky!) and everyone knows their role and responsibilities. Lauren was preparing her things for the movement to a biker safe house near Melbourne, so she wouldn't be anywhere near danger when all the factions met in the next day or so. Lauren approached Nathan who was busily writing his orders and consulting some manuals, totally engrossed in his study. She looked at him and it was he who first

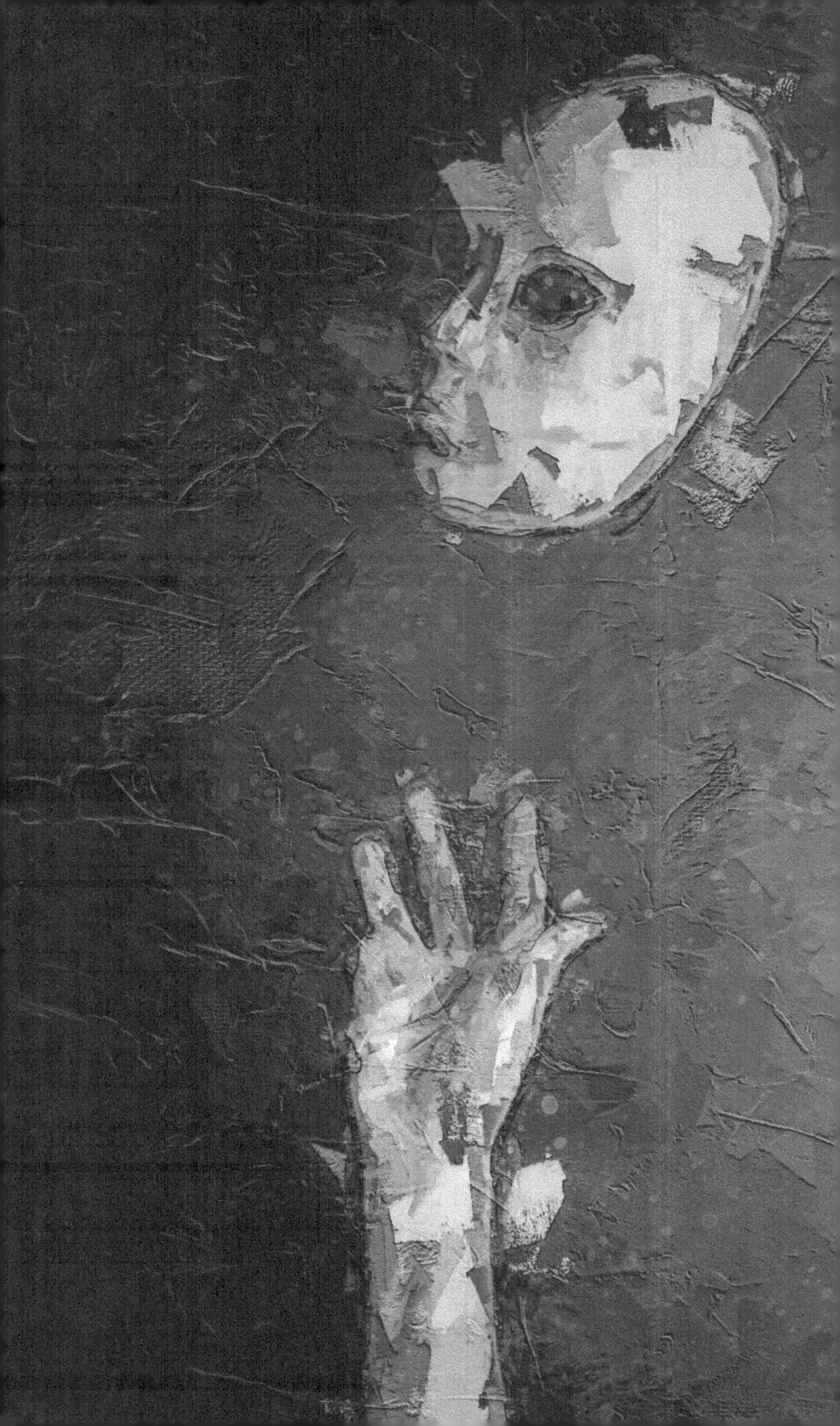

spoke, 'hey, Lauren, what can I do for you?' Lauren was completely surprised at Nathan's self-sacrifice and had never met another man like this. In her nights of solitude in the cabin, she had thought about all that had occurred in the last week. Last week, it had felt like a month of activity when compared to her usual sedate lifestyle! Lauren was more of a listener than a talker and had listened intently to what Nathan and the other men had recounted of their journey to Woomera and what they found. It gave her confidence that she would finally know about her father, his work, and its importance in the national framework. At times, she became annoyed as she wished her mother had provided the story of her father's life. If nothing else, she was confident that Garry would present the full story of Hamish MacMillan – eccentric scientist but a man whose heart and work was at the core of his nation's future and wellbeing.

Lauren leant forward and lightly kissed Nathan on the cheek and spoke. 'I can't thank you enough for what you have done and the closure you bring between me and my father. I know you and your friends have taken enormous risks in this pursuit of the truth and all I have to give you is my solemn thanks. Somehow, it doesn't seem enough?' Nathan was humbled by Lauren's succinct, heartfelt words and didn't want to dimmish her honest sentiment by blabbering on, so all he said was, 'It's okay, it's all about doing the 'right' thing and that is reward enough. There is so much wrong in this world and here was an opportunity to put something right, for a change.' One of Mad Dog's biker lieutenants had arrived with a tough, four-man biker escort to taken Lauren to the safe house, so she grabbed her things, made a cute waving gesture to Nathan, and followed the man out to the transport on the nth/sth road. Nathan thought of how Lauren had been put through the 'ringer' over the years due to the torment connected with her father and her piecemeal knowledge of him. He was sure she had heard many rumours and accusations that would not have been kind. At least now, she knew the truth, *good and bad*.

With all the activity that had been going on, morning had rolled easily into the afternoon and Nathan was just about finished with his preparations. It was now time to turn his attention to other important matters, such as Marcus Hayden and dinner with Caroline, later that evening. He laid out his clothes in the cabin and took a shower using the camp shower setup at the back of the crap-shack. All the while, Nathan was pondering on what would be said and considering all the angles. What would he do if Marcus denied his association with the *Agency*, and his asking questions? Was he just using Caroline to get to Nathan and what would be said if he completely denied the accusations? Nathan shaved, splashed on some cologne, and dressed, quickly. He checked and loaded the *Browning Hi-Power* and placed a spare magazine in his jacket pocket. Nathan walked out of the cabin with a determination he only used in the direst situations, and this was one of them. The van negotiated the country roads as if it were on remote control. Nathan was driving but his mind felt it was in a million places at once. He was thinking about the coming confrontation with all the opposing forces – especially Ma Baker and now Caroline and her new boyfriend, Marcus. How life had become so complicated in the last weeks. It was all coming to a head and life would return to normality but not for all...

Nathan had planned to arrive very early for the dinner and to catch Marcus unawares. As far as he knew, Marcus hadn't been informed he was going to be one of the dinner guests. The van was parked down the road in a siding that was semi-concealed with thick native shrubs. He cautiously walked the three hundred metres to Caroline's cottage and, upon his arrival, circumnavigated her house to see if it was vacant. There weren't any cars present, which was a good sign, so he crept forward until he stood outside the back door. Again, he listened. The only noise was a bird chirping high in a tree by the house. Nathan chose the back door as the lock had always been dodgy - he forgot how many times he had asked Caro to have it fixed. He produced a flexible plastic ruler and jiggled it inside the space between the bolt and the door frame. The door fell open and Nathan walked quietly inside. The house was vacant, so he re-locked the back door and positioned himself in the door side corner of the front room, between a bamboo louvered screen and the wall. He would not be seen until Marcus had fully entered the room. Nathan retrieved the *Browning* from his jacket and placed it flat on his thigh, once he had made himself comfortable in a chair. All he had to do now was check his phone for text messages and wait.

Marcus was only ten minutes away from the cabin and had run a few errands for Caroline, purchasing desert, some wine, and a few things like that for dinner. He also planned to give the house a tidy and mused that he was becoming 'Mr. Domestic.' Marcus was feeling like a 'free man,' and it felt like a burden had been lifted from his shoulders, now he had resigned from the *Agency*. What he would do for a living he did not know but he would worry about that later. At least he didn't have to perform anymore 'dirty' jobs. His frugal lifestyle meant he had plenty of savings and now he had someone with whom to spend it with. The weighty *Jag* slowed down to a roll outside of Caroline's place. Marcus skipped the few steps to the front door. He felt buoyed by the warmth of the day's sun and had a fondness for this cottage because it was here that he had turned his fortunes around. *Life was good.* The front door was unlocked, he entered and was heading for the kitchen when a cold and deliberate man's voice told Marcus to *'sit the fuck down.'* Marcus wasn't the type to be rattled but he was concerned he had been surprised, so easily. He stared across the room at the older man sitting in the chair with a *Browning* semi-automatic pointing at him and knew that it was Nathan Phillips. Marcus took a seat on the edge of the settee, but Nathan told him to sit back, deep into the sofa. 'Get yourself comfortable, because we are going to have a long chat.' Marcus thought he would lighten the situation and attempt to calm down Nathan, who by his own standards, looked very intimidating. 'No cause for concern, you'll get no problems from me, mate,' said Marcus. To which Nathan replied in a slow and menacing voice, *I'm not your fucking mate!* By the end of our tete-a-tete you had better convince me not to put a bullet in your brain and drop you in the abandoned shaft, I have picked out for you, ten minutes away.' 'Okay,' said Marcus, slightly agitated, 'there is no need for this "old school" show of force, what is it you want to know?'

Nathan asked what his intentions with Caroline were. 'I don't give two fucks if you are still with the *Agency*, but Caroline is family, and I won't see her used and hurt.' Marcus thought he may as well be honest. Nathan wasn't the sort of guy to bullshit to. If he slipped up in his responses, he would be *digging his own grave.* 'Okay,' said Marcus, 'when I first met Caroline, my initial intention was to pump her for information concerning you, your activities and your friends. But I instantly and, without equivocation, fell for the girl, and we have been inseparable ever since.' Marcus said Caroline had turned his life around and he had resigned from the *Agency* and was now unemployed. 'Here,' replied Marcus, 'I will send you the resignation text I sent to my boss.' Nathan told Marcus to retrieve his phone from his pocket very slowly and send the text. If he didn't get it in a few seconds, he would assume Marcus had texted an ally to come to his rescue. Nathan told him he would be occupying space in a cold, damp shaft before his colleagues would get here. The text was sent, and Nathan told Marcus to lie on the floor with his hands on the back of the head. Just a precaution as he quickly read the text. 'Okay,' said Nathan, 'this looks kosher, you can get up and take a seat but what have you told the *Agency* about me and my friends?' Marcus relayed how he had been brought in as backup to Madison Baker, who seemed to be running off the rails with this project. He said he had only been involved in the operation for a short period and hadn't even enough information to submit a report. His abrupt resignation saw to that. 'Okay, so you're not with the *Agency*, and you have a new, hot girlfriend. It might seem like a conflict of interest but what do you know that can help me with Ms Baker?' Marcus replied, 'nothing more than what you already know. She is an evil bitch that takes great delight in hurting people. One of the reasons I left the *Agency*, too many psychos. Give me the Army any day! I will say one thing, never trust her and always expect her to do the worse.'

Nathan seemed satisfied with Marcus' answers and his candour. 'You realise that this still does not make us friends. I will be watching you and the first time you hurt Caroline, expect swift retribution. It may not be me, but I have a network of colleagues that you can't even fathom.' Marcus could gauge Nathan's sincerity and his regard for Caroline. He was 'old school' which meant his values meant more to him than bucks and his word was priceless. Marcus replied, 'if I every hurt her I will deserve what is coming.' 'Besides all this,' said Nathan in a commanding tone, 'you will tell her the truth. Why you met her and how you have changed. The decision for you to remain as a couple will be entirely hers. And there is no debate on this.' Marcus could tell he had no room for manoeuvre and would have to comply with Nathan's instructions. As he was taking this in, a car door slammed outside, and

Nathan placed the *Browning* in his jacket pocket. The door suddenly burst open, and Caroline entered the room with a burst of vigour and a broad smile. 'I see you two have got acquainted,' as she addressed the two men. 'Yeah,' said Nathan, we've been having a long, interesting chat. Seems we both served in the Army and shit like that.' Caroline went and dragged Nathan out of his chair and took him over to Marcus, who, by now was standing, waiting to give Caroline a kiss. She placed an arm around each man. 'Isn't it wonderful,' she said, with a degree of pride and passion, *the two main men in my life, the best of friends?*' Nathan threw a steely glance at Marcus who was unfazed and coolly stared back. 'Great' said Nathan, somewhat sarcastically, *'what's for dinner?'*

Chapter 32

THE BEGINNING OF THE END...

Everything was in order. Nothing more could be done. All the equipment had been skilfully prepared. Explosive charges and weapons had been checked and re-checked. Nathan despised using the term 'with crack military precision' as he knew so many military outings were far from being 'crack' or 'precise.' Weapons were cleaned and cleaned again. Vehicles and motorbikes had been re-fuelled and expertly concealed. Sentries had been briefed. Every man there had surveyed his own equipment and made any adjustments, as necessary. Nathan had presented detailed orders to all who would be involved in the coming battle as well as describing their antics in central Australia. Like any good commander, Nathan had selected the ground of his own choosing for the

coming fight, and it was his home area as he knew it so well. The confrontation would take place in the scrub and shaft area to the east of the north south road and Nathan's back cabin. Now all they had to do was wait for the various combatants to come together. The main element here was timing. The plan would work if the opposition arrived at or close to, the same time. He had appointed competent commanders to deal with the various factions. Uncle Phil would deal with the Carlton Crew, Graham would manoeuvre the Creswick drug dealers, and Nathan would sort out Madison Baker and her cohort.

The time ticked away until it was early afternoon on the Saturday. Nathan had tasked Paul and the bikers to act as 'foxes' that would lead the hounds back to their lair. They knew the people they were chasing and that was the easy part. They had identified the haunts in Carlton and Creswick where the antagonists frequented. As far as Madison was concerned, a loose text message or a visual identification of one of his vehicles from a police camera would stimulate her interest and she would come running. Keeping distance from their pursuers was the hardest part and timings would be staggered due to the opposition being located in different geographical areas. As soon as they were being followed back to the back block area, Nathan would be alerted, and all would be on standby.

As it turned out, *the factions tumbled easy for the lures that had been set.* Uncle Phil had dropped hints to the waitress at the café he knew in Carlton to be a front for the Carlton Crew; he noticed he had gained their attention and took off on his powerful bike, a *Kawasaki Ninja H2*, but not too fast that he couldn't be followed. Graham was playing the same 'see me, catch me' game in Creswick. A loud word here and a drop of a name there at the local hardware store also had the same effect as Uncle Phil. Graham could see the young attendant take out his phone and make a call as soon as he overheard the mention of Nathan and Lauren's name and the fracas at the nursery. Again, Graham waited around until interested parties appeared and then headed out to the back block area. Paul was still driving Nathan's '67 *Fastback* in a circular route around Melbourne, especially in dense security camera areas. Paul was keeping his eye out for the standard operative vehicle and would be off like a jack rabbit as soon as they were on his tail. Unfortunately, the *Agency* was quicker than him. Two SUVs pulled up either side of the *Fastback* at the set of lights, lowered the rear windows and the rear passengers pointed their assault rifles at Paul. The door opened on the black *Ford Everest* that parked in front of the *Mustang* and Madison Baker stepped out, *a grin so wide on her face that she resembled Luna Park.* Paul knew *this would only mean trouble.*

Nathan was reviewing his plans for the coming engagement when his phone rang – No caller ID, again. He knew this would only be one person. 'Yes Madison,' was the reply, *what do you want now?* 'Hello Nathan, I have a friend of yours who wants to chat with you,' said a smug Madison and she thrust her phone into the face of Paul, who was now beaten and bruised. 'Talk,' was all she said. *'Nathan don't tell these arseholes anything.'* Paul's voice trailed away as she snatched back the phone and said, 'And to let you know I'm not kidding, your precious *Mustang* is now being recycled for baked bean cans. No charge.' 'Okay, what do you want?', inquired Nathan. 'Well,' said Madison, 'that is more like it, a bit more compliance for a change. You know what I want, the manuscript and Lauren Gale. Yes, we know about her. Not much gets past us. You give me all this and your mate lives - *that's the deal.*' 'Okay,' said Nathan, 'I will meet you at the back of my block in one hour. I am on my way there now. *Will that suffice?*' 'Perfect,' said Madison and she hung up. Neither party trusted one another, and Nathan knew Madison was wilier than a bag full of snakes. Nevertheless, she was headed to where he wanted her to be, and Paul had done his job, but this isn't how he wanted her brought to him.

Nathan was receiving updates from Phil and Graham on their situations and the likely time these groups would arrive at the back block area. Phil would guide his group to the far eastern side of the shaft area, that mostly comprised of the odd shaft and mullock heaps. Graham would concentrate his group on the southern side of the shaft area, which was very thick in vegetation and had a shaft and a small tunnel system. Nathan would lead Madison to the eastern side of the shaft area where there were more dangerous shafts and leaky tunnels and was the most dangerous part of the area. The plan was to *divide and conquer.*

It hadn't taken long for the Carlton Crew to get their act together. The dark Italian man had been cajoling his friends to action ever since their meeting in the restaurant and had kept them on a high alert level. Phil was making it easy for them to follow him. He would pull over to the curb and pretend to make calls on his mobile phone. This gave the henchmen time to catch up with one another in their cars, which were heavily ladened with weapons, ammunition, food, sleeping gear and clothing. Their plan was to stay out until the task was finished. There were now five cars following, not in a procession but a loose gaggle on the tail of Uncle Phil. The Italian man was feeling smug as he believed he would honour his departed uncle, his *familia*, but he was not prepared for what was about to go down...

'Okay, you're sure this guy was talking about Lauren and that jerk that beat me up?' said Tyler as he gave Brendan a rough shove and pushed him out the door of their crap house. 'Right, whatever you do, *don't lose this guy*, and let me know where he is at all times, thanks.' Tyler told Brendan of what was transpiring in town and barked at him to get on to his phone and summon their team together. Once assembled, his posse would assemble in town by the rotunda and follow the old grey-haired geezer to where Lauren was and exact some revenge on her friends. As he did so, he opened the boot of his sedan and checked the pump action shotgun that had been resting there besides a half-dozen boxes of shells. Tyler was getting excited at the prospect of taking revenge on those who had made him look like the small man that he really was. He also was very giddy at the idea of giving Lauren a good smack for her part in his beating. He believed he needed to teach people a lesson for the derision and angst he suffered. However, it was Tyler who was going to be educated and he didn't even know it... 🖋

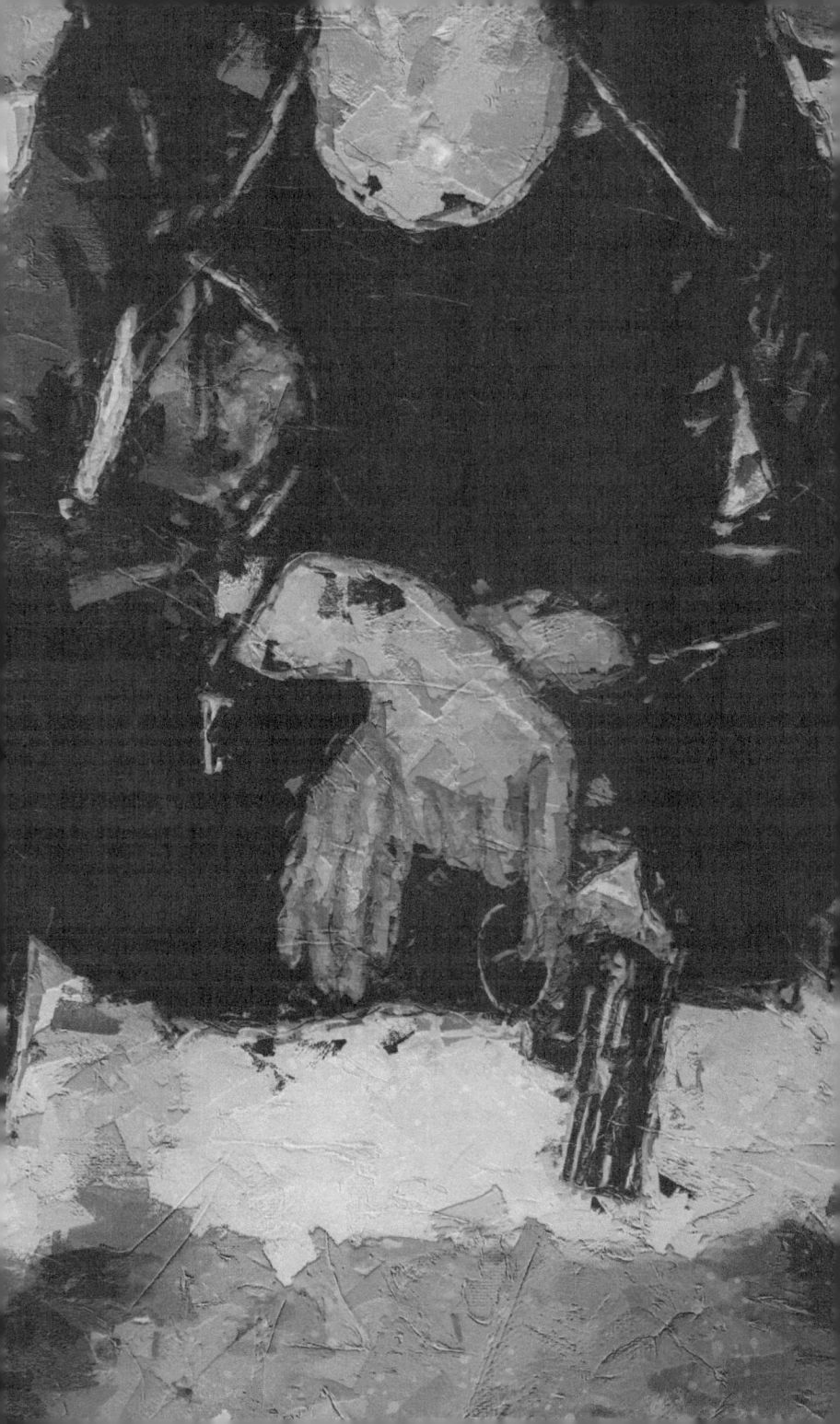

Chapter 33

SATURDAY'S ALRIGHT FOR FIGHTING...

Now was the time for action. As soon as the conversation ended with Madison, Nathan contacted all the team leaders involved, via their closed radio network and outlined the expected timing of when Madison Baker and her crew would arrive. Both Phil and Graham had contacted Nathan and they said the 'hounds' were on their tails, and they were both leading their quarries on a merry dance and could be out at the site, give or take ten minutes. Security cameras, of the camouflage hunting variety, had been positioned at likely points to detect and monitor the belligerent groups and to assist with co-ordination and control of the event. Nathan would wait another thirty minutes before he would get Phil to bring in his group first, then followed by Graham's group, ten minutes later and then Madison Baker. Nathan was energised by the way things were progressing. Although a variety of doubts and various scenarios continued to run through his mind, his measured plan to divide, distract and create diversion amongst the warring factions would have an excellent chance of success. Let the antagonists fight one with another in the belief they were waging war with Nathan and his cohort. However, they were *willing accomplices in their own destruction.*

At the same time as Nathan was finalising his preparations, Madison was sitting comfortably in the *Ford Everest* and was feeling quite pleased with herself. She was exalted in the belief that this operation soon would be over, and she had already texted her beauty consultant to give her a facial and to do her nails later in the next week. The constant running around had played 'havoc' with her nails and skin complexion; she would have her haircut the week after. She gazed back from the front passenger leather seat to study Paul, who was going in and out of consciousness and was constantly being propped up by one of Madison's thugs. The beating had been severe and a mark of how Madison treated people who crossed her. Madison commented, '*wakey, wakey*, Paul, we'll be out at the goldfields soon. I need you to be *compos mentis* for when we see your old buddy, Nathan. Don't die on me yet, *that comes later...*' Paul looked up through a puffed and bleeding eye, his eye socket was certainly fractured. He knew Madison couldn't keep her word and he was a goner. What he did know was as vicious as Madison was, Nathan was as clever. Just as Phil was looking back to make certain he was still being loosely pursued, he heard the codeword '*Long Tan*' in his headset. He geared down on the *Kawasaki*, made a wide U-turn in the street, and accelerated sharply towards Nathan's back block. The Italian man in the dark clothes signalled to his driver to follow, at pace and the accompanying vehicles followed their leader. By this time, Phil was accelerating and riding the bending country roads, sharply and expertly on his Japanese super bike. The Italian leader took this as a sign that Phil was trying to evade them, he could if he wanted to, but he was making the chase interesting. The leader *urged his driver, angrily in Italian*, not to lose Phil and the car's acceleration increased, markedly. When Phil was five minutes away from the back block, he passed on the codeword '*Von Ryan's Express*' to Nathan, who knew group one would be arriving almost immediately. Nathan quickly passed the word along, and everyone present at the back block area steeled themselves for the coming confrontation.

Bikers created a ring around the Nathan's 'killing zone' and once protagonists were allowed in, they would never be allowed to venture out. Phil had slowed down considerably on the dirt north/south track. Although he couldn't observe his support, he knew armed and angry looking bikers were concealed and anticipating in the bush. He rode the bike another 100 metres, abruptly pulled over, looked back at the pursuing Carlton Crew, and headed east into the scrub of the *Kong Deng* mining area. The Italians pulled up sharply on the gravel, rapidly exited from their vehicles and headed in the direction they last saw Phil running. The bush was thick, and the city men weren't used to moving efficiently through the scrub, they pulled at branches, stumbled, and cursed the vegetation. All a bit too hard when compared to the genteel Lygon Street pavements! Phil occasionally looked back and lightly laughed at the stumbling and bumbling of these men. Nevertheless, they were still heading in his direction. He slowed to make their pursuit easier and soon was at the mouth of a large mullock heap that had been turned into an entrance that led into a deep shaft, eighty metres later.

This shaft had a number of winding tunnels that ran off the main corridor. Phil took one last glance and made eye contact with the Italian in the dark clothes, who urged on his troops, at the same time,

Phil ran into the shaft corridor. It went from bright light to instant pitch-black darkness in seconds but ahead, Phil could see the glow sticks, attached to string thirty metres ahead. From behind, he could hear men running, *fast* towards the entrance. Phil ran to the glow sticks, which were strung out in intervals along parachute chord. The glow sticks went for another five metres in a straight line and then abruptly turned to the right, down another corridor. This corridor led to a small exit. As Phil ran, he gathered up the sticks by the chord, removing the illumination and his trail form the pursuing men. All the while, Phil was making his way out of the corridor, the Italians had continued with the hunt, turning on cigarette lighters and some small pen-torches they had, which had slowed their chase.

The pursuit was now slow as they weren't certain where Phil was or where they were being led to. Vito, who was in the lead group, spoke with an increasing vibrato of suspicion and concern to his uncle, 'Mario, I don't like this, *I think we are being suckered...*' Just as he spoke, a large explosion filled the corridor where the men were standing, rock, dust, branches, and rubble cascaded upon them. A few of the men at the rear of the lead group, managed to escape the carnage and exit the entrance, only to be fired upon by bikers who had boxed them in. The cave entrance had been destroyed by a very small, improvised charge primarily using ammonium nitrate. This chemical is found on many bush properties and can be easily accessed. It was this type of explosive used by Timothy McVeigh to destroy a U.S. Federal Government building in Oklahoma. As Phil exited the corridor, the explosive erupted, and the impact pushed him forward into the arms of Nathan who was waiting for him. *'Damn, that was a close-run thing,'* shouted Phil, who had been slightly deafened by the blast. *'One down and two to go,'* said Nathan. Both men jogged to position two. The firing had mostly died between the bikers and the Carlton Crew. Bikers now moved forward shooting anyone still alive and now concealing the bodies in the bush. Another group of bikers had removed any vehicles parked on the north/south track and the area looked as normal and tranquil as it had been before. The only exception now was the tomb that now encased Vito, his friends and Mario, the angry Italian nephew who used to wear all black clothes.

Nathan picked up his phone and rang Graham, who was taking a leisurely drive around the wooded hillsides around the greater Creswick area. He could see he was being tailed but it appeared that it was taking some time for Tyler's crew to get its act together and to gather in some force. Slowly, cars started joining the procession and Graham headed the drug posse towards the northern side of the back block area. Nathan asked Graham to keep this group dangling but slowly moving toward his location until Madison Baker had arrived. Just as he finished his call, his phone rang, and it was Madison asking directions to their meeting point. Nathan told her to drive to the southern side of the *Kong Deng* site, where she would locate a narrow dirt road that would lead her into a flat salt pan area, wide enough to park cars. This is where he would be waiting. Madison said she would be there in ten minutes. The trouble with Madison was that she had always gotten her own way. And she had always come up against lighter, less diligent opposition. Madison didn't realise it and she never would know or imagine, but over the years, she had been setting herself up for failure. She barked some instructions to her men, and they loaded their automatic weapons and sat upright in their seats, scanning the road ahead and busily conducting radio checks via their headsets. Paul sat a forlorn figure in the back of the *Everest*, not really sure how this was going to play out, but he was a realist and knew where it was all heading. *They were now only five minutes away.*

On a bushy mullock heap, three hundred and fifty metres away from the proposed meeting point, stubby fingers in camouflage gloves adjusted the windage and elevation knobs on the PSO-1 scope on the Russian

Dragunov sniper rifle to take in a number of acquired target distances. The sniper preferred to use his laser range finder than relying on the scope's and he recorded this information on a small note pad. Wind was not a problem at the moment, and he knew he could not be seen, as he was expertly camouflaged behind staggered layers of foliage. His bullets would only exit via a minute cavity through the bushy tiers, preventing any sign of smoke or flash. The weapon had been a souvenir of his tours of Iraq and Mark Simmons had managed to secret the weapon back home. He would provide 'overwatch' for Nathan during his meeting. It would be his pleasure. Phil would assume control of the operation whilst Nathan was meeting Madison. He would wait until the meeting was underway and then have Graham guide the Creswick drug-runners to the meeting point. At this point in time, they were only five minutes behind Madison's arrival.

Nathan walked to the salt pan and positioned himself at the range distance, he had agreed upon with Mark. He carried with him a large, but old looking yearly almanac that he would use to maintain the illusion that Madison was going to get what she came for. He stood alone on the grey and hard salt pan and pricked his ears for any sound. *This is where it could all go pear-shaped*, but he was confident in his ability and that of Mark's shooting accuracy. Besides this, his *Browning* was concealed behind his shirt, behind his belt in the small of his back. He also had other tricks up his sleeve... Off in the distance, he could hear the whirr of engines and started to see the odd puff of dust from the black SUVs that now grew large as they motored towards him down the track. Mark, in his sniper hide, passed on the information to Phil that the *Agency* people were on site and to keep concealed as they had put a drone in the air to get eyes on the target. Phil passed on the codeword *'Jed Clampett'* to Graham to now bring in Tyler and his crew.

The two dusty black SUVs pulled up twenty metres from where Nathan was patiently standing. A solitary vehicle stayed back 100 metres, still on the dusty, dirt track. Meanwhile, the noise of the drone could be heard, only slightly, over-head. Madison couldn't wait to get out of the car and raced out to confront Nathan. She stood five metres away. 'Hi Nathan, nice to meet you. Funny, *thought you would be taller?*' She paused, 'Just my way of brevity and softening the moment.' *'Oh, very funny,'* said Nathan. 'And I was misguided to ever think that you were of the fairer sex.' 'Okay, enough of idle chatter,' said Madison, 'Where is the manuscript and Lauren Gale, as we arranged?' 'Well,' said Nathan, 'until we sort out some issues, Lauren is in safe keeping, you'd do the same if you were in my shoes.' Nathan could tell right away this was not to Madison's liking. She turned around and nodded to the car and two burly men, dressed like contractor mercenaries, dragged a bloody and dishevelled Paul out of the *Everest* and dumped him ceremoniously at the right-hand side of Madison. 'I'm tired of your games, Nathan, produce Lauren and the manuscript or Paul gets it. Your choice.' Before Nathan could utter a word, Madison spoke, *'oh, to hell with it,'* and she pulled a brushed steel *Walther PPK* out of her jacket pocket and, without any warning or mercy, shot Paul in the head. Paul lurched to the side and hit the ground hard, as if he was shoulder tackling the dirt. Now, crimson ooze mixed with the grey powdery dust of the salt pan. *'Why the fuck, did you do that?'* screamed Nathan, who would've ripped out Madison's throat if he could have gotten closer without being shot. 'To speed up the process and to let you know I'm not playing games. *You will be next if you don't give me what I came for.'* Before another word could be said, Nathan stepped back and crashed down through a camouflage screen into a small foxhole, which had been concealed by dirt-coloured sandbags and chicken wire. A split second later, the *Dragunov* fired. Madison had been fortunate to move when Nathan stepped back, the bullet only grazed her shoulder and she scurried back to the safety of the *Everest* SUV. *'Damn,'* cussed Nathan, who thought it always seemed to be the way with these evil-to-the-core types, *they always ride on the crest of luck.* By this time, Mark had fired a number of shots and had shot out the radiators of all the vehicles and had taken out two of Madison's agents in the process. Nathan had picked up his Ruger that he had placed in the foxhole and was firing to where Madison had run for cover. Without hesitation, he threw two smoke grenades and darted out of the hole - *like he had the devil on his tail* and headed in a northerly direction, back to the bevy of mullock heaps in the centre of *Kong Deng.*

Once Nathan was clear, Mark collected his weighty rifle and kit, exited his hide, and made for an alternate firing position, two hundred metres away. An 'overwatch' sniper was not what Madison had anticipated. She knew Nathan had his contacts but didn't expect his assets to be in advance of her own team. Whilst she was pondering this situation, one of her men slapped a dressing and surgical tape on her bleeding wound. The pain must've been excruciating but Madison didn't flinch a muscle. She called out to all her men to collect plenty of ammo and to follow her. She divided her men into two groups and told one group to head to the right and circle around and meet them at the largest mullock heap, which was three hundred metres away. Madison was driven to bring down Nathan and her anger and determination was relentless. Nothing else mattered. For an older guy, Nathan could still move fairly quick, and he darted here and there for cover in the scrubby bush, only firing the odd shot to let Madison know the direction he was heading. He had vanished before they knew it. In all the calamity, he had still been monitoring his comms and heard Graham's codeword *'Beverley Hills,'* which indicated Tyler and his men had arrived and were being driven down, from the northern edge of *Kong Deng*, to the large mullock heap that all parties were moving to. The timing couldn't have been better as Tyler's group did appear to have heard the shooting from the south and, like the Carlton Crew were on a headlong charge to *capture or kill their quarry*. Nathan's plan was proceeding as he had planned. Now, two groups, unknown to one another, were converging fast onto the same point and were only just over one hundred metres away. Around the perimeter, bikers were starting to reign in the circle, tighter and tighter until the net was drawn in and closed - *without mercy*, around the opposition.

The large central mullock heap was around eighty metres in length and fifty metres wide, resembling a small dirt mesa, yellow and green. It also contained a number of small tunnels cut into its crusty sides and a deep and water flooded central shaft. Phil and Graham would engage the drug posse to the north but would monitor and quieten their fire to give Tyler and his group the incentive to rush the central dirt area. Nathan would apply the same tactic to Madison, whilst Mark was positioned in a hide to the middle and west of the large dirt heap. He could use his rifle fire to persuade any attackers to stay within the general area and assist the bikers to engage any runners who attempted to slip through the net. Of all the groups, Tyler's men were the least efficient and motivated. All the while they were on the move through the bush, Tyler was grabbing his semi-reluctant comrades and *dragging them forward, cajoling, abusing, and pleading with them* as they went. Like Madison, he was determined to dispense his retribution, this day. The whole firefight became very muddled and confusing to all, except Nathan, Phil, and Graham. They would fire bursts of shots at the parties, who were slowly making their way towards them. As it happened, Madison's right flanking team saw the first two members of Tyler's crew and opened fire on them, in the belief they were Nathan's men. This is what Nathan had planned and hoped for! Tyler's men returned fire and both groups moved on one another. Madison and her team were still headed for the large mullock heap and their pace quickened when they heard the rifle fire and automatic bursts from her men, she was ten metres away and about to link up with her flanking group.

A small, innocuous shrub lay to the right of the mullock heap. Inside the bush, a full twenty-litre fuel can of gasoline had been carefully placed and concealed. It was wrapped in barbed wire and contained nails, bolts, and any metal pieces available. Having seen Nathan, Phil and Graham seek cover in the corridor of the large mullock heap, Mark flicked the safety switch on the *Dragunov* to semi. He waited until the moment was right, when the combatants were close for the improvised 'dirty bomb' to have its maximum effect. The attackers kept moving forward upon each other until they were in the 'killing area.' Mark followed his marksmanship routine and fired a single, deadly round. An almighty '*boom*' rang out in the area and instantly five men were cut down, as if by an invisible and merciless scythe. The remaining combatants were dazed, and the battle ceased. Madison had taken a severe shrapnel hit to her right lung; *frothy blood was trickling out of her wound.* Her breathing was becoming laboured, and she realised assistance would not be forthcoming from her men, who, by now were limited to a few wounded assaulters. *Tyler had been killed outright by the deadly blast*, leading the charge and only one or two of his young comrades were still alive, but dazed and bloodied.

Madison sought the only cover she could identify and crawled, as best as she could, using three bruised arms and limbs to the corridor entrance of the mullock heap. The rifle fire re-commenced but it was the *Cossacks* who were finishing off any opposition, as their punitive ring tightly circled the area. Intermittent shots and screaming could be heard until only silence pervaded the old gold mining area. *No noise. Dust had settled. The battle was over.*

After seeking refuge in the entrance, Madison attempted to use her mobile phone to call for backup, only discovering it to be damaged and inoperable from the fracas. She placed her throat scarf inside her blouse to act as a makeshift field dressing, as her ugly injury was beginning to bleed profusely, but before she could think any further, *Nathan Phillips slowly stepped out from the shadows and receding smoke.* Madison looked up and desperately *raised her Walther,* but Nathan kicked it out of her drooping, weak hand. She dropped her tired arms, part in resignation but also because her blood loss was now taking its toll. *'Okay, you win,'* said Madison, in a belligerent voice, defiant to the end. 'I suppose you're going to come out with some old school, white guy, army bullshit, like *"Mess with best, die like the rest, or some other worn out cliche?"* 'No, not really,' said Nathan. And on that simple comment, Mad Dog walked forward into the corridor entrance and *stared vengefully down at Madison Baker*, who now lay frightened in a mire of her own blood and filth. Nathan walked out quickly without looking back. He initially heard a series of ghastly screams, but these were quickly followed by a dozen rifle shots from an AK 47. He didn't want it to end this way, but the *Cossacks* were owed for their losses, and their unflinching loyalty.

Mad Dog's men had been rounding up all the bodies, that also included the 'Carlton Crew' who had not perished in the shaft and were placing them where it would make an obvious statement to anyone in forensics - *even someone with a college certificate*. A major drug deal had been unfolding here on the central goldfields and a drug law enforcement operation had erroneously underestimated the ability and resources of the criminals. A fierce, no-quarters battle ensued, and this was the unfortunate, but inevitable outcome. Garry would masterly edit the footage from the camouflage security cameras and leak the story to the media. *Front page news.* The involvement of Nathan, his men and the *Cossacks* was sanitised as best as could be managed. The crumpled body of Paul Burton was left where he fell, an innocent victim in Madison's sordid saga; his life extinguished for information and anecdotes he may have had on the Creswick drug runners and the Carlton Crew. This will be the story circulated as well as the execution style ending of one of Victoria's former police officers, at the hands of Madison Baker.

It was now time to disburse all the parties away from the back block area before this all-mighty ruckus had been reported to the authorities and there were cops and *Agency* members raining down on them. All parties would drive back to their respective homes, headquarters, and haunts, via a number of back road and highway routes, and at staggered timings. There were brief rest stops to facilitate this masquerade and to prevent any group from being loosely connected. Nathan, Phil, and Graham were the last to leave. Graham would drive back to Ballarat and Nathan would stay with Phil, in Melbourne. The men were exhausted and didn't have anything to say. Their glances to one another said it all. *They had survived. Nothing more to be said.* The time for war stories and bullshit would come later. The plan had worked and barring any missed details, it would be hard to implicate them in this massacre. Sure, there would be files at the *Agency*, where Madison Baker had outlined who the players were in her investigation but her gross failure and corruption at the end would act as a 'black eye' for the *Agency*, who would attempt to hide their shortcomings and blame the disaster on 'rogue' Madison Baker and the various criminal elements in attendance. ✒

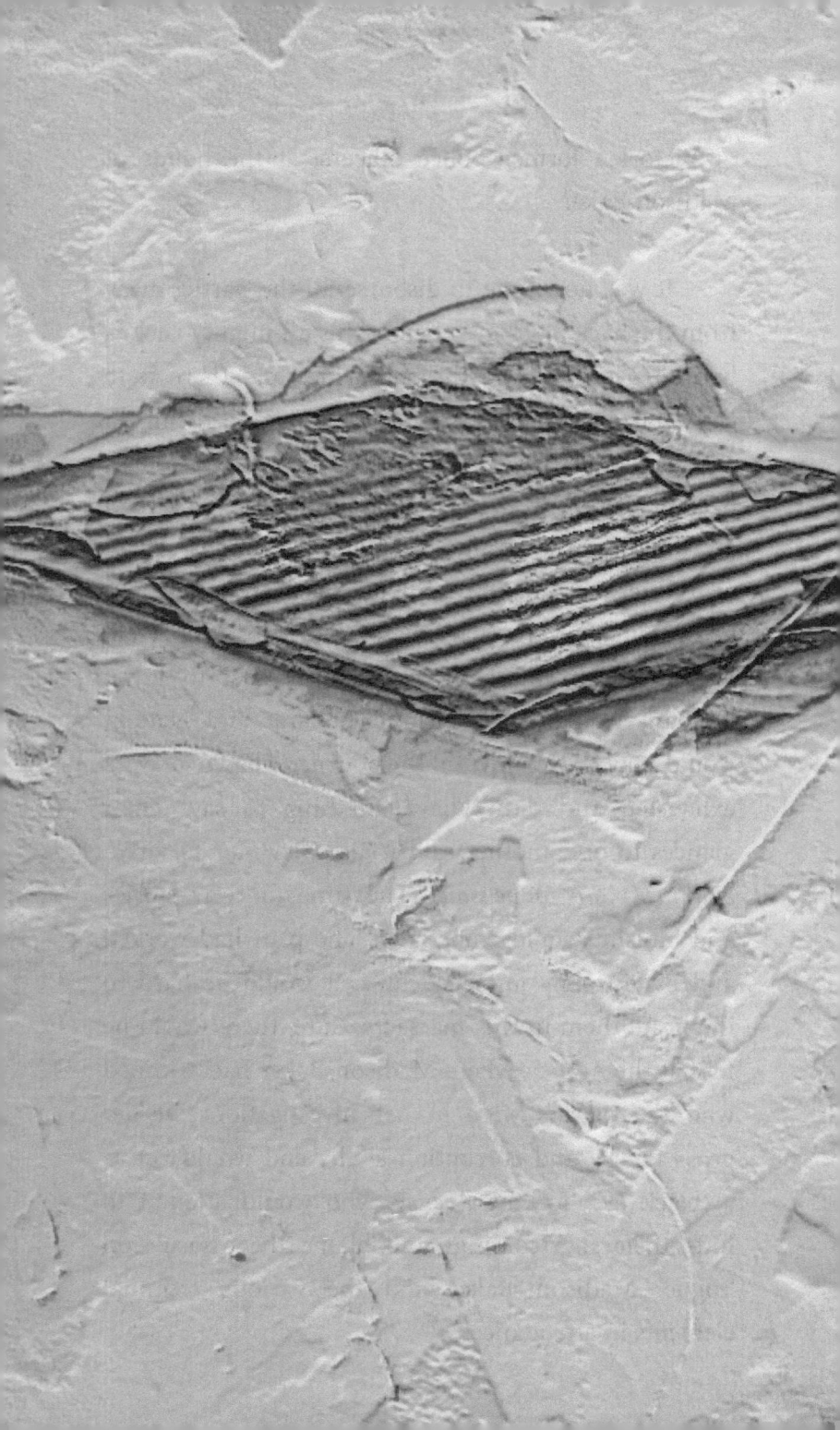

Chapter 34

DAMAGE CONTROL

The news of the demise of Madison Baker and her team came as a mighty thunderclap for the *Director*, who sat wearily in his office chair. It was Sunday but he had to try and get on top of the situation. In front of him, on his desk lay an initial report, which he read and re-read. The police had informed him that there were no survivors from the *Agency*, and they were in the process of conducting a thorough investigation. Any and all information would be forthcoming. Coupled with this disaster were the morning headlines: 'Drug Gang battle in Central Victoria.' 'Massacre in Middle Victoria – No Survivors.' *'Damn you, Baker,'* he thought, but he instantly softened his stance and reminisced and thought how Madison had been a 'good trooper' for the *Agency,* but her drastic and unorthodox methods eventually ended her life. For her failure, Baker was now taking the 'long sleep.' What made this situation all the worse were the calls in the press from those from the socio-political pulpit calling for a Royal Commission into activities from covert police and security groups such as the *Agency*. The civil libertarians and bleeding-heart liberals had been banging on about the abuse of power and secret goings on for years and it looked like they would be getting their way. '*Damn*,' thought the *Director*, 'I want be able to take a crap without Parliamentary approval.'

The *Director* sat looking across at his desk, his office and how this small space represented nearly a lifetime of work. He finally let out a deep sigh and knew what had to be done. Almost instantly, he felt better that the decision had been made. The *Director* opened a file that he had composed a number of years ago, especially if this situation ever arose. The file was composed of two parts, a letter, and a detailed exit plan. He checked the letter over, inserted the current date, and time, digitally signed it and forwarded it to the relevant Ministers and heads of Departments. He may receive an inquiry text or two but for the most part, it would be days before he would be asked to explain his decision. The title announced: '*Resignation*.' The plan he forwarded to his smart phone. Time to step down, time to move on and time to vacate to a place where the *Director* couldn't be extradited. He closed down his computer, turned off the office light, locked the door and walked out for the last time - *never to be seen again*.

The stinging, brutal slap across the face came as a surprise to Marcus. He didn't think Caroline could or would ever be capable of violence, but he had it coming, and he didn't really know how to respond. For an 'action man,' he was stunned. Caroline had collapsed on the bed, sobbing uncontrollably, gasping for breath, her nose running and tears cascading down her cheek. She was a physical wreck. Her condition reminded him of the look of immense discomfort on the faces of people after they had been exposed to tear gas. Marcus had decided to come clean and tell Caroline why he first met her and what were his initial intentions. He had planned to do this, even without Nathan's insistence. So much had changed after he had fallen, deeply and madly in love with her. Her loving influence had re-directed his life's course. *'How long were you going to play me like a puppet?'* roared an angry Caroline, *'how long were you going to screw me until you got your jollies?'* 'How can I ever trust you, ever again?'

Marcus sat down on the bed and moved closer to Caroline, who moved away by an inch, as if repulsed by his physical contact. Although she resisted, he grasped her two tiny hands in his and looked at her, with a sad and worried countenance upon his face. He began to speak, quietly and truly honest for the first time in years. 'My darling, I can never say enough to apologise for what I have done. The way I treated you was irreprehensible. I know this and it will take more than a few apologies to make up for what I have done. I won't insult you by just saying sorry. *I love you more than anything or anyone on this planet.* I want to be with you forever. Please allow me the chance to love you and to prove to you my eternal love?' He still gripped Caroline's hands and she wasn't resisting his contact, anymore. She knew she loved Marcus more than anyone she had ever met. He would have to earn her trust, but she was prepared to take a chance. Her tears began to fade, and she looked up at Marcus, fragile and innocent from the pillow she had been crying on. 'We need to talk about this more,' said Caroline and then she raised her tone, *'and don't think you're going to get out of this easy, buster!'* The couple kissed and Marcus cradled Caroline in his arms. He knew there would be some mighty bridge building ahead but at least he had the rest of his life with Caroline to make things right.

Garry had not fully anticipated the mighty furore that was created by his news story. He knew that it would be immensely popular with certain elements of society, those who possessed an innate distrust of Government, but the story had remained on the pages of the tabloids for the last week and featured nightly on the news and current affairs programs. It was not going away soon. His editor had been 'visited' by the Federal Police, especially concerning the intrusion into the Woomera Rocket Range and who was involved. Oh, the authorities huffed and puffed and threatened charges but nothing in the story linked Garry, Nathan, or David to the physical act of trespassing on Commonwealth Property. As they say in the Army, 'no names, no pack drill.' Partnered with this startling expose was the Federal Opposition's calls for a Royal Commission into the nuclear device, secret scientific testing, and the highly suspicious death of Prof. Hamish MacMillan. Indignant politicians were having a field day pointing fingers at one another across the parliament house floor; both parties were just as guilty and complicit as this conspiracy play had been acted out over many decades. Nathan had presented Garry with a story of the ages. He would most likely win some coveted award for this disclosure but telling the truth was what counted, no matter how distasteful. This was what was the most important thing in the nation's interest. Garry knew there would be other gripping and insightful stories, but this narrative would always be special, for the story, for the adventure, *and for the friendship between three men.*

Some of those involved in this drama were finding it harder to cope than others. It was incredibly difficult for Lauren to hold back the tears as she looked down at the small bronze tablet that bore her father's name, date of birth and date of demise, nestled in the many other rows of bronze tablets at the metropolitan lawn cemetrey. The simple metal plaque failed to do justice to a man who was a giant in his profession; it equally failed to announce the shortcomings of a father who was forever absent.

Overtime, the tablet would develop a healthy patina and resemble the other dark plaques that announced the names of people who once lived and breathed, but now, barely visited or thought of. At least it wasn't a glum day for the event. The warmth of early summer made the area slightly humid, as the sprinklers had done their work for the morning The new tablet rested besides a slightly older one, that of Lauren's mother and now, both her parents were laid to rest. She was a young woman who would get over the loss in time. Hopefully, Lauren would find someone to share her life with and move forward.

Nathan, who had been standing silently respectful to one side, decided to speak. 'What are your plans now?' he said softly and without any hint of prying or interrogation. Lauren raised her head, looked at Nathan and explained how she planned to go overseas on a long vacation. She would keep the business as this would fund her new adventures. After travel, she planned to study and embark on a new career. She paused, and then spoke again. 'I can't thank you enough for what you have done for me. I know you and your friends took a lot of risks and for some, they paid the ultimate price. However, you have presented me with an opportunity for closure, I thought I could never have. *Thank you*'. As she finished, she kissed Nathan on the cheek and they both turned and walked back to the car. He was glad he contacted Marcus to discover the whereabouts of Hamish MacMillan. In his zeal for redemption, Marcus managed to locate the body of the professor and have it returned to his daughter for burial. To Nathan, it sounded like Lauren had made a decent plan for her future. He would pop in on her, like a good friend does, from time to time, but he had a feeling in his bones this girl would be alright. 🖋

Chapter 35

EPILOGUE

The '67 *Mustang Fastback* drove slowly down the gravel and rock road to the front of Nathan's cosy cabin, at the front of his quaint bush block. He had been so appreciative of the crushing machine operator at the motor wrecker's who had decided not to destroy the classic car and alerted him. Nathan had given the man a healthy tip. The operator said he decided not to destroy the car because he loved *Mustangs* but also because of the way Madison had spoken to him dismissively. Just goes to show *you can achieve more with honey than salt!* The drive back to the block was only ninety minutes from the lawn cemetrey after he had dropped Lauren off at a friend's place in Melbourne. However, it had given him enough time for serious reflection. This whole saga had only started less than two weeks ago but it had been an intense fortnight. Good friends had been killed, secrets unearthed, and exposed, and new friendships made.

He felt tired, as if he had just had a tough workout but felt exhilarated as well. 'Shit', he thought, 'I'm getting too old for this'. Physically, it would take him a number of weeks to mend but as tough as he was it would take him months, even years to mentally recover.

As he alighted from the car, *Moochee* came saddling up to him, purring and rubbing her fluffy torso against his leg. He bent over and picked up his most favourite connection in the world. 'Oh, okay, so I suppose you want something to eat after tarting around with the local boy cats, don't you?' *Moochee* let out a loud purr and he walked with the cat inside the cabin. A barbecue and party was planned for later in the week, courtesy of Uncle Phil, at his Melbourne nightclub. All will be in attendance, including the *Cossacks*, Garry, Graham, Mark, Caroline, Marcus, and Lauren; even David was making the trip down from the border. They would remember fallen comrades such as Danny, Brian and Paul and toast their lives, comradery, and accomplishments. There would probably be the odd punch-on between bikers and someone will get teary, sobbing drunk, but it was all part of the healing process. Better to vent than keep it bubbling, deep down inside. For the meantime, Nathan was looking for some cat food and a tasty snack, probably a sausage roll or a donut for himself. The air felt cold in the early evening and although the days were getting warmer, the nights were still very cool out on the block. He decided to light a small fire in the stone fireplace, warm his crypt of a cabin and quickly consume his light meal in his leather recliner. *Moochee* jumped onto his warm lap, and, in a little while, as always, they both fell asleep, nourished and content in front of the obliging warmth of the tiny fire.

The End